FOREVER
AFTER

Also by David Jester

An Idiot in Love
An Idiot in Marriage
This is How You Die

FOREVER AFTER

A DARK COMEDY

DAVID JESTER

Skyhorse Publishing

Skyhorse Publishing books may be purchased in bulk at special discounts for sales promotion, corporate gifts, fund-raising, or educational purposes. Special editions can also be created to specifications. For details, contact the Special Sales Department, Skyhorse Publishing, 307 West 36th Street, 11th Floor, New York, NY 10018 or info@skyhorsepublishing.com.

Skyhorse® and Skyhorse Publishing® are registered trademarks of Skyhorse Publishing, Inc.®, a Delaware corporation.

Visit our website at www.skyhorsepublishing.com.

10 9 8 7 6 5 4 3 2 1

Library of Congress Cataloging-in-Publication Data
Names: Jester, David, author.
Title: Forever after : a dark comedy / David Jester.
Description: New York : Skyhorse Publishing, 2017.
Identifiers: LCCN 2017014307 (print) | LCCN 2017021406 (ebook) | ISBN 9781510704435 () | ISBN 9781510704367 (softcover) | ISBN 9781510704435 (ebook)
Subjects: LCSH: Grim Reaper (Symbolic character)--Fiction. | Death--Fiction. | BISAC: FICTION / Fairy Tales, Folk Tales, Legends & Mythology. | FICTION / Occult & Supernatural. | GSAFD: Black humor (Literature) | Humorous fiction. | Fantasy fiction. | Occult fiction.
Classification: LCC PR6110.E79 (ebook) | LCC PR6110.E79 F67 2017 (print) | DDC 823/.92--dc23LC

Cover design by Lilith_C

Print ISBN: 978-1-5107-0436-7
Ebook ISBN: 978-1-5107-0443-5

Printed in United States of America

To my mother,
For your belief, your support, your forgiveness, and your love.
I'll never forget you.

PART ONE

SOUL REAPER

1

In the darkest corner of the dimmest bar in the dankest town, a man sat in silent rage, his only company a half-filled tumbler of whiskey and a lifetime of regrets.

He mumbled under his breath, pure hatred spilling out of his lips and seething into hollow gray. He spat and he cursed and he grunted. He stomped his tattered trainers on the sticky floor. He shook his head in bitter insolence. He slammed his fist onto the table.

On the other side of the musty room, beyond a fetid assortment of stools, chairs, and odors, an apprehensive bartender watched the actions of this deluded man out of the corner of an ever-vigilant eye. He could see the man was hurting, he could see he had a story that he probably needed—and certainly wanted—to impart, but he didn't want to hear any of it. He wanted the angry man to drink up and piss off so he could close up shop without any confrontation, putting pay to a long day.

The drunk staggered to his feet; the bartender sighed inwardly. He stumbled forward like a man who has only just learned to walk, his gait unstable, his feet kicking through molasses. He crashed into the bar and used it for support, flopping his pliant torso over a surface the bartender had been polishing for an hour.

"You married?" the drunken man chewed up his words and spat them out over the bar. Fresh spots of spittle glistened on the polished wood.

The bartender offered him a brief glance and an uncommitted shake of his weary head.

"Best way to be," the drunk slurred, flopping an arm onto the bar. "Wish I was never married," he said reflectively.

He tried to rest his head on his hand, and after a few slips and a close call with the hardwood surface, he finally found flesh. He stared longingly over the bar. The bartender focused on cleaning a glass in his hand.

"Name's Neil," the drunk propped up his other arm and offered his hand to the bartender. It wasn't taken. He retracted the gesture but retained his stare. "Want to hear a story?"

The bartender didn't acknowledge the inebriate presently drooling droplets of whiskey-soaked saliva onto the sticky varnish.

"Not the talking type, huh?"

The bartender replied without making eye contact, "It's been a long day, mate, and you're very drunk. Why don't you finish up and head home?"

Neil retreated. He threw his hands forcefully onto the bar, bruising his palms.

"My money not good enough for you?" he yelled. A deluge of alcoholic odor ejected from his mouth.

The bartender didn't respond. He didn't even wipe away the stray spittle on his cheek. His eyes remained fixed on the pint glass in his hand, a glass in danger of turning back into sand if he cleaned it any further.

Neil looked ready for action; the anger had boiled up inside of him. He glared at the unresponsive bartender and thrust his finger angrily over the bar, threatening an abusive lecture. Then he paused, halted, and instantly cooled down.

"Fuck this!" he spat in exasperation, deciding there was no fun in arguing with a human wall. "I'm going for a piss."

He took his glass of whiskey with him as he mumbled and stumbled his way to an ammonia-drenched bathroom.

At the urinal, still cursing under his breath, he used his right hand to drink while his left aided with the task of urination. Dipping his nose into the glass, he savored the smell of the alcohol and eliminated the stench of stale piss and shit fermenting in the room beyond the calm amber liquid.

With his attention fully on his drink and his mind on other things, Neil's heart nearly jumped out of his chest when, from his periphery, he noticed a young hooded man standing next to him. He felt his body jump inwardly as his organs tried to leave his skin.

He turned to face the newcomer with an erratic fluttering in his chest. "Where the fuck did you come from?" he blurted.

The man in the next urinal answered in a mechanical voice without lifting his head. "I'm sorry if I scared you."

Neil felt his heart settle. His tensed muscles relaxed.

"You didn't," he assured, not wanting to expose his previous panic.

"Can you stop pissing on my shoes then?"

"Shit," Neil snapped, steering the offending arc of urine away from the young man's sneakers and aiming it back toward the urinal. "Fucking, shit," he said, laughing slightly, "you should have, I mean—fuck," he chuckled.

"Apology accepted."

Neil urinated with a smile plastered on his face. He finished in a hurry—too bored and careless to wait for the final drops to release, happy with them soaking into his pants. "So, you live around here?" He turned to the next urinal, but the strange man with the wet trousers had disappeared.

Neil shrugged to himself, wiped his hands on his trousers, and headed back out into the bar. He spied the man whose shoes he had soiled at the far end of the room and sauntered over, shooting a look of disdain at the indifferent bartender on the way.

The back of the room was lit only by a small bubbling fluorescent, positioned above a tacky, dusty, and generic landscape painting on the wall. The man was reading—the title of the book was short and pointlessly generic enough to indicate a mass-market thriller.

Neil sat opposite the reader, plonking his weight down heavily, audibly sighing and grunting as his backside crushed against the thinly padded bench.

The man didn't look up; the bartender clearly wasn't the only person intent on ignoring Neil.

Neil coughed to clear a glob of dehydrated mucus from his scorched throat, and then, in a scratchy tone, asked: "You not drinking?"

The reader casually turned a page in his book before replying: "No."

Neil stared at his averted eyes. His intuition had drowned in a sea of alcohol, but enough of it remained to warn him against close contact with the man. There was something strange about him, something off. He didn't seem the aggressive sort, he didn't look like he possessed any anger at all, but there was *something* behind those impassive eyes. Or maybe it was the fact there seemed to be nothing behind those eyes that fired so many warning signs in Neil's mind.

"Go on," Neil pushed, ignoring his intuition and finding that the sparse warnings capitulated against the remotest sense of resistance. "It's on me. What you having?" He looked toward the bar, ready to shout an order.

"No, thank you."

"You sure?" he persisted, still trying to catch the attention of the bartender, who had now moved onto cleaning a spotless shot glass.

"No."

"Whiskey? You want some whiskey?"

Still the reader refused to glance at the alcohol-drenched face peering expectantly at him. "No, thank you," he said placidly, turning another page—the sound of the folding paper audible in the relative silence.

Neil drew his attention from the bar, deflated. Out of eyeshot, a relieved bartender continued to clean a pre-polished glass. He took another sip of his whiskey, disappointed to see that the sloshing liquid was nearing the bottom of the glass.

"So, where did you come from?" he quizzed. "I didn't see you here before."

The reader turned another page and didn't utter a word.

"You married?" Neil continued, undeterred. "I bet you're not; you look too smart for that." He bent forward. His right eyebrow creased downward, the corner of his mouth twisted distastefully. "Marriage is for suckers, right?" he said in a gravelly pitch.

"If you say so," came the placid reply.

Neil nodded and leaned back on the seat. "I'm married," he stated.

"Makes sense."

"Ten years," Neil continued, not registering the comment.

"That's a long time," the reader said, turning another page.

Neil nodded to himself, staring reflectively into the middle distance. "Most of it bad," he explained. His face twisted in disgust. "And now she's fucking my best friend. Doesn't that just make you sick?" he inquired. "I'm Neil, by the way." He offered his hand over the table, a pleasant look on his sweaty face.

The reader looked over his book for the first time. His eyes stared blankly at the extended hand before dipping back to the pages of the paperback. "I'd rather not."

Neil withdrew his hand and shrugged his shoulders. "Not the touchy-feely type, huh? My wife was like that. *Fucking bitch.*" He spat venomously. "But she'll get what she deserves."

He reached inside his jacket and fiddled around, his fingers prodding and probing. When his hand reemerged, it was grasping a small handgun. He turned the weapon this way and that. His chunky, sweaty fingers toyed with the sturdy weapon.

The reader looked up, acknowledged the weapon, and then returned his attention to the book.

"Three hundred and seventy-five this cost me," Neil said, his inebriated eyes gleaming as they drank in the sight of the gun. "It's worth every penny. You know what I'm going to do with it?"

"I have an inkling."

Neil nodded sternly. "They're both at it now. My wife and my friend; fucking like dogs just a few doors from here. I'm going to give them what they deserve. I don't give a fuck about going to jail. It'll be worth it."

He drank the remains of his whiskey and slammed the empty glass down angrily on the table. A drop of amber splashed the side of the glass and began a depressing descent to the bottom.

"I just need a bit of Dutch courage," he grunted as the harsh whiskey rolled down his throat.

The reader slowly nodded.

"You not scared?" Neil quizzed, flashing the gun in front of him, making sure he had noticed it.

"Not really."

"It's fully loaded. Six shots. This *is* a real gun, you know."

"I noticed that."

Neil stared at the unimpressed man, trying to catch a sense of fear or anxiety hidden behind those dead eyes. He looked hard, studying the lifeless orbs, but found nothing. If he was hiding any fear, he was hiding it well.

"Fucking weirdo," he spat.

He climbed lazily to his feet and steadied himself on the table after his legs threatened to give way. He stuffed the gun into his jacket, shot one final look at the side of the bartender's head and then disappeared out of the pub.

When the doors of the pub slammed shut in the drunkard's wake—after the bartender breathed a huge sigh of relief, muttered a thankful curse under his breath, and allowed his mind to prepare for sleep—the only customer remaining in the bar calmly

closed his book, deposited it into his pocket, and walked toward
the exit.

Neil staggered down the street, spitting distasteful comments as
his mind whirled with madness. He paused under the hazy glow
of a streetlight—looking like a Dickensian villain in the ethereal
halo—to paint the pavement with a glob of sticky saliva before
continuing on to his destination.

Through the front window of one of the terraced houses, he
watched two silhouettes dancing together in the cozy radiance
of a dozen candles, their naked forms entwined in the flickering
warmth.

"Fucking bastards," he spat. "*Bastards!*" His shout was loud
enough to twitch a few curtains in the street, but the lovers dancing in the orange glow didn't flinch.

Shaking with anger, Neil kicked open the gate to the property
and stormed to the doorway. Behind him, unseen in the shadows, the reader with the apathetic eyes watched as Neil dropped a
shoulder and charged the door, snapping it free from a flimsy lock
and stumbling onwards into the warm house.

A scream from the house echoed into the street. Curtains
twitched; lights snapped on like lines of luminous dominoes; fingers hovered over final digits on multiple phones. The stranger in
the shadows calmly walked forward.

The screaming woman dragged her voice back to her throat,
gathered her senses, and glared at the intruder. "Neil!" she pulled
away from the tight embrace of her naked lover, clawing his reluctant hands away from her exposed breasts.

The disappointed naked man didn't seem as startled by the
intrusion. "What the fuck are you doing here?" he asked, his eyes
on Neil, his hands still trying to instinctively grasp the flesh next
to him. "It's not what it—"

"Don't even try to lie to me," Neil interrupted, his voice sharper in the moment, the slur of inebriation overpowered by adrenaline.

He raised the gun, pointing the trembling barrel at his wife and his best friend, giving them an equal share. "I know what you've been up to. I've always known. I'm going to give you both what you deserve."

His wife moved forward, shoving her lover's stray hand away from her thigh. "Neil, don't do this. Calm down. There's no need—"

"*Don't you fucking tell me to calm down, bitch!*" Neil's finger grasped tighter on the trigger as the anger coursed through his veins. "Ten years we've been married!" he yelled, waving the gun around like he was conducting an orchestra. "Ten *fucking* years!" He turned his disappointment toward his former best friend. "How can you do this to me?"

"Look, mate—"

"No!" Neil snapped, the gun now madly rolling around his palm, the barrel threatening everyone and everything in the room. "I'm not your fucking mate, not anymore. We've been best friends since we were six, we've known each other most of our lives. *I've* never done any wrong by you. *I've* never stepped out of line. *I've* never even *looked* at any of your girlfriends," Neil was emphasizing his comments by pointing to himself, forgetting he was holding a gun. His potential victims obviously wondered if this was their chance to rush him, to tackle him to the ground, to save themselves from a possible execution and a certain lecture. There was no need.

Neil had begun to relate a story of how he had forgiven his friend for breaking his Power Ranger when he squeezed the trigger. The resulting blast shook the small room to its foundations. In the street, everyone was now awake and alert.

The rattling resonance of blasted gunpowder and the stench of blood, defecation, and cordite was still in the air when Neil came to his senses. He found himself looking down at his own bloodied body; his hand still cradling a smoking gun, his temples tapped with entry and exit wounds.

"What was that?" he asked calmly.

"Looks like you shot yourself."

He looked up to see the silent man, the man who had been reading a book in the bar while he waved his gun, just standing there.

"You?" he said softly. "What is this? What's going on?" he paused, contemplating his current clarity. "Why am I sober?"

The previously silent man simply shrugged. "Death seems to have a sobering effect on people."

He held out his hand, and, after staring at it for a few seconds—trying to soak in what the newcomer had just said—Neil grasped it and the two men left the house.

When the deafening residue of the blast had disappeared and the sound of police sirens was hovering on the horizon, Neil's former best friend was the first to break the resulting silence.

"Well, I never saw that coming."

His partner in crime couldn't withdraw her eyes from the lifeless body of her former husband. The chill creeping in from the open door suddenly felt all too poignant. She was cold and shaky. She felt exposed and ashamed.

"What should we do?" she asked, a little hysteria creeping into her voice.

"Well, I don't know about you, but *I'm* still horny."

In the tranquil waiting room for the recently deceased, the untroubled and uninhibited souls of the dead awaited their destination. A plethora of former people—a mixture of the sinful and the slightly less sinful—all contently gazed into the middle distance.

Neil sat in complete silence among those quiet souls for several minutes before finally turning to the man who had accompanied him on his journey and asking the question that had been niggling away at him since they arrived. A question that had further bothered him after witnessing other confused people enter the waiting room, each accompanied by a man or a woman who, like his accomplice, seemed to know what they were doing and where they were going.

"Are you my guardian angel?"

The apparent angel had been staring disinterestedly toward the front of the room, where a short female receptionist sat behind an open desk, calling out names and room numbers.

He laughed softly at the question.

Neil smiled politely, but still wanted an answer. "Are you?"

"No."

Neil nodded solemnly and turned his attention toward the front. A short, stubby man guided a confused youngster down a corridor where they both disappeared through an unseen doorway. Moments later, the short, stubby man emerged with a slip of paper in his hand and a smile of contentment on his face.

"You *are* an angel though?" Neil wondered.

"Something like that."

The receptionist called the room to attention by clearing her rattling throat over the loud speaker. "Michael Holland," she said, looking up expectantly.

The man next to Neil stood.

"Is that you?" Neil quizzed. "Is that *us,* I mean?"

Michael nodded.

Neil stood, feeling a twinge of trepidation for the first time since entering the room. "Where are we going?" he asked as Michael led him down the corridor toward a beckoning black door.

Michael shrugged his shoulders and the last words Neil heard before entering the room were: "I have no idea."

The smile of contentment Neil had seen on the face of the stubby man was moments later also plastered on the face of Michael Holland. It was a smile of relief, of a day's work completed.

He took his slip of paper to a small computer terminal embedded in the wall near the reception area. When prompted, he typed his serial number onto the touch screen and inserted the paper into the slot provided. A series of electronic beeps followed before the details of Neil Simon's life flashed onto the screen.

His date of birth, his date of death. The cause of his death was listed as "Accidental Suicide." His destination as "to be decided." In the end, that was all it came down to—four snippets of information, leaving Michael feeling that he got more out of their life than they did.

Moments later the details dropped away, replaced with a notice stating, "Thank you. Your account has been credited," before the screen returned to default, retaining the slip of paper.

Michael walked past the waiting room without a glance. He felt the sneering eyes of the receptionist on his right shoulder; the snobbish glares of fellow reapers on his right. He made for the exit, but before he could slip out and back into whatever part of his world he chose, he bumped into someone who regarded him with equal degrees of snobbish sneering.

The tall, foreboding figure stood defiantly in front of a line of teenagers all wearing expensive clothes and somber expressions. As Michael took an instinctive step backward, the spindly giant shifted forward, looming over him.

"Anything good this evening, Michael?" he asked. His sunken eyes glared down at Michael like a warden studying a new arrival.

Michael didn't like the man, but he couldn't help but feel meek in his presence. "Hey, Seers. No, not really," he answered submissively.

Jonathan Seers stepped back. His bandy legs shifted sideways to expose the line of sullen teenagers that had all but vanished in his shadow. They all looked up at their warden expectantly.

"I gate-crashed a party," Seers announced smugly.

He grabbed the boy at the head of the line, his thick, long fingers tightly grasping his shoulder-length hair. He pulled him forward with a hard yank and held him in front of Michael like a prized turkey.

"Freddy here turned eighteen today," Seers explained as the boy capitulated to the overbearing presence still grasping his hair. "He wanted to be popular. Wanted to give his friends a night they wouldn't forget. He tried to buy some pills." He pulled harder on the teenager's hair, lifting his tiptoes off the floor and holding him up by the mangy locks. "Smart-ass ended up with a batch of rat poison from a dealer who didn't take too kindly to being talked down to."

Seers grinned. Michael feigned a smile.

He yanked the boy backward, back into his prominent shadow. The boy toppled and fell over his own heels, but he seemed relieved to be out of the grasp of the derisive behemoth.

"Another exciting day in the Heights," Seers gloated, the smirk still smeared on his bony face. "Maybe you'll join me someday."

"Maybe," Michael replied without conviction.

Seers grinned one last time and then shoved his way past Michael into the waiting room. Michael held his ground until the last of the followers had sulked their way past. In the waiting room he could hear the greetings and ass-kissing that Seers received. Even the glum receptionist was up on her feet with an adoring smile on her face as Seers worked his way around the room like a king addressing his loyal and adoring subjects.

Michael whispered under his breath, "Fucking prick," before scooping the hood of his jacket over his head and walking out of the little piece of purgatory.

2

On streets rife with despair, where the pavement was murky with ash from a million smokers and the gutters clogged with the wares of the downtrodden—condoms, cigarette ends, needles—Michael walked with his head down and his hands stuffed deep into his pockets.

In life he lived in mediocrity, never achieving success or comfort, but was content with his underaccomplishment. He had been happy with what he had: his one-bedroom apartment, his frozen meals-for-one, his weekends down the pub. In death he found himself in a metaphorical hell, on the lowest rung of society, mixing with the worst of the worst.

A shoulder, moist with body odor and thin with malnourishment, brushed past him on the street. The man didn't apologize to Michael, didn't even acknowledge him.

Michael sighed and shook his head.

Ahead, the street was alive with skimpily clad women offering their bodies for the price of a fix. Their flesh tight to their bones, bruised and blackened; their eyes sunken deep in their skulls; their lips a mixture of cracked, dried, blue, and diseased, all covered over with lashings of lipstick that shone a defiant shade of black and red against their pale skin.

"Want me to show you a good time?"

"Hey cutie."

"What, you not even going to look at me?"

Michael brushed past without raising his head. It was better not to acknowledge them. Better to avoid their Medusa stares. Not because they exuded a powerful seduction over him, but because they depressed him. They reminded him just how low he had sunk.

These were the women he knew now; these were the women he worked with. He had reaped the souls of their friends and soon he would reap them. His old life had been a conveyer belt of beautiful women; he had been popular with the ladies, they had loved him and he had loved as many of them as he could. Now they sickened him.

He slalomed through an assortment of beggars, prostitutes, and clusters of those who could have been both but were too inebriated to be either.

Michael dreamed of the day when he could work in a place like the Heights. Where the streets were paved with gold and not splattered with vomit. He wanted to collect the souls of the successful and educated. To mingle among the intelligent, the well-bred, the well-off, and the overprivileged.

In a back alley, a darker slice of this dark town, Michael paused. A motionless man lay slumped up against the wall like a broken puppet. The sleeve of his right arm had been rolled up, his pale flesh exposed to the cold. A needle hung loosely from a vein at the top of his forearm. A small trickle of blood ran down from a pinprick opening, stretched wider under the pull of gravity.

Michael removed a small electronic device from his pocket and glared at it with a twinge of curiosity on his face. The figure stirred slightly, cackling a vomitus groan. Michael nodded, stuffed the electronic timer—his database of the dead and soon to be—into his pocket, and continued down the alley, stepping over the intoxicated man.

These were his streets, these were his people, and every one of them disgusted him.

He entered a grimy apartment through a stained, flaked, and graffitied door. There were crushed beer cans and the telltale stains of piss, expectorant, and vomit outside the door. It stank of sickly putrefaction, and that smell didn't much improve when he opened the door and entered the two-bedroom dwelling.

He had lived in the apartment since his death. This was his heaven, his hell; the place he had been confined to. A definitive example of a bachelor's pad, it was dark and gloomy, and it stank of stale body odor and melancholic masturbation—most of the smells provided by Michael's roommate in eternity, Chip.

Chip was slouched on the sofa when Michael entered, a stumpy, hairy man who appeared to be of hobbit and Neanderthal parentage. His face was small and compact, his features squeezed together by a vice: a flat head, flat chin, protruding forehead, bulbous nose. The color of his skin was hard to decipher; in reality it was probably a ghostly pale, but with the layers of dirt and masses of hair—which didn't seem to grow from anywhere specific, but rather just seemed to stick all over his sweaty skin like loose hair on soap—he looked apish.

His protruding lips loosely held a joint. The billowing smoke rose into apathetic, red-lined eyes that watched Michael as he sauntered over to take a seat opposite.

"Are you not working tonight?" Michael wondered, half glancing at the television, where a talent show played on low volume. A pompous judge was displaying his distaste for a devastated singer.

With a thick trowel-like hand, Chip removed a small bag from his pocket, thrusting his hip upward to jam the hand into the material. He pulled the top of the drawstring bag and emptied the contents onto a nearby coffee table where they were acquainted with a half-eaten slice of pepperoni pizza, an outdated TV guide, and a cell phone that had run out of battery three weeks ago.

Michael watched the assortment of teeth cascade from the bag. They bounced against the solid top like sleet before settling in ragged piles on the dusty surface.

"Finished," Chip declared, managing a proud smile as he gestured to the teeth with a wave of the empty bag.

Michael stared absently at the piles.

He had been dead and confused for thirty years, but even as little as seven years ago, this would have surprised him. Back then he hadn't known Chip, hadn't known that tooth fairies even existed, and if he had, he certainly wouldn't have expected them to look like Chip, otherwise he might have entertained the idea of an eternity spent living with one.

Chip spent his nights patrolling the same area as Michael, but where Michael took souls and left empty corpses, Chip took teeth and left money. It was his job to take every spent tooth from every child throughout their adolescence, but it was only the first tooth that mattered, the rest were just complimentary. The teeth were taken back to the Collector Headquarters where they were ground, analyzed, and destroyed, but not before the organization had collected and filed the child's DNA to maintain a database that the government would kill for, but one they didn't even know existed.

"I told you to stop bringing those back here," Michael said. "It's fucking disgusting. Can't you drop them off at the office?"

Chip didn't seem to be in the mood for trudging the two miles to his workplace, he barely looked capable of making it to the toilet without tripping over his own stupidity. "I'll do it tomorrow," he said indefinitely. He took a long toke from the joint as though to emphasize his lack of mobility and then he offered the burning stick to his friend.

Michael watched the ember spill smoke into the dim room. The simpleton face of his grinning roommate appeared expectantly through the hazy, ragged lines. He shrugged, conceded, and took the joint, settling back to watch television as an entire country cheered the antics of a dancing dog, knowing that he was just a few tokes away from understanding their enjoyment.

"How was your pickup?" Chip said half-heartedly, his smiling eyes on the television, enjoying the performance as much as the squealing audience.

"Demented."

"Drugs?" Chip wondered, the scent of degeneracy piquing his interest.

Michael turned distastefully away from the television; there wasn't enough dope in the world. "Adultery," he explained. "He tried to kill his wife for having an affair, ended up killing himself."

Chip laughed, a little too enthusiastically. He slammed his fists into the side of the couch. "Classic," he said, his voice strained with hysterics. "You have a great fucking life, mate."

Michael twisted his face and leaned back, sinking into the chair as he tried to let the dope take over him before the memories and the regrets of when he really did have a great life took over.

3

"I'm telling you—" Any story Michael told, anything he had to say, always took center stage. That night, he had been joined by his closest friends, Del and Adam, one either side of him at the bar, both, as always, enthralled by what he had to say. They hovered around him like a revered deity. "—If you ever get the chance to fuck twins, you've gotta go for it."

They smiled simultaneously as Michael ducked forward to take a thirsty swig from his pint of beer. The pub wasn't full that night, but there were enough people, enough conversation, to fade out the pop music that blasted an offensive drawl from a jukebox.

In one corner of the pub, a group of men hovered around a pool table, drinking, joking, laughing, and shoving each other in masculine acts of aggression between shots. In another corner, a group of a dozen women, from their late teens to their early forties, celebrated the start of a boisterous hen party—their symphonic voices halting only to lap up cheap cocktails.

Between the two largest collectives, among the drabs of men on the pull, women looking seductive and teenagers looking nervous, were Michael and his friends.

"You really did it, Mickey?" Del wondered.

Michael shrugged impassively. "Would I lie?"

Adam grunted and shook his head, a sign of upmost respect and jealously. "And both of them think you're only dating them?" he wanted to know.

Michael nodded proudly, winking at his friend over the rim of his glass as he took another long drink.

"Nice one, Mickey." He slapped his friend lightly on the shoulder. "Which one was better in the sack?"

Michael shrugged and then pondered the question. He put his half-full glass down on the bar and ran a thoughtful finger across the rim, wiping a fleck of froth. "Hard to say," he said. "They both had subtle differences. Susie was a little hairier downstairs, a little *too* hairy for my liking. That shit was like Velcro when we finished."

Del and Adam recoiled in synchronization. Michael grinned and called to the bartender, holding up three fingers and pointing to his pint.

"She had a better body, though," he continued. "A little slimmer around the waist, tighter ass." He drew her form in the air with his palms. "Nicky had bigger tits, but Susie also had the energy and flexibility. I'm telling you, they may look identical on the surface, but once you get underneath, it's like shagging a split personality."

Adam looked momentary solemn. "Never mind both," he said with a weighted sigh into his glass. "I'd be happy with either of them."

Del and Michael laughed boisterously at their friend, who wore a cheeky smile.

"We need to get you laid," Michael told him.

"Agreed," Del toned in. "Sick of your fucking moping. Would you be happy with a prostitute?"

Adam looked offended. "I ain't paying for it."

Michael sighed. "Then *I'll* fucking pay for it."

He shook his head. "There's something not right about paying for sex."

"Fuck it," Michael said with a shake of his disagreeing head. "It's a service. They're the trashcan and you have something you need to empty."

"Nice image mate," Del said.

The three men laughed together and then turned around on their stools, facing away from the bar where an elderly bartender had just finished pouring their drinks.

Michael's stare was immediately pulled to the hen party. He caught flirtatious glances from a couple of the drunken women. One he deemed too old, an unhappily married woman looking for a drunken fling. The other, in her midthirties, was better looking, but too drunk. He had no problem with drunk women, but there was a line, and it looked like she was about to throw up on it.

He turned his attention to the pool table where the group of men were still enjoying their game; all of them were silently watching the smallest of the group, who was eyeing up a long shot on the black.

They were all dressed in tight-fitting leather jackets—strewn with cheap patches and emblems—that struggled to engulf their large frames. They were all bigger than Michael, bigger than his friends. They looked like they wouldn't move if asked; they probably wouldn't have moved if someone drove a car through them.

With a sly smile tweaking the corners of his mouth, Michael asked, "Fancy a game of pool?"

Del snapped a short and mocking laugh. "You seen those guys?" he said, appalled at the suggestion. "They'll break our fucking necks just for asking."

Michael shrugged off the comment and jumped down. "We'll be fine," he declared confidently. "Come on."

Del and Adam followed apprehensively behind their friend as he strode toward the table.

The small man had sunk the black to equal quantities of applause and distaste. He was receiving a mixture of curses and high-fives from his friends when Michael interrupted them.

He stood in front of the table, waited until he had everyone's attention, and then addressed the biggest man there: a bearded man made purely of muscle and fat, with sweat patches staining his T-shirt and tattoos coloring his bulbous arms.

"You guys finishing any time soon?" Michael asked him.

The big man looked Michael up and down derisively. He sucked in his protruding stomach—concealed under a stretched, sweat-stained T-shirt and angled by the flaps of his sleeveless jacket—and shifted forward, hugging the floor with his heavy boots.

"Fuck off, kid," he spat.

Inches away from the big man, Michael felt like he was choking on his odor, a morbid concoction of sweat, tobacco, and beer. Despite the smell, he shifted forward until he could feel the moistened touch of the biker's stomach against his own.

"Kid?" Michael said, smiling wryly. "Just because I'm smaller than you doesn't make me younger." He paused to reciprocate a curious cross-examination. "Although judging by those wrinkled biceps of yours, I probably am."

A wave of hushed silence passed through the group as everyone drew in sharp breaths.

Del mumbled apathetically from behind his friend, "Here we go again," and the silence erupted into chaos.

The big man swung for Michael, but Michael saw the monstrous arm working its way backward long before it had time to connect. He ducked out of the way, feeling a rush of air dust his nose as the thick fist swept by. The big man toppled with the force of his own missed swing, just managing to save himself from hitting the floor.

The youngster who had potted the black to win the game moved at Michael with a pool cue in his hand and a determined grimace on his face. He moved around his tumbling friend and swung the cue at Michael, who threw his hands into its arcing flight to protect himself. The cue smacked his palms with a dull sucking sound, slapping a vicious whip against the flesh. He ignored the burn in his palms, closed his hands around the thin end of the cue, and yanked it out of the youngster's hands.

With the cue raised above his head, he took a quick step away from the table and flashed the weapon at the others, who were preparing to launch into an attack. Grinning like a madman, he twirled the cue through his hand and over his head, using it like a baton in a parade.

"Every fucking week," Del muttered as he watched.

The big biker straightened and moved for Michael. Michael swung for him and caught him square in the jaw with the tip of the cue. The chalked end grazed the bottom of his ear before snapping against his cheekbone. Michael pulled it back for another swing as the big man recoiled, but before he could launch another attack, the other men were upon him, their fists and knees jabbing away at his stomach and thighs, their hands grasping for the weapon in his hand. Del and Adam reluctantly threw themselves into the brawl to help their friend, pulling the men off him before they had a chance to do any serious damage.

The fight expanded into the rest of the room, as customers ducked and ran out of the way to avoid catching any of the wildly thrown punches and kicks.

It lasted for a few minutes, but for some it felt like hours.

When the fighting had ceased, two of the bikers had fled. The biggest one lay partially unconscious at the foot of the pool table, having found himself the main beneficiary of the boot, fist, and weapon attacks. The other two were wearily bent double on the floor, contemplating a return to the fight whilst keeping one eye on the exit should the fight return to them.

"Well, that was fun," Michael beamed, admiring his handi-work.

Del and Adam had both received broken noses and bloodied faces for their trouble. Adam was having a hard time standing and felt like he was about to unleash his guts onto the floor via his mouth and anus simultaneously, but Michael seemed to have been perked up by the fight. His eyes were quickly swelling, his nose and lip were both bleeding, and his shirt was torn, but he was happier than when it had started.

The sound of police sirens filtered through to battle-weary ears, which hissed with constant whines or didn't work at all.

Michael casually walked to the bar, returning to his pint. "Drink up," he told his friends.

The bartender, who had phoned the police during the chaos, stood in wait. "You shouldn't have done that," he told Michael with a stern but concerned expression on his face.

"You shouldn't have called the cops," Michael told him, still smiling.

"You just pissed off a very strong gang."

Michael shrugged and downed his drink in one go, spilling half of it down his shirt as his swollen lip failed to get clean purchase. He finished with a relishing sigh and a smile that beamed even wider.

"They weren't that strong, right guys?" he said, turning to his two friends.

Del shrugged nonchalantly. "We've had worse."

Michael waited for his friends to finish their drinks with equal gusto before they all exited the pub, leaving it empty barring the broken bikers crawling and groaning on the floor—the rest of the patrons had left at varying times during the brawl.

Outside, the sounds of sirens were heavy in the air. The lights of advancing police cars ascended into the night sky, flashing at the darkness like a dazzling and distant firework show.

"Split up and fucking leg it!" Michael hollered.

They turned in different directions and fled the scene. Michael scuppered across the road, ducked into an unlit backstreet, and then dove down an opposing alleyway. He enjoyed the adrenaline of the chase as much as the fight and was still grinning broadly when he breathlessly slumped down on a step deep inside the alleyway—the road, the pub, and the police cars, all out of sight.

He looked around in the stale darkness, assessing his poorly lit location. To his right, the back way to another stretch of alley was blocked by an overflowing Dumpster. Behind him, on the cold step where he took refuge, a grime-covered door shielded the back entrance to a liquidated fast-food restaurant.

The light was dim, the source distant and obscured, but it was prominent enough for him to make out the small cuts on his knuckles and the pencil-shaped bruise on his palm. The light wasn't strong enough for him to see the person next to him. When he pulled his attention away from his hands and looked up, the sight and proximity of the figure on the small step gave him a juddering fright.

He jumped and recoiled, turning toward the man but leaning away. In the dim light, he could see he was a lot older than himself, maybe middle-aged, maybe more; a glimmer of grayness glittered on his stubbled chin and flecked the hair above his ears, a multitude of wisdom lines creased his forehead. He was smiling; his piercing eyes glimmered from underneath a furrowed brow that questioned Michael's surprise.

"What the fuck!" Michael spat, breathless. "Where did you come from?"

The man lowered his brow, maintained his smile. "Quite a fight you put up back there," he stated simply, ignoring the question.

"What?" Michael was unsure if he was about to be raped and mutilated or if he'd just stumbled upon an innocent weirdo.

"I was wondering." The grayed man faced forward, seemingly interested in a sheet of moldy newspaper that clung to the pavement like statically charged cellophane. "How does an aspiring art student learn to fight like that?"

"Aspiring art . . . " Michael shook his head. "You saw what happened in the bar? How?"

The man tilted his head this way and that. "I fear you wouldn't believe me."

Michael stood, backed off slightly. "What's going on here? Are you part of the gang? Did the bartender phone you? Did he put you up to this?" He clenched his fists and left them dangling by his side. He was prepared for a fight, even though the old man didn't look like the fighting type.

The man remained seated. His confident and calming gaze met Michael's agitated, trepidatious features.

"Not a setup. This is an offer," he explained. A serious expression crossed his face and cancelled out his smile. "*Although*, as your assumptions were not *entirely* incorrect. I have to be quick."

"What the fuck are you talking about it?"

"I have been studying you, headhunting if you like. I work for a very highly respected organization, and I think you would fit right in. We are on the lookout for individuals such as you."

Thoughts of MI5 popped into Michael's head but were dismissed just as quickly as they arrived, replaced by something far more likely and far less interesting.

"Are you a fucking pimp?"

The older man laughed—a sound both spine chilling and comforting. Michael took another step back.

"I am something you can't even comprehend," he explained when the laughter had faded from his voice.

Michael shook his head dismissively. "Fuck this." He turned and ducked into the alleyway, exposing himself to any potential enemies on the street ahead.

The man stood behind him. He opened his arms imploringly. "Clearly you're not in a talkative mood," he said, raising his voice as Michael scuppered into the alley. "But I dare say you will be soon enough."

Michael stopped in his tracks, taking a few steps backward until he could see the man again. "I don't think so, mate." He addressed him face to face, raised a threatening finger, and thrust it menacingly at him. "I don't know who you are or what you want, but I don't want to be any part of it."

He left one last look of diastase with the stranger before turning around and heading into the increasingly bright lights of the street ahead. The sound of sirens was now extinct but the lights of distant police cars, still parked outside the bar, lit up the sky a few streets ahead.

Further down the alleyway, next to a pair of Dumpsters, a collection of broken cardboard boxes and a clutter of empty beer cans, two men were waiting for Michael. At the sight of him, they popped their sluggish selves from the wall and slowly advanced toward him.

He saw their silhouettes before their faces, as their bulky frames staggered forward. He prepared to fight or flee, depending on the severity of their intentions, but he relaxed somewhat when their faces were close enough to make out.

They were bikers from the bar. He had left one of them bent-double and beaten. No doubt he had dragged his crippled body away from the scene before the police had arrived. The youngster who had swung for him with the pool cue before fleeing the scene when the violence erupted, was with him.

"Hello, boys. Ready for round two?" Michael said cockily.

"Nice moves back there, kid," the older one commented. "But you pissed off the wrong people."

He lunged forward unexpectedly, catching Michael by surprise. He wrapped his body around him, snaking his arms around his chest and using the clasp to pin Michael's arms uselessly by his side.

Michael was still smiling. He opened his mouth to offer a mocking retort when the youngest one sucker punched him in the stomach.

He felt the air rush out of his lungs, felt his body jerk in opposition. He bent over from the impact, dipping at the waist. His captor forced him upright, held him tighter.

The younger biker, his face a picture of concentration, his tongue poking out of the corner of his mouth, lowered his head and delivered punch after successive punch to Michael's midsection.

Michael coughed something out in mocking reply, but was surprised to feel his words strangled into silence before they escaped his throat. He felt something cold and wet soaking his shirt and his pants, running through the material and dripping down his legs.

The youngster stopped punching him. His tongue returned to his mouth, his body straightened, his determined gaze lifted to meet the perplexity on Michael's face. Only then did Michael see that he was holding a knife. The sickening sight of the blade, covered in blood, was an extra thrust through his heart.

His captor let him go and he immediately fell to his knees, suddenly overcome with panic and pain as a dizzying madness crept into his mind.

The older attacker planted a boot into his spine, stabbing his steel-pointed toecaps in between his shoulder blades. He laughed and spat onto the back of Michael's head.

He said something, but Michael didn't hear it. His world was spinning, his ears imploding, his body drifting. He felt himself being pushed to the floor, but barely felt the abrasive concrete as his face was forced against it or the crushing weight of the man behind him as he walked heavily over his back and away from the scene.

He managed to turn himself over, taking the pressure away from the wounds in his stomach and exposing them to the air and the fresh drizzling rain that had begun to pierce the night sky.

Through hazy, quickly fading eyes, he saw the stranger from the alleyway approach. He watched as his smiling, grayed expression beamed down at him.

"You ready to talk now?"

PART TWO

SEEING DOUBLE

1

Inside a decrepit diner, at the corner of a street deep in recession country, where the surrounding shops were bordered up boxes of their former selves and the pedestrians ambling by did so with a melancholic swagger, Martin Atkinson sat alone.

His fingers tapped dull melodies on the chipped, glossed surface of the center booth. The heel of his right foot bounced up and down repetitively as his calf muscles worked out their angst.

Martin was anxious, ill at ease, and very agitated, but most of all, he was hungry.

In his grubby fingers, black with dried dirt and yellowed from the tips of a thousand cigarettes, Martin twirled a packet of ketchup. He checked his watch. He licked his lips. He eyed the counter, the window, the floor. He checked his watch again.

A waitress appeared behind him, her hollowed steps introducing her approach. Martin relaxed slightly, his sensitive nostrils pulling in the aromas from the food she carried.

She placed a mountain of food in front of Martin's twitching features and noted his delighted expression as his eyes pored over the cuisine.

"Full English," she said as he watched the food, making sure it didn't get up and leave before he had a chance to dig in. "Extra bacon. Extra sausage. Extra black pudding. No beans. No tomato."

She paused—he was drooling; she was intrigued, and a little bit disgusted. "That okay, love?"

"Perfect," he said with a liquid swirl to his words as his salivating mouth chewed them up before offering them. "Thanks."

She gave him a practiced smile, ignored his strange behavior, and returned to her station behind the counter.

When Martin sensed the waitress was no longer paying any attention to him, he dove into the plate of food like a child jumping into a ball pit. He relished the texture and the sound of tearing meat as his teeth ripped strands of bacon and charred sausage to shreds. The food barely stayed in his mouth long enough for him to relish any taste.

Occasionally, he lifted his head to check behind the counter and out the window. He was weary of being watched, of being judged; as far as he knew, no one was paying any attention to him. He didn't see the car parked opposite the street, didn't see the darkened figures behind darkened glass as they surveyed his animalistic behavior.

His stomach growled and groaned with contentment when he left the diner. He felt at ease now that his hunger had been satiated. He took a deep breath of fresh air, lit a cigarette, and set off down the street at a leisurely pace.

With a light breeze at his back and the suggestion of sunshine on the horizon, he decided to take a shortcut through the park. He relaxed even more under the tuneful whistling of flocks of birds and the distant barking of unseen dogs.

An exaggerated cough from behind disrupted his peace, stopped him dead in his tracks. He turned around with a smile still beaming on his pudgy face.

Two men stared back at him, both of them wearing three-piece suits despite a growing afternoon heat. They didn't look friendly; they didn't look aggressive. Their faces were blank, devoid of emotion, not even the slightest hint of a smile on the corners of their mouths. Their eyes and the emotions beyond were shaded with pitch-black sunglasses.

"Can I help you?" Martin asked, feeling his smile slowly slip from his face.

"Martin Atkinson?" one of the identical men quizzed.

"Who wants to know?"

In a voice very similar to the first man, the second man replied: "We do."

"That's why we asked," One clarified.

Martin felt ill at ease. He felt like he was seeing and hearing double, and he was sure that neither of them had good intentions.

"What do you want?" he asked, hearing the trepidation in his own voice.

The suited men looked at each other, their faces in perfect sync as they turned to exchange a glance and then turned back to a bemused Martin.

"We've come to help you," Two said.

Martin took a few steps backward and glanced around. No one else was near.

"I don't need your help," he told them.

Over his shoulder, he could see a thicket; he could see the welcoming claws of darkness inside the dense accumulation of trees and foliage. He backed up toward it, noticing the two men following his every step.

"I suggest you leave me alone," Martin warned. He could feel the cooling shadow of the trees on his back, "For your own safety."

The two men followed him regardless.

"We can't do that," One said.

He was among the trees now. He kept going, happy to see the two men duck into the darkness with him.

He stopped and turned to face the other way, his back to them. "How do you plan on helping me?" he wanted to know, feeling confident and safe inside the shaded darkness.

The two men looked at each other. They fired a synchronized look over their shoulders. They returned their eyes to Martin, watching as the leafy trees painted shadows on his broad back.

"We want to rid you of your curse," One said.

"We're going to kill you," Two added.

Martin snapped his head back toward them, exposing a set of sharp teeth and a jaw that stripped back to his ears. He lifted his hands, preparing to attack. His fingers had been replaced with elongated pincers—tipped with razor-sharp claws. He waited for the terror to explode in the eyes of his attackers, waited to revel in their fear before ripping them to shreds.

Their faces were still emotionless. They didn't react, at least not how Martin expected they would.

Simultaneously, from underneath immaculately pressed jackets, they exposed black handguns fitted with silver suppressors. Martin sensed the danger and threw himself toward them, but it was already too late.

There was a short staccato blast; a light show in the darkness.

Martin, the agitated, anxious man with a belly full of meat and a mind full of shame, was reduced to an angry, agonized wreck on the dusty, dirty ground before being executed. Put down, like the wounded animal he was.

2

"I have an appointment for twelve with Doctor Khan."

"Please take a seat."

Michael was the only one in the waiting room. It was a fairly small room. Opposite the reception desk, to the right of the only window, four chairs were lined up against the wall. The doorway leading to the doctor's office was on Michael's right as he took his seat.

There were a few magazines on a small coffee table shoved between his chair and the next. He glanced over and read a few of the titles with little interest. He noted magazines on gardening and interior decorating, magazines whose entire customer base seemed to be medical waiting rooms. There were also the obligatory pamphlets on health and a picture book to keep the children entertained. Michael frowned them away and sat upright, his attention on the receptionist, whose attention was on a stack of papers in her hands.

She was pretty, which was a rarity in this part of town. She also had a job, another rarity—a sign that she probably didn't live around here. Years ago, Michael would have been all over her, but this was the eighth time he had sat opposite her and he had barely said more than a few words to her, none of which had referenced anything other than his appointment or her job.

He watched her blue eyes pore over a file, watched her thin lips unconsciously mouth the words she read, watched a smile tweak a fine wrinkle at the corner of her mouth when she read something she found amusing. She picked up the stack of papers and bounced them on her desk to align them. She yelped in discomfort as one of the papers slid against the nib of her forefinger, opening up a wound that dripped crimson onto the desk.

She glanced up at Michael, met his gaze with her beautiful eyes. Michael smiled back; she turned away. She lifted the wounded finger to her lips and opened her mouth to expose a powerful set of canines, out of place on such a small and delicate face.

Michael turned away, inwardly disgusted. He knew, of course. When the angle was right, and the door was open, he could see behind the reception desk to a mirror in the doctor's room—a mirror she had never appeared in. It bothered him, turning some inner part of him against her, but it didn't surprise him. No one in the office was alive, patients and doctor alike.

The door to the doctor's room opened and Michael turned to greet whoever opened it, but there was no one there. He saw straight through into the doctor's office, saw the folded legs of the doctor poking out from under her desk. The door closed, the handle lifting up and down as if clicked in place by an invisible hand.

Michael felt a cold air brush past him. He sensed someone in front of him and then heard that someone's footsteps as they crossed his path, walked to the other end of the waiting room, and then left through the main door, which opened and closed in the same ghostly manner.

Michael turned to the receptionist again, the blood sucked dry from her finger, her garish teeth hidden behind beautiful lips. She was staring straight back at him with a soft smile on her soft face. She answered his quizzical expression: "The world needs a bogeyman, right?"

He shrugged, "Does it?"

Before the receptionist had time to reply, a buzzer sounded on her desk, followed by the static-shrouded words of the doctor: "You can let Mr. Holland in now."

The receptionist beamed at Michael, her true nature hidden behind an endearing smile that wouldn't hurt a fly. "You're up," she said happily.

In the adjoining room, Michael sat down opposite the doctor, immediately withdrawing his gaze when he felt her penetrating eyes boring into his.

The room was light, bright, and far from inviting. He felt cold within the confines of it. It was clinical and sterilized; he would have preferred claustrophobic and dark.

"Mr. Holland," Doctor Khan began. "How are you today?"

Michael dragged his eyes to the doctor. He could never meet her gaze for long, so he divided his attention between her eyes and an encyclopedia of doctorates and degrees on the wall behind her.

She was an accomplished psychiatrist; she had been in the business longer than Michael had been dead and alive combined. She was the go-to woman in the district, spending her time treating a multitude of patients between four offices across the county.

She was a pleasant woman, clearly very professional and certainly very sought-after, but there was something about her that Michael found intimidating. A beaming smile constantly graced her face; a smile that hid her own thoughts and exposed those of others. It put him on edge.

"I'm fine," he said guardedly, adding: "I think."

"If you were fine, you wouldn't be here."

He shrugged his shoulders dolefully.

The doctor looked away, just as Michael's ill ease at her penetrating eyes grew to discomforting levels.

"So, what's bothering you?" she asked, pretending to look over a few notes on her lap.

"Do I really need to tell you?"

She made eye contact again, briefly this time—her eyes doing all the smiling for her face. "No, but I prefer it that way."

Michael wasn't going for it. "It would save a lot of time if you just did your thing," he told her.

"Because the art of psychiatry is about building a relationship."

"I mean, why do you even bother communicating with your—" Michael paused, hesitated, and then frowned. His eyebrows narrowed disapprovingly at the grinning psychiatrist.

Unprompted, the doctor said, "No, but I wanted to prove a point."

"Did you have to do—" Again Michael stopped himself, but this time he wasn't frowning. He shifted agitatedly on his chair, glanced this way and that around the spaciously isolated room, and then finally relaxed, albeit with feigned comfort.

"Okay," he said. "We'll do it the normal way. No mind reading. It's off-putting."

The doctor seemed pleased. She made a few notes. Michael stared absently at the nib of her pen as it scrawled its shorthanded squiggles.

"So," she said, slowly lowering the pen while Michael's eyes followed. "How are things at work?"

He raised his eyes to meet hers. "A nightmare," he explained with a reflective nod of his lethargic head. "I'm still on the bottom rung, working with the worst; the scum of society."

"Aren't all people equal?" she wondered. "You deal with death all the time; you should know that better than anyone."

Michael shrugged his shoulders apathetically. "Dead, everyone is the same. It's their lives that depress me. Some of them have so little to lose that they see death as a minor distraction." He slumped back, lowered his gaze. "Last week I picked up a drunk driver. He drove straight into a wall and died on impact. When I found him, he was so fucking cheery that I wanted to kill him again." He sighed heavily and wrapped his arms across his chest.

"Isn't it good to see that?" Doctor Khan wondered. "Doesn't it make a nice change?"

Michael shook his head for a few seconds before answering. "You come to expect a certain something from the dead. A mix of anger, fear, and loss. It's a happy ritual they all abide by. It's the only part of the job I feel comfortable with, as disturbing as that may sound."

"Is this man the reason for your visit?"

He shook his head, unfolded his arms, and leaned forward listlessly. "I want to know what I'm doing here. That's why I'm here; I want you to tell me. I should be dead."

The doctor didn't flinch, didn't lower eye contact. Michael had hoped for a note of sympathy, something different from the norm, but he got the answer he had been expecting: "You chose to work. You chose to live on."

He sagged back in his seat. "Fine."

"Immortality not good enough for you?"

He shrugged nonchalantly. "At the time it sounded like a good idea," he explained. "But I expected a little, I don't know, just . . . more. I guess."

"More?"

"Naked virgins and free whiskey on tap," Michael explained with a wry grin. "A constant state of euphoria, a body that never feels pain or disease."

"It didn't live up to your expectations then?"

"No. I'm on the assembly line. I live in filth. Last week, I had the biggest hemorrhoids I've ever seen. It was like a grape vine growing out of my ass," he shook his head disconsolately. "How the hell do dead people get fucking piles?"

"It is a complicated world."

"*Too* complicated. None of it makes any sense, and every time I ask about something, every time I complain, you know what they tell me?"

The doctor nodded. She had said the same thing to him before.

"In time you will learn," she recited.

"Exactly," Michael spat distastefully.

"And they are right," Doctor Khan told him. "This world has to be experienced to be understood. You may think thirty years is a long time, but in the scheme of things, *here*, it isn't."

"So they keep saying."

"It's true. I've been around a long time and *I'm* still learning."

Michael deflated in the chair. He hadn't gotten what he wanted, and once again he was going to leave just as clueless as he was when he arrived.

The doctor continued. "My advice to you, Michael, is to relax. Stop wondering, stop asking questions, and just let it be."

"Fine," Michael said with the stubborn and unconvincing tone of someone who certainly wasn't going to relax and definitely *was* going to ask more questions.

He stood, straightened his jacket, smiled appreciatively, and turned to leave.

Doctor Khan called to him before he exited the room: "And lay off the dope."

3

On the night of his death, Michael had experienced the same contented sobriety that he had since glimpsed in the eyes of so many of the recently deceased.

That night, when the final raindrop splattered on his pale face and his soul slipped out of his body, he had felt empty. He had felt like he was the body his soul had left, and not the other way around.

The man who had spoken to him before his death and then watched him die extended a hand.

"Samson," he offered with a smile.

Michael looked at the proffered appendage and then at his own lifeless body. "I'm dead?"

Samson withdrew his hand, tucking it into his jacket. "I'm afraid so."

"You knew this was going to happen?"

Samson nodded apologetically.

"So what now?" Michael clambered to his feet and looked around the dim alleyway. There were no bright lights at the end, no ethereal melodies. "Is this it?"

"It doesn't have to be if you don't want it to be," Samson said cryptically. "That's what I'm here for. My offer still stands."

Michael took a step back and rested a hand on his forehead. Dying and then being offered a job was a lot to take in at once, but what bothered him was that he wasn't stressing over it; his conscious had been sedated.

"Does it always feel like this?" he asked. His eyes picked out the glinting police lights in the distance as they sparkled against the freshly fallen rain. "Death, I mean."

"I guess so," Samson said.

Michael turned to the older man. "You don't know? Didn't you die?"

Samson shrugged. "*Technically* I'm dead. But I didn't die."

"I don't understand."

"It's not important." Samson carefully stepped over Michael's dead body and put an arm around the shoulder of his "living" one. "Come with me," he said.

They walked out of the alleyway and into the street where the rain beat a rhythm on the road and the streetlights spilled their sickly glow onto the pavement.

They walked slowly past the closed shops, quiet bars, and simmering houses, beyond the pub where old alcoholics drank their sorrows away; the nightclubs where the young danced and drugged the night away. They passed a beggar on the street who looked up at them both, shook a tin cup that rattled with the lonely sounds of a solitary coin, and then groaned when they passed by unsympathetically.

They walked for ten minutes before Samson spoke again. "You like this part of town?"

Michael laughed scornfully. "It's a fucking dive. Never seen anything so disgusting in my life." As though to add emphasis to his statement, a short, fat man stumbled out of a pub further up the road with an empty pizza box in his hand. He vomited all the way down his hoodie with the ease and comfort of a baby, then, finding the pizza box empty, he began to eat the vomit, mistaking it for spilt pizza topping. "We come here for a bit of down-an'-out," Michael added, sneering at the drunken man who had now stumbled into the street, still chewing on a slice of regurgitated pepperoni. "A laugh. A rumble. A slag."

"You know these streets well, though."

"I guess so."

Samson nodded as if he already knew.

They crossed onto the bridge that marked the west end of the town. Things became a little brighter on the other side, as the council estates turned into middle-class suburban homes for the blue-collared workers of the district.

There was someone waiting ahead of them in the middle of the bridge, his attention on the blackness below, his head hung low. Michael watched him until he felt Samson's hand gently squeeze his shoulder.

"This is the deal, Michael," he said, stopping him. "I give you immortality. I give you another life, an infinite one. I give you a job, reasonable pay. You give me your commitment and dedication."

Michael nodded, waiting for more.

"What do you say?" Samson asked.

"What job?" Michael asked. "I don't understand. What do I do? Where do I do it?"

"You collect the souls of the dead. Like I did with you tonight."

"Like the Grim Reaper?"

Samson smiled broadly. "Something like that, but there isn't just *one* grim reaper, there are thousands in this country alone."

"So why do you need me?"

"I need you here." He opened his arms around him, gesturing to the town as a whole. "I need you to work Brittleside."

"You're shitting me."

Samson slowly shook his head.

"But this place is the fucking pits. What do I get in return?"

Samson opened his mouth and then snapped it shut again, looking a little puzzled.

"Oh, right, the immortality," Michael recalled.

Samson grinned.

"But how does it work? I mean, will I be a ghost?"

"Your other life, your *other self,* will still be dead. But you can live a normal life as you did before. Your friends and your colleagues may be a little," he pondered for a moment, "*different,*" he said with enough emphasis to make Michael feel uneasy. "But everything else will be the same. You can function like a normal person for as long as you want."

"But I'll be dead. My friends, my family . . . won't they know? Won't they go to my funeral?"

"*That* Michael will remain dead. His friends, his family, his job, and his memories are with you, but are redundant now. *This*

Michael," he said, gesturing to him, "will be the same to you and to everyone that matters, but to everyone that *doesn't,* he'll look like a completely different person."

Michael thought about this for a moment. He had never experienced such clarity in his life, but there was a lot to take in. A lot of thoughts threatened to cloud that clarity. "And my name? I mean, this is only a few miles from where I live."

"Keep your first name. Your surname we can change in time, when it matters."

"To what?" Michael said quizzically.

Samson shrugged. He seemed to be growing impatient. He peered over Michael's shoulder, toward the middle of the bridge. He checked his watch and then beamed at Michael again.

"The surname's not important," he said. "Whatever you want."

Michael nodded acceptingly.

"So, do we have a deal?" Samson said, stealing another look over Michael's shoulder.

Michael turned around to see what he was looking at. "I guess so," he said, seeing a solitary figure hugging the railings and peering into the blackness below.

When he turned back around, Samson was gone. He looked around, studied his surroundings. He wasn't anywhere, and there was nowhere he could have run to so quickly.

"Is that it?" Michael asked no one in particular. "What do I do now?"

Seemingly hearing him, the man in the middle of the bridge shouted back. "It's too late. You can't stop me now!"

He began climbing onto the railing, steadily lifting his legs until he was positioned on the other side. He leaned cautiously back onto the railing, his legs inches from the edge.

"I wasn't trying to," Michael called out, finding himself walking toward the man.

"Too late!" he yelled.

Michael walked closer. The stench of cheap alcohol clawed at his nostrils when he came to within a few feet of him.

"You seriously going to jump?" Michael asked.

The man turned around, glaring drunkenly; his eyes flooded with tears. "Of course! And don't you try to stop me!"

Michael held up his hands defensively.

"My life is a joke," the alcohol-drenched despondent droned. "It's pointless!"

"It can't be that bad, mate," Michael said as warmly as he could. "Come on, let's go and have a coffee. It's on me."

The man turned to him. Initially shocked and angry, a gradual sense of pleasant surprise swelled on his face. "Why do you care?"

"Because I know what you're going through. Life can be a bitch, trust me on that. But there're ways around it. Ways to beat it."

"Really?"

"Sure," Michael stepped forward, smiling all the while. "Even in the bad, there's plenty of good. You just have to learn how to see it."

"I like the sound of that."

Michael was inches away. He reached out for the railing, slowly, as not to alarm. "Now come on, let's go and have a drink, get you warmed up and cheered up, huh?"

The man smiled. "Okay." He released himself from the railings and slowly turned, facing back toward the bridge.

"What's your name, by the way?" Michael asked.

"Me? I'm—" his foot slipped on the rain-soaked lip. Michael saw the horror explode on his face as he felt himself falling backward. He reached out for the railing; Michael reached out for the flailing hands. Neither connected. The man fell backward. The final thing Michael saw were feet kicking aimlessly in the dark before his body disappeared into the blackness.

He ran to the edge to look down, hoping the suicidal man had managed to somehow grasp onto the ledge. A heavy splash below indicated otherwise.

"Shit," Michael spat, staring into the gloom. "What a fucking shame."

"Ian," a voice from beside him said.

The jumper was standing next to him, a look of serenity on his face as he joined him in peering over the side. "My name is Ian," he repeated. "What's yours?"

"Michael."

"Nice to meet you, Michael. Want to go for that drink now?"

4

Michael cut a sullen figure as he somberly trudged toward the center of town. He took the route that led from its top to its center, a twisting road that led down a steep hill and was boarded by a line of poorly maintained houses and hollowed-out shops and businesses.

He lifted his head to acknowledge the people he passed. A part-time prostitute; a full-time drug addict. A kid without a future; a mother without a care.

Further down, he saw his old friend Del walking toward him. He had his arm snaked over the shoulders of an attractive, intelligent-looking woman. They were both smiling, happy with each other's company, as they strode up the sloping pavement.

He hadn't seen his old friend for years and in that time he had aged, but he had aged well. He was still a good-looking man; his youthful sprite had been replaced with wizened handsomeness. The years had treated him well.

He didn't live in Brittleside and wasn't on Michael's radar. He had moved to a better place to live a better life and he had someone to live that life with.

Michael passed them with a glance and a longing smile, allowing it to linger for longer than he intended. Del gave him a nod in return, a brief and friendly recognition to acknowledge a stranger. He didn't see the friend he had spent most of his youth with, he didn't see the spirited young man who had nearly gotten him killed on a number of occasions and yet loved him like a brother; he saw a stranger, a random, insignificant nobody.

When he brushed past Michael, the sullen reaper released a drawn-out sigh, allowing the memories that had rapidly reformed at the sight of his old friend to fade into his breath and disperse.

The main street that snaked through the center of Brittleside was a boarded up shadow of its former self, or so Michael had been told many times. It was how he had always known it to be: rundown, empty, grimy, and dilapidated. He didn't doubt that at one time the buildings had been open and the street had thrived with life and activity, but the only differences between now and thirty years ago were an extra board or two.

He checked his timer anxiously. He was late. He was rarely late, but when he was, it didn't usually matter. The dead had nowhere to go, and they couldn't go anywhere when he wasn't around to guide them. There was nothing stopping him from going home and leaving a spirit of the recently deceased to wander aimlessly around his own place of death, and it had been known to happen to far more experienced reapers than Michael. But the people at the top, whoever they were, wouldn't be impressed. He needed to make as many good impressions as he could, otherwise *he'd* be the one stuck patrolling those streets, left to wander aimlessly around the spot where he allowed his eternal soul to die the night he agreed to immortality.

He picked up his pace when he saw the entrance to the park. A nighttime rain and a light morning shower had left the grass sprinkled with tips of dew that clung to the bottom of his jeans as he walked, soaking them by the time he reached his destination.

He saw the body first. The man had been shot a dozen times, his wounds filled with drying blood that had painted the moist grass red.

He checked his timer again. On it were the vague details of every death he had to deal with in the coming days, every soul that was about to commit itself to the afterlife. The rest, the semantics of death, came through an intuition that coursed through Michael like a second soul. There were exceptions, of course—only on rare occasions could he anticipate murder, where the free will of others was involved, and that rarity faded to an impossibility when the hand of immortals, or nonhumans, played a part.

In thirty years, he had been to fewer than fifty murders, and he had only foreseen two of them: a drug deal turned violent and a drunken domestic that had resulted in a beaten wife stabbing her abusive husband. For the others, the timer flashed him a warning moments before the event, giving him a matter of minutes to get to the scene to transport the soul. Of course, it didn't matter if he was late. More than once he had taken his time to drag his weary self to the scene after being woken by the dreaded chirp of the timer.

He glanced around. He expected to see the soul hovering over his body, but there was no one there. If he had wandered off, he would return. Like a murderer to the scene of the crime, they always came back, but Michael couldn't afford to wait around. He had been around enough murder scenes to know that people had a way of ignoring him; it wasn't that he was invisible, they could see him and he was sure they had, but they seemed almost entranced by his presence. He could step back, blend in with a waiting crowd and chat amongst the people there, but if he was found standing over the body looking suspicious, he was ignored.

It made his job a lot easier, but he still didn't like to hang around. There was much emotion around death, and when it came to murder, that emotion was usually unbridled fear and morbid curiosity, two of the human emotions that made Michael feel uneasy.

He peered into the forest, lit from all sides by the breaking afternoon sun. In the undergrowth something writhed against a mass of fallen leaves. It popped up a curious head, sniffed the air, and then bolted up a tree.

The soul couldn't have gone far. It was resigned to a restricted radius. Michael didn't know the exact rules, another aspect he wasn't sure of, but he had enough experience to guess at the proximity. He searched that proximity three times, even peering under bushes and up trees, despite the fact that spirits couldn't interact with their environment enough to climb or hide. He still couldn't find him.

Taking one last glance at the body, Michael halted his search and prepared himself for the inevitable long day ahead.

There were a few people in the waiting room when he arrived, reapers preparing confused and sedate souls for the afterlife and whatever lay beyond those black doors. Michael recognized a few faces, colleagues he had seen many times throughout the years, most of whom he never spoke to. It was a depressing, dull business that created depressing and dull people. There were exceptions, of course, Seers being one, but they were even worse.

Michael nodded a smile in the general direction of the seated population, a generic greeting that covered all bases. He went up to the receptionist sitting alone behind her desk—a short, miserable woman who wore a permanent scowl on her wrinkled, aged face.

"Looking lovely today, Hilda," Michael said without feeling.

She had been writing, but stopped when Michael approached. She lay down the pen and sneered at him. "Cut the bullshit, Holland."

Michael thought about resting his elbows on the desk and leaning in, but he didn't like the idea of being so close to her. There was a chance her breath was poisonous—her eyes almost certainly were. He could feel them boring into him as she spoke.

"As charming as ever, I see," he said, sticking his hands into his pockets.

"There's only two feet of desk between us," she said with a glare. "How about you keep up with the smart talk and I show you just how charming I am."

Michael grimaced, "Fair enough."

He looked behind him, checking that no one was paying any attention. "I have a problem," he said softly, keeping his voice low.

Hilda shook her head disinterestedly, looking back at her desk. She was clearly eager to continue her work and for Michael to leave her alone. "Discuss it with the shrink. I'm not interested."

Michael shook his head. "Not that kind of problem."

The hint of a smile crept onto her bitter lips. "Is it the hemorrhoids again?"

"No." Michael raised his eyebrows, studied the hideous figure momentarily. "How did you . . . never mind." He shook the thought away, took another glance around to make sure he wasn't being watched. "Look, I've lost someone. A soul. I was due to pick him up fifteen minutes ago, maybe more. He wasn't there."

Hilda raised her eyebrows inquisitorially. "Are you sure it was the right one?"

"Positive."

"Because you've made that mistake before."

"This guy *was* dead; he *was* the guy. And can you stop mentioning that please?"

"We still talk about that, you know," she said fondly, recalling the time when Michael tried to escort a living soul through the doors of purgatory. "It helps us pass the time. In fact, you've come up quite a lot in our conversations; office talk would be so dull without you."

"Thank you, you're so kind," he replied bitterly. "Now, can you please fucking help me?"

Hilda reluctantly lowered her head to the glaring blue screen in front of her.

"Name?"

"Martin Atkinson."

Michael handed over his timer. Hilda's eyes scanned the small layout for a few moments. She placed it to one side. Her grubby fingers, sprouting hair around the knuckles and holding grime underneath the fingernails, pattered away on the keyboard.

"Murder?"

"Yes."

"Were you there on time?"

Michael shrugged his shoulders unconvincingly. "Sure."

Hilda paused, lowered her frantic fingers, and looked up at Michael. "Once more with conviction," she pushed.

"No, okay?" Michael conceded, knowing he was going to find himself the subject of many more banal office conversations in whatever Hilda classed as her office with whichever unlucky idiots she classed as colleagues. "I was a little late. *More* than a little actually. An hour or two, maybe."

"Did your appointment with the shrink run over?" Hilda quizzed slyly.

"None of your business."

"I guess there was a lot to talk about."

"Look, I didn't have my timer. I didn't see," he groaned. "Can you please just get on with it?"

He was growing increasingly agitated. A few of the guardians behind him had heard the conversation and were trying to suppress giggles. Their faces were alight with hilarity when he turned to look. Mistakes were rare, but they happened, and when they did they gave everyone something to laugh about, something to make fun of. Something to break the monotony.

He sagged on the spot, sighing heavily. He didn't particularly care what the others thought of him, but he also didn't need more reasons for them to think less of him.

"Okay," Hilda declared with a heavy exhalation, enjoying the barely audible giggles far more than Michael. "One soul, missing. Unknown method of death."

"He was shot. A few times," Michael explained calmly.

Hilda raised her eyes from the screen. "Are you a doctor?"

"No."

"Unknown method of death," she reiterated, her attention back on the computer.

"*He was shot.* I saw the fucking bullet holes."

Hilda handed him a printout from the computer. "Unknown method of death. Bureaucracy is a bitch, ain't it?" she asserted with a grin, clearly enjoying herself. "Now, hand that in. No credits for you this time. Any more failed souls and you'll have to report to the boss. We can't have the world filling up with ghosts, now can we?"

"Whatever," Michael said dejectedly.

"Have a pleasant day."

"Go fuck yourself."

The waiting room wasn't quite heaven or hell, and it wasn't limbo or purgatory. It seemed, as far as Michael could gather, to be a mixture of both. He bypassed the waiting room without a glance and ducked inside one of the many uniform doors.

The room beyond was dark and seemed to go on forever. Michael took two steps and stopped before a small desk, the top of which lit up at his approach. A buzzing machine, almost organic in its frenetic mechanical nature, levered out of the tabletop with an incessant whirring sound before halting with an expectant click. A small shutter flipped open across its surface like a Jack-in-the-Box preparing for a jovial surprise.

Michael placed his timer inside. The shutter closed, the machine whirred. A succession of electronic sounds followed, overlapping the background purr.

An automated voice leapt from the invisible walls, bouncing around the room like an echo with no origin.

51

"Failure to collect souls will result in a warning and deducted pay," the gender-neutral voice announced in monosyllables. "Repeated mistakes will result in demotion."

Michael sniggered under a snarl. "You can't demote me any fucking further," he mumbled under his breath.

"The deceased remains unaccounted for," the voice continued.

The whirring stopped, one final beep, like the sound of an arriving elevator, sounded and the shutters of the noisy box sprang open, revealing Michael's timer.

Michael took the device, dropped it back into his pocket, and exited the room before the automated voice could offer its preprogramed message of salutation.

5

Martin Atkinson's body festered where it lay, feeding the maggots and have-a-go scavengers on the edge of the park. The whereabouts of his soul was as big a mystery to Michael as the people who killed him. Human victims were clear, their hidden lives, their potential deaths, and their darkest secrets were usually revealed just as quickly as their eye color or their accent. But the undead, of which there seem to be so many, were as opaque as the night.

"Good morning!"

A smiling vicar passed Michael on the winding footpath, nodding pleasantly as his incense-scented aroma wafted by. Michael didn't return the greeting.

He didn't believe in God or religion when he was alive and still wasn't too sure in death. The vicar, a man who had never glimpsed the afterlife and had spent the majority of his adult years preaching about a martyr he would never meet and praying to a God he wasn't sure existed, probably knew more about the afterlife than Michael—a man who had been dead for thirty years.

Michael liked religious people; it took a certain type of dedication to devote your life to an ideal and it usually created a pleasant and peaceful character, but Michael knew Reverend Edwards, and there was nothing pleasant or peaceful about him. The only good thing about his existence was that it would be over within the decade.

He sat down on a bench and watched the vicar disappear out onto the street, waving to people he passed on the pavement, chatting jovially to the ones friendly enough to stop.

Michael turned away in disgust. The reverend had a history. He had more skeletons in his closet than Ted Bundy; the holiest man in town had, in his youth, gotten away with rape, robbery, and assault, and currently spent his days dreaming up plans to get into the pants of his eleven-year-old stepdaughter. A few years from now, he would find a way into her pants, right before she found the machete he hid under his bed and used it to hack him into Michael's hands. If Michael still had his job by then, that was—he couldn't be certain of anything in a world he barely understood.

The dark ones had an energy that was unmistakable and made them easier to read. They stood out likes flares in the darkness. Their deaths and their lives had a bigger impact on the lives and deaths of others, thus weaving an illuminating web.

Michael watched Jonathan Marks with something resembling awe and contempt. The youngster was a hundred feet away. He was on his way home but had been approached by three bullies heading the other way. The leader of the group was Dean Moore, a short, bulky kid with bright-white hair gelled into meticulous spikes on his head.

Dean pushed Jonathan to the ground, and the laughter of the three bullies filtered through to where Michael sat. Dean's was the loudest laugh of them all.

When the feeble victim was on the ground, he threw his hands in front of his face to protect himself before any punches or kicks had been thrown. This yielding posture was enough to incite more laughter, followed by a barrage of kicks and stamps.

Jonathan's dad was just as bad as Jonathan's school friends. The laughter, the taunting, the occasional beatings. His dad was also a poacher and a drunk. Jonathan planned to steal his dad's keys when he passed out drunk, use them to unlock his gun cabinet, steal his shotgun, and then slip it under his bed for the night. In the morning, he would hide the gun under his coat, walk the two miles to school, and then shoot every kid who had ever bullied or taunted him.

It was a simple plan and one that would give Michael a lot of work and a lot of credits, but there were many variables at play. The only thing that was certain was that Jonathan had the means and the motive.

Michael didn't want the business, he wasn't that desperate for credits, and he certainly wouldn't get enough of them to warrant bearing witness to such an event. The town was bad enough as it was; he couldn't bear living among the sorrow and the spectacle that it would become should Jonathan find the right moment to go through with the act.

He wasn't the only youngster whose life was on the line. Dean Moore, the guy driving the majority of the kicks into Jonathan's crumbled body, was also in Michael's sights, with a little more certainty over his future.

The brutish bully was a closet homosexual who had sexual fantasies about the people he beat up, including the aspiring sociopath presently on the receiving end of his frustrations. Like a six-year-old boy who taunts and mocks a girl he fancies at school, Dean used violence to express feelings he could never relate vocally.

He repeatedly engaged in mutual masturbation with another boy in his class, a boy who walked the thin line between *the bullied* and *the bully* and didn't want to slip, didn't want to become what his classmate Jonathan had become. There was a strong chance Dean would try to further his fantasies with this boy, and if he did, his sexual inclinations would be exposed, leading him to take his own life with the help of a bottle of his father's whiskey and a box of paracetamol. On the plus side, should his future converge with the twisted one of Jonathan Marks, then liver failure would prevent him from the romantic irony of being murdered by the hand of his tormented sweetheart. If he did die before Jonathan went on a rampage, then that could prove to be a catalyst that stopped such a rampage from happening in the first place. The paths had been laid out, the connections made, but free will, luck, and factors Michael couldn't even begin to comprehend meant it wasn't always easy to predict the life and death of his subjects.

A middle-aged couple, their faces alight with the peppy glee of contentment, trudged past. They walked parallel to each other, a foot of pavement separating them. They tried to look nonchalant, uninterested in each other, but they were clearly paying more attention to each other than the dogs they walked or the park they walked in. They were telling the world that, yes, they may know each other, but they weren't exactly best of friends and certainly weren't indulging in a sadomasochistic affair. An affair that would bring the cherry-faced woman close to Michael's door when she forgot the safe word and her lover continued to strangle her.

Michael eyed them up as they passed, a complimentary smile dropped his way by both, but he doubted they even noticed him. There were few variables at play there, and Michael was almost certain of the outcome and the resulting impact it would have on their respective families.

He sighed heavily and stood to leave, cutting through the center of the park, keen to avoid the outskirts where Martin Atkinson's body was probably moments away from being discovered.

He shot a glance at the bullies and their victim as he moved to within ten feet of them. None of them paid any attention to him. Dean was still calling the shots as he stood over his anguished victim.

"Now, let's jump on top of him!"

"Wait, why?"

"We'll wrestle him! Come on, that'll show him!"

Michael barely suppressed a smile as he moved past with quickening steps.

"*Dude*, that's not wrestling."

6

Daytime television—where the banal, the pointless, and the idiotic combine to create a torrid and unmemorable concoction of watered-down humanity that isn't fit to show to those who choose their TV time.

Angela Washington loved it. She loved the mindlessness of it all. The topics unfit for human consumption that became fantastical during the day when all the kids were at school and she could stand and do the ironing while looking down, in her own modest and introverted way, on those worse off and less intelligent than her. It made her smile, even when she had nothing to do but housework, and that was the most important thing.

When the doorbell sounded, she was still smiling. She put down the iron, still fizzing a vapored dragon breath into the already humid living room; untied her apron, tainted with trails of flour and eggs from cakes currently rising in the oven; checked her appearance in the mirror above the fireplace, flicking a saturated stray hair from her forehead; and went to answer the door, humming happily to herself.

She wasn't expecting anyone but had a few friends and neighbors who liked to drop by unannounced.

Through the peephole, she could see two figures standing at the door, their height and size seemingly uniformed. She sighed, anticipating salesmen or Jehovah's witnesses. She opened the door regardless, deciding it was too late to rudely turn her back, having exposed her silhouette through the smeared glass in the door panel.

The men at the door were wearing black suits, black ties, black shirts, and black tinted sunglasses. Their arms were folded behind their backs in a formal manner.

"May I help you, gentlemen?" She couldn't see any briefcases, bags, or leaflets, but also couldn't see their hands. Nor could she gather their intentions from their blank stares.

"Angela Washington?" One asked.

"Yes," Angela answered politely.

The two men exchanged a blank stare and then looked back at Angela. Her left hand still lightly grasped the door frame, her right toyed with the back of her tight ponytail.

"May we come inside?" Two wondered.

Angela swapped a stare between the two men. "Why?" she inquired.

"We have a few things we need to discuss," he replied.

Angela ducked her head between them and threw a gentle wave to her neighbor across the street, passing by with his small Jack Russell tugging maniacally on the lead two feet in front of him. He threw a wave back and hollered a friendly greeting.

The two men watched the neighbor closely, only turning back to Angela when he had escorted the dog down the driveway and was trying to usher him into the house.

"What are you trying to sell?" Angela asked courteously.

They exchanged a look again. The man on the right, the first to speak, turned around to make sure the neighbor had vanished inside with his ferrety canine.

He turned back. "Salvation," he said darkly.

The curiosity on Angela's face trembled, leaving barely a smile left to supplement her Stepford charm.

They stepped forward as one, pushing Angela back and barging roughly into the house. They slammed the door shut behind them and took up parallel positions in front of it.

Angela stumbled backward across the hallway, almost losing her balance. She looked concerned. Her eyes were alive with terror.

"What do you want?" she begged. The fear was evident in her trembling voice; the smile had been wiped clean off her face.

"Your soul."

They both produced pistols and whipped them in front of her, aiming the menacing barrels at her tearful face.

She backed up until her ankles were restrained by the bottom step of a narrow staircase. "I don't understand," she said with lips quivering. She looked from gun to gun, barrel to barrel, dead face to dead face, horrified at what she saw.

Both men hesitated a moment. They looked ready to pull the triggers but they paused, keeping the guns aimed at the shaking homemaker.

"Angela Washington?" One asked. "Aged forty-five. Housewife. Divorced. Three kids?"

"Yes! Yes!" Angela cried, throwing her hands into the air in maddening desperation. "What do you want? Please, what do you want from me?"

"I guess we were expecting a little more . . . " One replied, trailing off.

Angela was hysterical. "A little more?" she asked, something other than hysteria and fear crept into her voice and onto her face. Her trembling body became rigid; her frightened face took on a different emotion.

The two men looked at each other.

"Hair?" one of them asked.

The other nodded in agreement.

"I don't know what you're talking about!" Angela screamed.

Again the intruders exchanged stares. This time they lowered their weapons and for a moment their concentration waned into curiosity.

"You think we've made a mistake?" One wondered softly.

Before Two could answer the question posed by his doppelgänger, Angela launched herself at them both. Her face had been transformed in its entirety, the smiling mother of three now a snarling animalistic killer bent on blood.

Her neatly arranged sparkling white teeth were hideously large, protruding through her snarling lips like the serrated edge on an unsheathed knife. Vicious claws, capable of opening a man like a tin can, dominated her delicate hands, hands that merely moments ago were baking cakes and ironing clothes.

She tackled one of the intruders, wrestling him violently to the floor, his head and back slamming against the carpeted foundation. His lungs heaved out every inch of air under Angela's powerful body, which transformed by the second.

With her jaw still protruding from her neck as if being inflated from behind, she tried to take a bite out of his throat, but succeeded only in tearing the fabric from his suit as he twisted away. He grasped her by the shoulders and tightened his grip on her flesh, but he could feel it growing in his palm, getting stronger and stronger with each passing moment.

His hands slipped from her flesh, his body yielded against her sudden strength. She growled in excitement, a snarling hungry glimmer in her eyes which still appeared human, but glowed with a monstrous radiance. She opened her mouth, eyed his throat, and dove in for the kill.

A hissing sound preceded a barely audible thump and the beast jolted to a stop, stuck atop the fallen intruder like a rigid cowboy on a beaten horse. A torrent of blood gushed forth from an exit wound in the torso of the she-beast, spraying over the spectacled face of the man in the black suit—his sunglasses shielding the viscous crimson from his eyes.

The thing that had been Angela Washington jerked violently on the straddled man. It coughed a splutter of blood from its fearsome jaw, wheezed through damaged lungs, shuddered as its lifeforce spat out of every muscle, and then slumped forward, eclipsing the man beneath.

There was a struggle, then Two managed to pull himself free, tossing the beast aside like a hefty, sluggish rag doll. His colleague stood above the crumpled, muscular figure with his gun still raised.

"That was close," Two said, scooping globs of blood from his face and flicking them onto the floor. The blood left a sickly sheen on his hand, which he wiped onto the seat of his trousers with a grimace.

"Very," One agreed. He lowered the gun that had blown a hole straight through the beast's chest.

"Messy as well," Two added, removing his sunglasses and using his sleeve to clear the sickly smears from the lenses.

"I had no other choice."

"You could have pushed her off first."

One shrugged. "Perhaps," he said unconvincingly. "I'm sorry."

"Apology accepted."

"Send me the dry cleaning bill."

"Will do."

They stepped back and peered at the corpse. It was still recognizable as human, but only just. The transformation had been quick but it hadn't finished, so parts of Angela remained. Her stomach, partially clad with fragments of a pink blouse that her growing torso had all but destroyed, wasn't hers, but nor was it that of a beast. Her ears, hair, and forehead had retained the style of the attractive single parent.

The body twitched, still holding onto the last remnants of life. Her killers didn't flinch.

"How long does it take for these things to fully transform do you think?" One asked as he surveyed the mismatch of human and beast.

Two shrugged unsurely. "We were warned they could turn quickly but beyond that . . . " he trailed off.

"You think we could bring down a fully formed one?"

"With those?" Two said, nodding to the gun in One's hand. "Sure. Silver bullets seem to be working so far."

"And if we run out?"

"Wooden stake?"

"Isn't that vampires?"

Two shrugged his shoulders. "I'm sure we'd figure something out."

"We could try normal bullets, see how they react," One proposed.

"To what end?"

"I guess I just want to know."

"And if they don't work and keep coming? How are we going to stop them before they rip us apart?"

One thought about this for a moment and then shrugged. "Just a thought."

Two removed a device from his chest pocket. He wiped away a drop of blood that had worked its way onto the screen.

The beast that was Angela Washington writhed, groaning in agony. Her body tried to transform and let go at the same time.

"Come on," Two said. "We better finish up."

7

Michael gave a solemn shake of his head as he looked down at the corpse. First Martin Atkinson and now Angela Washington. Two bodies; no souls.

The woman before him looked no older than forty-five. She had a kind face and gentle features that reminded Michael of his mother. A mother who had cried relentlessly over the death of her son, not knowing that he continued to exist, in one form or another, just a few miles away.

He bent down and checked the frail corpse. She didn't look like she could hurt a fly, yet she looked like she had been fighting before her demise. She had been executed. Shot once through the chest and then once through the forehead.

He checked his timer.

"Right on time," he told himself. "Where the fuck are you?"

He had already checked the house and the garden. Ghosts rarely left their bodies so soon after death, but he checked anyway—she was nowhere to be seen.

In the Dead Seamstress, a dark and cozy shack-like pub on the edge of town—hidden underneath a former newsagent's and accessed through a backstreet and an ominous staircase—Michael attracted immediate attention.

Rusty chimes above the door jangled an eclectic tune when Michael entered. Everyone inside peered up from their drinks and conversations. They all looked at him, gave him a quick once-over, and then resumed their activities.

The bar was staffed solely by an aggressive little man who had to stand on a stool to see over the top. He glared at Michael as he approached, his unibrow arched toward the top of his swollen nose.

Michael greeted the bartender. Michael had noticed the man constantly looked like he was moments away from growling or humping his leg.

"Mickey," he replied with a simple nod.

"What's all this about?" Michael asked, indicating his scrutinized arrival.

Scrub grunted to clear a glob of thick phlegm from his throat before swallowing the offending expectorant.

"Everyone's a bit on edge."

Michael waited for an explanation, but didn't want to push for one when it didn't come. "Fair enough," he said. "Give me a pint, would you?"

Scrub hopped off the stool and scuppered over to pull a pint glass from a dusty rack where a milieu of insects and dust mites gathered.

"You ever thought of getting the floor raised?"

Scrub turned and glared at Michael, his tiny face peering up at him like a demonic imp.

"What you tryin' to say?" he said aggressively.

Michael held up his hands. "Never mind."

He saw Chip sitting in the corner of the room, huddled forlornly over a pint of dark ale. Naff, their mutual friend, was sitting next to him, looking a little happier and prouder—his neck straight, arms folded across his lap, a tumbler of whiskey on the table in front of him.

"So, what's all the commotion about?" Michael said, turning back to Scrub and trying again.

To Michael's surprise the little man was staring back at him, waiting expectantly for their eyes to meet like a mythical murderer in a horror film. Michael nearly jumped out of his skin when he turned to see that grim face peering back.

"We have mortals in," Scrub said grimly.

The little bartender watched the final drops of beer slip into the top of a brimming pint glass. He took it away from the pump and plonked it down on the bar, not budging from his stool the entire time.

"Again?" Michael said, taking a sip from the foamy top.

"Something here attracts them."

"I can't imagine what."

"Third time this week," Scrub continued, undeterred. "Walking in here like they have the fucking right. This place isn't for *them*, it's for *us*. This is *our* haven; they have no right to—"

"You feel strongly about this, huh?"

"Mortals piss me off," Scrub explained succinctly.

"Is that because you never got the chance to be one?"

"Possibly. Not like I would want to be one anyway, filthy fucking—"

"I'm sure it will be fine," Michael interjected, keen to stop the onslaught. "Pour me a whiskey as well, would you?"

Scrub groaned bitterly and relented, firing a fierce glare in the direction of the mortals before grabbing a bottle of whisky and a dusty tumbler.

Michael had seen the intruders on entering. They stood out, cleaner, happier, friendlier than the locals. But they were currently being stared into submission by a roomful of angry undead men and women. It wouldn't take long before they finished their drinks and left. It would be forgotten about in a few weeks.

The last time mortals had found the pub hadn't been as easy to forget. They were so outraged by the state of the floor, the glasses, and the clientele that they immediately tried to vent their rage on TripAdvisor. As soon as they left the pub to find a Wi-Fi signal and voice their displeasure to the world, they forgot where they had been and what they had been doing.

Michael took his drinks and sauntered over to his friends.

"Chip. Naff." He acknowledged the pair as he sat. Chip sluggishly lifted himself up from the table, giving Michael a place to rest his drinks. "How's things?"

Chip groaned.

"Same old, same old," Naff said. "Heard you had a few issues today."

"Already?" Michael rolled his eyes. "Word travels fast."

"I work in the records department, mate. It's our job to keep account of, well, *your* job."

Michael smiled meekly. He drank the whiskey, enjoying the burn as it traced a heated path to his stomach. He slammed the glass down, instantly feeling better under the visceral glow of the alcohol.

"What about the grumpy fucking tooth fairy here?" Michael nodded to Chip, who was holding his head in his hands, weighed down by his own boredom. "Surely you can't keep track of what he's doing and still let him continue doing it."

Chip livened up at that. He lifted his head and gave Michael *the eye*. "Hey!" he snapped.

Michael stared straight back at him. "You drink and smoke all day."

Chip's eyes rose to the ceiling in thought. He nodded, scrunched up his mouth. "True," he conceded.

"We cut him some slack," Naff offered. "Or rather, *I do*," he corrected. He received a thankful, but half-assed glance from Chip before the tooth fairy resumed his slumped posture. "And the tooth game is different," Naff continued, shaking off the uncharacteristic gratitude. "What he doesn't collect will only be picked up by someone else. If you miss a soul, no one is there to claim it."

"I didn't miss it," Michael said defensively. "It wasn't there to collect."

"Did you look properly?"

"It's not a fucking coin down the back of the sofa, for fuck's sake," Michael snapped.

Naff held up a hand. "Chill," he said calmly, "I'm just saying."

Michael calmed down in the heat of an impending argument. "Fucking hell," he said softly into his pint, hunching his head over the rim of the glass. "It's been a shitty day," he grumbled soberly. "I lost another one before."

"Another *soul*?"

Michael nodded solemnly. "Angela Washington," he clarified. "Shot just like the other guy. I showed up a few minutes after and there's no sign of her." He took a long, slow drink, delaying the story of his own misery. "If I knew it was going to happen, I could have been there, I could have seen it. I would know what happened to her, where she went."

"It's never that cut-and-dry. Even if you had foreseen it, it's not always that clear and definite. You can't spend your life following around the potential dead on the off chance that this is their time."

"But sometimes it *is* clear, sometimes there is only one outcome: all roads lead to me. And even when it isn't so clear," he gave a simple shrug, "I like to see what happens. I like to keep track, to know the outcomes, which possibility the universe, fate or whatever, chose. And if someone's going to rob me of a death, I like to know who, so I can enjoy the moment more when it's *their* time to die."

"Bit harsh."

Michael groaned and gave an apologetic nod. "I know. I don't mean it, I don't really care, truth be told. If someone finds the path and the possibility that doesn't lead them into my hands then great, good for them. I'm just being an unnecessary bastard. It's been a long day."

"Angela Washington," Naff said with a thoughtful frown. "That name rings a bell. She's a werewolf, right?"

Michael shrugged.

"I remember reading her file. I'm sure she is."

Michael shrugged and took another long drink. "What're you talking about?" he wondered.

"What are the odds?" Naff quizzed. "The first guy was a werewolf. I was on duty at the time, I checked his file. Two people show up dead on the same day, both shot and both are missing their souls. This can't be a coincidence."

"I don't care," Michael said apathetically. "Whatever it is could cost me my job." He checked his watch; his eyes sank at the sight. "I should have reported in after that," he explained. "I couldn't bear to face them. The ridicule. Or worse."

Naff was looking increasingly animated. Even Chip had started to pay attention.

"But don't you find it weird?" Naff pushed.

Michael stood. "No," he said simply. "Let it be. I'm going for a piss."

Naff wrinkled his nose. "I prefer to hold it in until I get home," he said, reluctantly changing the subject. "It's hell in there, and trust me, I've been to hell. Less fire, more piss, but I can take them in equal measures."

"Too many shakes," Chip said suddenly.

"What?" Michael asked.

"They say shake it once or twice that's okay, shake it three times and you're playing with yourself." Chip recited some of his encyclopedic knowledge of the obscure, pointless, and disgusting. "Judging by the floors, we have a lot of excessive masturbators in here."

Michael paused with an open mouth, ready for a reply, but shrugged it off for sanity's sake.

"I don't understand that phrase," Naff said as Michael worked his way around them with increasing speed, trying to get away from the conversation.

"What's not to understand?" Chip wondered, seemingly perking up now that the topic had to do with urine and masturbation. "One shake: fine. Two shakes: fine. Three shakes: not fine."

"But what constitutes a shake? Is it one movement up and down, thus spraying yourself? Or is it left and right, spraying the floor and the poor idiot standing next to you?"

"You're putting too much thought into this."

"Well, what do *you* do?" Naff wondered, taking a sip of his drink.

"I wipe my cock on the hand towel."

Naff nearly choked on his drink. Michael left the table, and his friends, with a smile on his face.

8

Michael awoke with a hangover. The perils of drowning his sorrows had caught up with him. His head ached. His stomach groaned. His mouth tasted like he had spent the night gargling toilet water.

His mind ran through the night's events, or at least as much of it as he could remember. He remembered drinking glass after glass of whiskey in the Dead Seamstress. He remembered stumbling out into the street in the early hours.

He rolled over, scrunching up his face when the movement threw a dagger to the back of his brain. He sensed someone above his bed, saw their large form silhouetted against the amber glow from the closed curtain on the other side of the room. He slowly peeled his sticky eyes apart, and at first he only saw a blur, but then his eyes adjusted.

"Jesus Christ!" he spat, rocketing upright.

His head exploded at the movement, his blood pressure plummeted. Sitting by the side of his bed, awkwardly positioned on a chair barely big enough for Chip, was Michael's boss.

"Not quite," the large figure replied calmly.

"Azrael?" Michael spat in astonishment, wondering if he was still drunk and seeing things.

"Indeed."

"Shit."

"Indeed."

Michael dropped his head tiredly into his hands. He furiously rubbed his eyes with his palms and fingers and used the base of his hand to knead some life into his skull.

He said, "What are you doing—" but then stopped himself. "Can you give me a moment to get dressed?"

"As you wish."

Azrael, the Angel of Death, calmly walked to the kitchen, leaving Michael to rouse himself in the bedroom. His huge body bounded gracefully through the grimy flat, almost floating with an ethereal decorum.

He paused by the fridge and knelt down to open it; his eight-foot frame towered over the large appliance. He looked through the contents with a murmur of curiosity. He picked up a tub of what appeared to be coleslaw, sniffed it with a startled grunt, and then shoved it back on the top shelf, unimpressed.

When he closed the fridge door, he glimpsed Chip standing on the other side, entering the kitchen with his grubby hands scrubbing sleep out of his bleary eyes.

Chip didn't notice the Angel of Death poking around in his fridge; he brushed straight past him and drifted toward the couch in the living room as the demon watched him, perplexed and amused.

Chip settled into the couch with his eyes still half-closed. He picked his nose and wiped the offending contents onto the arm of the sofa. He jiggled his grubby fingers inside his ears. He sniffed his armpits, and the smell woke him like a tub of smelling salts, his head jolting back and his eyes springing open. Only then did he see Azrael watching him on the other side of the room.

He dived onto the floor as if his legs had lost their rigidity and his body had spasmed.

"Good morning," Azrael boomed.

Chip dragged himself back onto the couch, his feet kicking cartoonishly on the floor as he hauled himself up. He peered over the arm of the couch at Azrael, ducking down slightly as he prepared to hide or run.

"Is it?" he asked, agitatedly. "I mean, of course it is! Good morning to you, sir." He slapped on his best smile, but simply looked constipated. "Can I get you something? A drink perhaps? Coffee?"

He made a move to stand but seemed to have decided his legs wouldn't hold him and sat back down.

"I'm afraid it goes right through me," Azrael countered.

Chip tilted his head from side to side, bouncing it on his neck like an ornamental dancer. "That's the point of a morning coffee, isn't it?" he inquired. "Helps clean the pipes."

Azrael shook his head. "I mean literally." He opened his robe, exposing his skeletal frame. He closed it again before Chip had time to thoroughly examine the contents.

"Holy shit," Chip spat, more impressed than scared. "Well . . . " he said slowly, staring distantly at Azrael's robe, "how about some toast?"

Azrael frowned and waited for Chip's gaze to meet his. When it did, it suddenly flashed a smile. "You're an odd little fellow, aren't you?"

"You're not the first person to notice."

The Angel of Death nodded curiously. "You work at the tooth factory right?"

"Freelance collector, kinda." Chip shrugged. "How did you know?"

"There's a bag of teeth in the fridge."

Chip hopped to his feet. "I was wondering where I'd put them," he declared, opening the fridge and removing the teeth, leaving another broad and simple smile for the Angel of Death as he passed.

"Are you here for me, by any chance?" he wondered. He was halfway back to the couch, obviously ready to run to the front door if the answer was affirmative.

Azrael simply shook his head, relieved that he wasn't.

"Oh, thank God," Chip sunk into himself with relief. "Well, nature calls. Do excuse me." He headed out into the hallway, talking as he went, "Apparently I don't need coffee this morning."

Michael passed his friend in the hallway and strode tentatively into the room, his hands clasped behind his back, his thumbs twirling nervously. He crossed to the living room and gestured for Azrael to take a seat. The Angel of Death took one glance at the sofa and shook his head.

"I'll stand, thank you."

Michael nodded calmly and rested against the back of the sofa, half seated, his arms folded across his chest. "So, to what do I owe the pleasure?" he asked.

"This is not a visit of pleasure," Azrael replied soberly.

Michael sunk his head into his chest and splayed his feet out further in front of him, sinking into the cushions on the back of the sofa. "Of course not," he said sullenly. "You're sacking me, aren't you?" he spoke into his chest. "I always wondered how they'd do it. Going from immortality to dust isn't easy; you wouldn't want to give the job of revealing that to just anyone. I guess sending down the head man, so to speak, makes things a lot easier for everyone involved."

He sighed heavily, pushed himself off the sofa, and looked Azrael in the eyes. "You know what? I don't care. This immortality business has been nothing but a confusing mess. I'm sick of people not answering my questions. I'm sick of still not knowing if there is a God, and I'm sick of being told *'you'll learn,'* because I won't fucking learn. If I ask a question, I want it answered, otherwise what would be the point of asking? I don't want to be told I'll figure it out for myself in a few decades or centuries, 'cause by then I won't give a toss about the fucking answer, will I?"

Azrael didn't flinch through Michael's rant. He remained standing, his eyes fixed on him.

"So how does this work?" Michael wondered, prepared to face death for the second time. "Will it hurt? Will I *go* anywhere?"

Azrael waited until a silence veiled the emotive atmosphere. "I'm not here to kill you," he said eventually. "I'm here to help you."

Michael tilted his head to one side like a perplexed dog. "I'm not losing my job?"

"No."

"Oh," he said, feeling a sudden rush of embarrassment and regret. "Then everything I just said . . . "

"Forgotten."

"Thank you," Michael said, genuinely pleased.

Azrael nodded sternly.

Still feeling embarrassed, Michael leaned on the counter next to his boss, his presence dwarfed.

71

"This about the missing souls?" he wondered.

"Yes." Azrael eased Michael's discomfort by shifting from his stationary position and walking across the room, taking an interest in studying his surroundings. "As you may know, both of your failed collections were werewolves. And although the souls were not collected by you, they *were* collected."

Michael perked up. "Someone else on my patch?" he asked, wondering if help had been drafted to scrape the shit off the shovel in Brittleside.

"No one sent by us."

"Oh."

"We believe your lost souls, those of Angela Washington and Martin Atkinson, are being used for," he paused, stopping next to a small ornament of a tiny, cutesy fairy that Chip had bought and then dressed with the clothes from a G.I. Joe action figure: blue overalls and an AK-47. "*Problematic* experiments," he concluded.

"Problematic experiments?" Michael folded his arms over his chest and allowed his body to slink against the counter behind him. "Is this another one of those things you're going to answer in a ridiculously vague way and then say nothing more about?"

Azrael grinned. It was an unusual sight, like seeing a hated teacher or a revered politician cry. "The experiments are hazardous to our business and they have the potential to shift a great deal of power into the wrong hands."

Michael nodded knowingly. "That's a yes then. How do I fit into this exactly?"

Azrael picked up what he thought was a small, fluffy toy ball. He tossed it idly from hand to hand while he looked at Michael, who didn't want to tell him that the ball was actually a collection of Chip's naval fluff that the fairy had persistently refused to discard.

"They started in your area." He seemed to catch a whiff of something unpleasant. He lifted the ball to his nose and recoiled when he caught the full scent. Michael barely suppressed a smile as his boss returned the offending ball to the bookcase.

"We believe they will continue here. We need you to find out exactly what is going on."

Michael shook his head in disbelief. "You're joking, right? I don't even understand my own job. I barely understood what you just told me, what do I have to—"

"This is your patch," Azrael interjected, a touch of menace flavoring his tone. "I have been watching you. I believe you are capable."

Michael shrugged and turned away, dejected. "So, can you fill me in a little more?"

"In time you will learn," Azrael mocked with a broad smile.

Michael nodded exaggeratedly. "Of course I will."

He watched his boss depart the room. He left through the front door, bypassing a merry Chip, who was cleaning his sinuses with a series of grunts and snorts.

"Un-be-fucking-lievable," Michael muttered in his absence.

A foreboding figure sat alone in a quiet and well-lit office.

He drummed his thick fingers, wrinkled and worn, on the solid surface of his desk, pounding a gentle, dull rhythm into the room.

He sighed and leaned back in his chair, which squeaked and strained against his heavyset frame. He spun gently, watching the office whirl by before his eyes as the chair rotated on its revolving axis.

The office was impressive to most—a tall bookcase of the finest dark oak, lined with first editions of priceless books, never read and barely touched; walls adorned with expensive paintings, a self-commissioned portrait, doctorates and degrees; an assortment of fine whiskeys, brandies, and wine, encased in a cabinet alluringly visible through a thick sheet of glass.

He lowered his head when the chair settled. His eyes fixed on the far wall of the office where a long window took center stage.

The upper sections of the room beyond were visible. The sparkle of numerous lights, the only indication of any activity in the expansive room, rose into view of the window.

The phone on his desk bleeped. He stared absently at it as a green light flashed and a familiar voice introduced two familiar people. Moments later, One and Two walked into the room, side by side as usual. He remained seated, waiting for them to come to him.

"Hello, boys," he greeted. "How's things?"

"Good."

"Fruitful."

The pair paused in front of the desk, looking down at him expectantly. A chair stood behind and between them, but neither of them took it.

"You have something for me?" the seated man asked expectantly.

One pulled out a large cylinder. A spiral of activity buzzed inside the crystallized glass like a horde of raving fireflies. He had been walking around laxly with the glass in his pocket, but after removing it, he took great care with it, placing it carefully on the desk.

"The first two on the list," he proclaimed proudly.

The seated man picked up the vial with equal caution. He lifted it in front of his right eye, spying the glowing mystery inside like an adventurer beaming at a new discovery through the lens of a telescope.

"Perfect," he declared with a touch of enchantment as he placed the vial gently back on the desk. "Any problems?"

"No, sir."

"None at all."

"Police?" he quizzed.

"No, sir."

The seated man nodded slowly, impressed but not willing to show it. "What about the reaper?" he pondered.

"Clueless, sir," One offered.

"One of the worst in the country, sir. A good choice," Two added.

The seated man looked content. His eyes flicked back to the vial, drawn in by the radiant effervescence, like a moth to a flame.

One and Two exchanged an awkward and unseen glance followed by a nod.

"We were wondering, sir," One asked, drawing his attention away from the vial.

"Yes?"

There was an uncharacteristic pause, brief but noticeable. "Why werewolves?" he asked.

He replied with a heavy exhalation. He stood and waddled around to the other side of the desk, pulling the attentions of the two men with him as they watched every step.

"The werewolf mutation is like no other," he lectured slowly. "It literally is the stuff of legend, only it isn't passed on by mere bite or scratch. The rituals, the *crossing over* if you like, is—well." He waved a dismissive hand into the air. "It's complicated. Cloak-and-dagger nonsense. The point is, anyone can be killed by a werewolf, but only the chosen can be turned."

"Like vampires?"

He snapped a jubilant finger at the questioner. "Exactly! Only more powerful and with fewer weaknesses. They possess amazing strength and resilience. They can adapt to any climate. They can hide their true selves at will, assimilate perfectly into normal society, and, unlike vampires, they are not harmed by daylight." He bounded around on legs that had previously looked wary, his enthusiasm on an adrenaline rush as he lectured the two men with the gusto of a professor.

"They have a pack mentality," he said importantly. "A willingness to fight for their own kind, to live *with* and to die *for* their brothers and sisters, blood or not. They are the perfect weapon. If one could harness their power and find a way to manipulate it, then they could create the strongest army the world has ever seen. Can you imagine that?" he cried.

The two men looked back blankly. If they *could* imagine it, it clearly didn't excite them as much as it did him.

"Wouldn't it be easier to study the actual werewolves, sir?" One asked. "Rather than their souls?"

The older man tilted his head this way and that. "Perhaps," he conceded. "But we've tried that already and the tests are proving to be . . . ," he rolled his tongue around the word. "*Difficult*. Let's just say it isn't easy to manipulate a three-hundred pound beast. They can be quite aggressive."

"I can imagine."

"So, instead we try to own them," he pushed on. "We give the souls a vessel that we control, a mind and a body that we have already manipulated. One that will do as we say no matter how painful it may be."

He strode over to the window on the far side of his office. The two men followed behind, standing on either side of him as all three looked down onto the expanse fifty feet below the office.

Two men dressed in white coats pottered about a room the size of a football field, slaloming through an assortment of computers, terminals, and large vats that seemed to glisten and throb under the activity of a hundred wires. Inside the machines, naked forms of human structure lolled about in gelatinous fluid like mannequins, lifeless and soulless.

The old man beamed as he surveyed his creations. "This is where the next generation of soldier will be built," he informed the suited twins. "Empty-headed idiots, with no purpose other than to kill and obey, will be bred in those vats."

One said, "This place looks familiar."

The older man nodded knowingly. "This, gentlemen, is where you were born."

"Ah," One acknowledged without a hint of irony.

The creator took a step back, admiring the spectacle of his creations as they studied their birthplace. "And, with your continued help, many more powerful weapons can be created. Once we build a strong force, we, or whoever chooses, can use that force to reproduce, to create even stronger soldiers—to breed an unstoppable force. There will be no limits to its, and to our, potential."

He returned to his desk, to the alluring vial glowing on its polished surface.

"Whoever chooses?" One queried.

He laughed haughtily. "I'm not an idiot," he declared with a wry smile. "I'll leave the conquering to someone else. I'll be looking for the highest bidder."

On his haunches, scrunching through darkened woods with Naff and Chip scuffling by his side, Michael checked his timer and sighed: "We're a little late."

Naff groaned. "It's hard to be punctual when you can't see where you're fucking going," he moaned.

Chip stumbled over something. He flung a barrage of whispered obscenities toward the ground and then scurried to catch up with his friends.

"Why would they come out here anyway?" the tooth fairy wanted to know.

"Wolves live in the woods," Naff said matter-of-factly.

"This is a *werewolf*," Chip argued, turning to face Naff, whose form was grayed in the darkness. "*Technically* human. Humans don't live in the woods."

"Hermits do," Naff countered.

Chip tutted in mock revilement. "So, let me get this straight, we're looking for a deadly werewolf hermit?"

"Well—"

"Shut up," Michael interrupted impatiently. "I can hear something."

The group paused as one, pricking their ears to the night.

"You're going mad, mate," Chip said after a moment's silence.

Just as Chip raised a sneer and closed his mouth, a middle-aged man, as skinny as a pole and as naked as the day he was born, ran a horizontal path on the pass ahead of them. An ethereal glow lit him in the darkness and followed him like a contrail.

"Holy shit," Naff spat.

Michael stood, slapping his hands together. "That's him."

Chip also straightened, staring perplexedly at the quickly disappearing trail. "Is there a reason he's naked?"

"He probably turned before he died," Naff explained.

Chip nodded slowly. "I hope so. Otherwise this could get weird."

They ambled forward, toward the trail, which had already dispersed into the breeze. The naked man appeared to their left, lit up like a Christmas tree within the midnight foliage.

He darted up to them, gliding smoothly over the unseen obstacles. "You gotta help me," he begged, his eyes wide. "There are some men," he said, gesturing behind Michael, into the darkness. "They killed me. They're trying to kill me again."

"Makes sense," Chip said softly.

Michael turned around and searched the darkness. Through the blackness, he could see the glimmer of torchlights bobbing up and down like buoys in a tarred ocean.

"I've gotta get out of here," the naked man said quickly, his wide eyes darting around. "They're fully armed."

"Guns can't harm you now, mate," Chip announced.

"They have other things," the naked man said with a manic wave of his hands, trying to indicate something he couldn't comprehend. "They tried something after I died. A probe."

Chip took all of this in. "They're probing and killing people?" He turned to Michael and grabbed his cuff. "I'm with the naked guy, let's get out of here."

Michael shook off the fearful tooth fairy, his eyes visibly sneering at him under the spiritual glow. "We're undead," he reminded his friend. "They can't hurt us."

"What about the missing souls?" Naff intervened, suddenly looking concerned. "If they can hurt them, they can hurt us."

"Trust me, I'm alive enough to feel someone probing me," Chip joined in.

Ahead, the two torches violently flickered and then straightened out. Two loud pops scratched the air and then exploded as a quick succession of bullets rocketed past the group.

A sickening thump tore a chunk of bark from a nearby tree and spat a cluster of sawdust at them. Chip twitched as a bullet whizzed past his ear with a high-pitched scream. An army of anxious rodents beat a path of retreat from their hideaways on the forest floor.

"Let's go," Michael said, ducking instinctively at the sound of trouble. He turned on his heels and scarpered, his two friends and the naked man in tow.

In a clearing, the two men in black, their clothes and demeanors at one with their surroundings, lowered their guns and exchanged glances.

"Did we miss?"

"I definitely shot the little hairy one."

"Undead?"

"Maybe."

"Reapers?"

"Maybe."

"Should we report back?"

"No."

"Chase?"

"They're gone now. We'll deal with them later."

Chip casually looked around, his hands stuffed lazily into his pockets, a scowl on his face. "So, this is limbo," he said, unimpressed.

The waiting room was empty but for two teenagers who clung tightly and lovingly to a large, bemused man who looked half embarrassed and half annoyed.

Hilda had watched the group enter, her perpetual scowl morphing into something even less endearing when Michael strode up to her and dropped his palms on her desk.

She looked beyond Michael, over his dipped shoulder, and spoke before he had the chance.

"Who's the naked guy?" she wanted to know.

Michael twisted his head around. The man in the forest, who appeared as James Waddington on the timer, was scanning his surroundings with the awestruck intrigue of a child on his first holiday.

Michael turned back to Hilda. "A job," he said simply.

Hilda nodded slowly, a slyness creeping onto her grotesque face. "So, you finally caught one," she mocked. "Well done." She peered back over his shoulder. James was now striding around the waiting room. His manhood bobbed about unashamedly with every wide stride.

"Why's he naked?"

"I didn't ask," Michael told her, refusing to go into detail. "I need to speak with Azrael."

Hilda nodded, reluctantly dragging her eyes back to Michael. "He said you would say that." She looked at her desk as though reciting from something scrawled onto the surface. "He told me to remind you that this is your job and he can't help you any more than he has," she finished with a flushing smile.

Michael stepped back with a sigh. "But he hasn't helped me," he pleaded.

Hilda shrugged. "What do you want me to do?"

He turned away, annoyed. James Waddington had now made his way to the hallway.

"James!" Michael called, stepping toward the naked dead man. "Here."

James looked up with a simple smile and then trotted toward the reaper like a content canine.

"I'll process him later," he told Hilda. "I need to take him back, sort a few things out."

She opened her mouth to object, her senses heightened by the possibility of establishing authority, but at that moment, Seers stepped out of one of the processing rooms and her anger was stolen by adoration.

Michael sighed inwardly, lowering his head to the floor.

Seers moved toward the sullen reaper and loomed over him. The florescent light above his head drew a shadow that engulfed both Michael and James despite only being a foot taller than them.

"What do we have here?" he asked.

Michael looked up at the grinning expression plastered on the face of the respected reaper. He drank in his presence and then spat it out with a simple answer: "A complication."

Seers nodded deliberately, his eyes passed from James to Michael, seemingly ignoring Naff and Chip, who were trying to use each other as shields.

"Always seems to be the case with you," Seers stated.

Michael felt a welling of anger inside him. Seers was intimidating—he was at the top of his field, a position Michael could only dream of attaining, and he was respected by everyone who met him—but he was also a condescending, patronizing prick, and Michael had things to do.

"Do you need something Seers?" Michael spat.

"From you?" he rolled his head back slightly and laughed a brassy laugh, theatrics from a man who liked to be noticed. "I very much doubt it."

"Then get the fuck out of my way!"

Michael barged past him, almost knocking himself off his feet in the process. Seers merely turned and watched him go, amused at his antics. He turned to Naff and Chip, both of whom were rooted to the spot. When he met their gaze, they snapped out of their trance and skipped forward, keen to take the longest route around Seers as possible.

"Jesus Christ, he's a big fucker," Chip muttered as the group strode into darkness.

9

The whistling agony of the kettle drowned out the constant noise from the street outside. At its peak the banshee screams of the forty-year-old appliance could rival any pneumatic drill.

Conversation between Michael and Naff stopped. All eyes, including those of James and Chip—currently trying to work an equally antiquated video game system in the living room—turned to look at the kettle.

The screaming died, the kettle whipped a mechanical click, and then conversation resumed as though nothing ear-destroying had just occurred. Even James Waddington, previously unaccustomed to the kettle, continued on as normal.

Michael began pouring hot water into three cups. "You have to help me," he told Naff as he measured out the steaming liquid before returning the clunky kettle to the stove. "Azrael said that this problem started with *your* department."

Naff accepted a cup from Michael, warming his hands on the heat that transferred through the ceramic. "I don't really want to get mixed up with this, or with Azrael."

Michael handed a drink to Chip, leaving James out. The recently deceased man had initially been deterred at not being able to drink coffee until he saw the coffee—cradled in a grimy jar like the moist droppings of a swamp monster.

In the kitchen, Michael said, "Apparently you already are, and if you don't help me, it won't look good for you will it?"

"That sounded like a threat."

"Fuck off, that wasn't a threat."

"It certainly sounded like one."

"Do you want me to threaten you? I can threaten you if you want me to threaten you."

"I don't think—"

"I'm not going to threaten you."

"That wasn't what I was going to say." Naff put his cup down on the counter. "I can't do this, I really don't think—"

Michael interjected. "Do you really want to piss off the Angel of Death?"

"Now *that* was a threat," Naff snorted. He picked up his cup and slipped the rim to his mouth. "But you have a point."

They took their drinks to the living room.

Chip had managed to work the game. He found the correct station on the television, tuned it in, worked out a kink in the power cord and unearthed both controllers—a task he usually faltered at during one stage or another. He was preparing to play a game with James, the screen slowly loading, but the arrival of his roommate had come during an argument.

"Spirit or not," Chip said, "I don't want your naked ass cheeks on my couch."

Michael took a seat opposite the couch, and Naff plonked himself down on a hard-backed chair opposite him.

"I don't think they're *actually* touching," James said, lifting himself up to double check. "I mean, they are, but, well, do they even exist?"

Chip clearly wasn't in the mood for existentialism. He shrugged that one off, letting the dead man rest his buttocks in peace, adding, seconds later: "And for fuck's sake, keep your legs closed."

"How you feeling?" Naff asked James, for want of anything better to ask.

James smiled back. "I feel . . ." he paused, shrugged. "Content, I guess. Happy."

"Were you happy when you were alive?"

"I guess so. I mean, I had a lot to live for. I had a family, a beautiful wife."

"Turning into a dog every month must have been a downer," Chip chimed.

"Well, yes, but—"

"You can control it though, right?" Naff butted in. "You can change when you want?"

"I can, but sometimes, during a full—"

Chip hadn't finished. "Waking up naked in the woods, covered in blood, and not knowing if you've spent the night raping sheep or eating them."

"Well—"

"And if your kids found out, God, imagine that," Chip stated almost dreamily, allowing his voice to drift into the heavens for a moment's thought. "And when the police find your body, all naked and torn, left alone in the woods. Everyone will think you were a fucking lunatic. Or a sex fiend."

"I don't think your wife would be too pleased either," Naff added.

James looked immediately dejected but still maintained a sense of calm.

"Leave the guy alone," Michael jumped in. "I don't think there's any depression in death, but keep it up and I'm sure you'll find it."

James grinned at the reaper. He received a nudge from Chip, gesturing for him to press a button on his controller. Chip leaned forward and prepared himself for a game before another loading screen cut in. He groaned and flopped back.

"So, you're the Grim Reaper then?" James asked Michael.

"Not *the* Grim Reaper, just one of them."

James nodded like he understood, not letting on that he didn't. "Are you all grim reapers?" he said, indicating to Chip and Naff.

"I'm a tooth fairy," Chip said.

James laughed, only stopping when he saw that no one else had even raised an eyebrow.

"He's being serious," Naff offered.

"Oh. And you?" he asked Naff.

"Records department. It's—" Naff opened his palms to begin a lecture and then quickly closed them again. "It's complicated."

"And boring," Michael added. He turned to James, "Tell us what happened out there in the forest."

Chip groaned, sensing that he had just lost his playmate.

"Okay." James placed the controller down on the floor, much to the dismay of the small man next to him. "I have a little place out in the woods for when I turn. During a full moon I can't control it, I can't stop myself from turning and I have no control when I do. I tell my wife I'm going on a business trip." A flicker of emotion entered his eyes and then departed. "It's just a tiny shack really. I don't spend much time there and it keeps me away from the center of town after I turn. I was there this afternoon, preparing. I took off all my clothes and lay down on the bed."

"Was the naked thing necessary or just for dramatic effect?" Chip wondered.

James glanced at Chip with the look of someone who wasn't sure if he was talking to a joker or an idiot, not realizing it was probably both. "They rip and tear, and what's not ripped and torn is usually covered in blood, mud, or shit by the morning."

Chip nodded. "Fair enough," he said, indicating that James had his permission to continue.

"So, I was lying in my bed waiting. I heard a car pull up outside so I went to investigate."

"You get many visitors there?" Naff interrupted.

James shook his head. "First time I've seen anyone else. When I looked, I saw two men climbing out of a car and heading my way. I didn't know what to do, I thought maybe they were police, I didn't know, but I panicked. I couldn't really hide from them. I mean I make so much noise and I can't control it. So I just ran."

The attention of the room was on him.

"The next thing I remember is being hot, like a pinprick of heat all through me, no pain at first, and then a massive surge of agony." He looked off into the distance as he recounted. His hands worked up and down his body as he remembered the agony that had coursed through it during his demise. "I slowed, staggered. I realized they had shot me. I saw the wounds, but then they shot me again and again. I fell, then . . . " he shrugged. "Next thing I know I was up and running again. No pain. No heat."

"You were dead," Naff stated the obvious.

James nodded. "Apparently. I couldn't run, though—something pulled me back, forced me to stay. Luckily the men weren't near and weren't rushing." He pulled his eyes back to the group, to Michael. "Then I saw you guys."

"Did you get a look at the two men?"

"Not really. They were both tall, muscular. They wore dark suits, dark sunglasses. Same height. Same hair. Same build."

Michael looked a little unsure. He turned to Naff, "Any ideas?"

Naff shook his head. "Could be anyone. We can rule out the police, though. Whoever did this knew what they were doing and they had information about who they were doing it to."

Michael nodded, "Okay, great, now what?"

A pitiful morning sun wrapped its faded rays around the deforested urban jungle, providing little light to the world awakening to face, with great reluctance, another day on its dismal streets.

A woman tottered along the path with a high-heeled shoe in each hand. Her face was a testament to a night on the town: her mascara smudged, her hair matted, her short skirt riding up her thigh to expose a faux tan line and the ghostly flesh above.

A serendipitous dog scavenged the street for food, finishing a half-eaten kebab before stumbling across an opened, barely touched chocolate bar. Dinner and dessert within three flicks of a mangled tail.

In a second floor apartment, above a sparse business either closed down or on its way, a bedraggled tenant poked his face through thick curtains, checking to make sure that yes, the morning had started and no, he hadn't died in his sleep and escaped another miserable day.

From his vantage point at the tip of an alleyway across the street, Michael watched the man in the window blink away the sunshine, groan, and then duck back behind the curtain.

Behind him, James Waddington broke a silence that had only previously been punctuated by the catcalls of domestic violence and the urgency of police sirens in the adjoining streets.

"I feel exposed," the recently dead man complained.

Chip looked him up and down. "You're naked."

"It's not that, it's just—"

Michael turned his attention away from the bed-and-breakfast opposite. The small man operating reception was just visible through the main window and had now picked up a paper and was flicking through the sports section.

"No one can see you," he interrupted.

"No mortal anyway," Naff corrected at the back of the group, hovering in a shadow provided by an overhanging drain pipe. "There *are* a few exceptions, though."

James was pacing back and forward, trotting to and fro like an agitated horse in a stall. "Don't I need to be somewhere else?" he wondered, not looking at anyone in particular. "I feel like I need to be somewhere else. Are we going soon?"

Chip watched his nervous movements with something resembling awe and amusement. "Is he mad?" he asked.

"I feel like I'm going that way," James answered for him.

Chip turned to Michael, the beacon of knowledge in those situations. "I thought they needed to stay near their bodies," he said. "Is that why he's . . . ," he glanced at James and then lowered his voice. "*Losing it?*"

Michael frowned at Chip. "He's fine. And they can go where they want when they're with me."

Chip wasn't convinced. "You think it's safe to bring him here? They can see him, and the last time they saw him they tried to kill him." Chip looked confused, he scrunched up his ugly little face. "*Again,*" he finished meekly.

"I'm not going back to work until I catch these guys," Michael told his friend. "Just go down there with him." He gestured deep into the alleyway, which narrowed toward a rusted metal door beside two gray dustbins. "Stay low; keep him hidden."

"Crawl into the alleyway with the naked man," Chip said distastefully. "Sure, why not."

Chip motioned for James to follow him. They walked to the end of the alley and ducked behind the bins, concealed but for a thin slice of naked flesh.

Michael watched the two go, turned back to the window of the bed-and-breakfast, and then checked his timer.

"Five minutes," he said.

Naff took a step forward, sliding up alongside his friend, his eyes also now on the window of the small establishment across the street.

"Why did you get an early warning on this guy and not the others?" He eyed up the man through the window. "Are you sure he's a werewolf?"

"I don't know. I didn't see him. I saw someone else, brief, but enough for me to get suspicious."

"And if it's not him, if it's not *them*?"

Michael shrugged impassively.

Naff stuffed his hands into his pockets. He looked around with a casual boredom and then wondered. "You ever deal with so many deaths this close together before?"

Michael gave a brisk nod. "A few years ago, a dodgy batch of pills was circulating the pubs and clubs. I took in six poisoned kids in one weekend. I've seen murders. Drug deals gone wrong. Escalated domestic violence. Had one fifteen-year-old kid kill his grandmother when she refused to lend him ten bucks. Never anything like this."

Naff nodded, looking slightly worried. "What are we going to do if they do show up?" he wanted to know.

Michael grinned from ear to ear, a telling grin that Naff didn't appreciate. "Don't worry," he said confidently. "I have a plan."

"Great."

When a silver vehicle slowed to a stop in front of the bed-and-breakfast, Michael knew he was witnessing the arrival of his targets. The car was an immaculate, expensive machine; its tinted windows shaded the occupants within. It was out of place in a town like Brittleside. The tinted windows were a common theme with the town locals, but they were usually fitted on broken relics barely fit for scrap and came with crude paint jobs and sound systems more expensive than the car that contained them.

The two men in black suits clambered out of the car, as if to further dispel any suspicions that Michael did not have. He watched them stand momentarily by the front door of the B&B. They checked their surroundings, failing to see Michael and Naff, who had now shifted to the back of the establishment and were peeking through the slats of a gate at the side of the house.

Michael heard the owner greet the two men, and he heard them reply, their voices muffled through the brickwork.

"That doesn't make any sense," the baffled owner stuttered, sounding anxious.

"Are you Alan Richards?" One said, repeating his initial question.

"Tell me who you are first."

"Friends," Two said simply.

The owner took a step back, swapping his glance cautiously between the pair. Michael assumed the owner was used to having strangers drop by, but these two were stranger than strange.

"Friends!" he spat, indignant. "How can you be my friend if you don't even know my name?"

"Is it Alan Richards?" One said without fault.

At that moment, Michael entered the room from the back of the house, stepping in from the kitchen door at the other end of the spacious room. The B&B owner was now cornered between three intruders.

"What's going on here?" Michael said to attract attention.

All eyes fell upon him, including those of Naff, who casually, and reluctantly, trotted into the room behind him.

"Alan Richards?" One asked Michael.

"Who wants to know?" Michael said with a flick of his head.

"I bloody well would," the real Alan Richards said. "What the hell is going on here? Who are you?" he asked both sets of intruders.

A noise from beyond the room alerted them; they all turned toward the door to the living room to see a woman enter. Her face was etched with a pleasant greeting at first, one practiced through years accompanying her husband in the hospitality business, but when she saw the three strangers standing in front of her, with questioning and intimidating glances on each of their faces, her happy eyes widened.

"What's going on?" She looked beyond the suited men to her husband, and the fear in his eyes told her something was wrong. Michael and the two men watched silently as the woman sidled up to her husband and was taken under a protective arm. He whispered something reassuring to her and then stared at the intruders, flashing each of them a threatening stare that they all returned.

Michael ignored the owner and strode straight up to the two men. Standing in the center of them, he peered up into both pairs of sunglasses. "Who are you?" he asked them.

"None of your concern," Two stated.

"Unless you're Alan Richards," One added.

There was a brief pause, followed by Two querying: "Are you?"

Michael nodded and lowered his gaze. "Yes."

He watched them simultaneously grasp for their pockets, but he didn't react. He watched them both produce pistols that glimmered and spread the dim sunshine that crept in from the large windows, but he didn't flinch. Only when the bullets were ejected—the thick thuds of gunpowder expanding in the small room—did he move. He flung himself backward, toppling over a sofa and flipping dramatically on the floor.

The men turned their pistols on Alan Richards and popped a staccato of bullets into his surprised face before he had a chance to assess the situation and get out of the way. His wife watched in horror and opened her mouth to vocalize her terror, but her words were sucked back into her lungs when a string of bullets pierced her forehead.

The men then turned their guns on Naff, ejecting the remaining bullets from the magazine into him. There were six shots in total, all of which hit Naff in the chest, but he didn't budge. He remained standing, his hands stuffed casually into his pockets, a look of disinterest on his face.

A glimmer of emotion, shock, perhaps awe, appeared on the faces of the two men. They swapped glances, making sure they both felt the same way, before turning back to Naff.

"You're not mortal?" One asked.

"Uh huh," Naff casually shrugged his shoulders. "This was your great plan?" he asked Michael.

A pained sigh lifted from the floor. Michael pulled himself to his feet with his hands grasping his chest and a twisted expression on his face. "That fucking hurt," he spat through gritted teeth.

He turned to glare at his friend; they exchanged a knowing look that was then shrugged off by Naff. Michael pulled out his timer, checked the display, and then stuffed it back into his pocket. "Right on time for once," he declared.

"You're immortal, as well?" One uttered redundantly.

Two pulled out a timer of his own and checked the screen, looking perplexed. His colleague glanced over his shoulder. Michael waited patiently.

"The woman," Two said softly. They both raised their eyes, noted the soul of the departed woman lingering at the back of the room. They looked at each other and offered a reciprocated shrug.

"We've been looking for you." Two slipped the timer back in his pocket and raised his gun at Michael.

One declared: "I think you have something that belongs to us."

"Give it to us."

The two assassins made a point of pressing their guns closer to Michael, aiming in the center of his chest. Michael met their threats with a wide grin and crossed his arms over his chest.

"You didn't think that through, did you?" he asked cockily.

They exchanged glances again; a thought seemed to pass between them before they returned their gazes to the reaper.

"We may not be able to kill you," One told him. "But we can find plenty of ways to hurt you if you do not give us want we want."

Michael nodded, "What *do* you want?"

"The soul," One told him. "James Paddington."

"Waddington," Two corrected.

"Waddington," One repeated with a nod.

Naff was still motionless at the back of the room, looking bored. Michael shot a glance at his friend before relaxing his own casual posture and facing the men, signaling he was up for a nego-tiation.

"Fair enough," he said as genuinely as he could. "I couldn't give a shit what happens to him, but first you tell me why." He glared at each of them in turn, expecting something to flicker behind their staunch apathy. Nothing budged.

"Why werewolves?" he pushed. "Why steal their souls? What could you possibly want with them?"

"I'm afraid we cannot divulge that information."

"It is none of your concern."

Michael sighed loudly. "I'm getting fucking sick of hearing that."

"Hand over the soul and we shall be on our way," One declared.

Naff stepped forward from the back of the room, suddenly interested. "And why do you look so much alike?" he wondered, his eyebrows arched inquisitively as he strode to Michael's side and studied the doppelgängers. "You twins?"

"Close."

"We are clones."

They both smiled simultaneously, as though to emphasize their statement. Naff looked a little less interested and took an instinctive step closer to Michael.

Michael moved forward, leaving Naff to battle his disturbances without the shoulder of his friend to lean on. He looked at them both closely and they let him, taking pride in their status.

"Weird," Michael said under his breath. "Every little detail."

"So how come you're not constantly speaking over each other?" Naff wanted to know.

"We're genetic doubles, we are not the same person."

Naff looked bemused; he opened his mouth to issue another inquiry and then slammed it shut when Michael offered a different line of questioning.

"So does that mean you're both mortal?"

"Yes," one answered proudly. "Of course—"

"*Shit.*"

Michael planted his hands, one on each of their shoulders, and grasped tightly. Instantly, the color drained from their faces. They fought back, tried to wriggle free, but their strength rapidly ebbed from their bodies. Their limbs quickly became incapable of resistance; their lungs incapable of breath.

They slunk to the floor like rag dolls, dropping out from beneath Michael's grasp. Their cold, lifeless bodies coiled around his feet.

He stepped back, brushed his hands together and happily announced, "That was easy."

Naff inspected the corpses with a gentle shake of his head. "It scares me that they gave you guys that ability."

Michael tapped his friend jokingly on the shoulder. Naff jumped instinctively and then cursed under his breath.

"Just be thankful they didn't give it to someone like Chip," he said.

Naff shuddered. "Good point."

Michael bent down to inspect the dead duo. He reached into the pocket of Two and withdrew a timer. It didn't look much different from his own; he could have easily confused the two devices.

"What do you think?" he asked, handing the device to his friend, who had only just finishing pondering a world where Chip could kill anyone who annoyed him or didn't buy him a drink.

Naff took it, turned it this way and that, inspected the screen, toyed with the buttons and the menu. "Remarkable," he said after a few moments, his eyes wide. "This is *our* timer," he held it up like a trophy, "*our* technology."

"Copy?" Michael wondered, still on his haunches as he searched through the dead men's pockets for any further clues.

Naff shook his head. "No. Straight off the line. I'd say someone somewhere was missing a timer."

"Why would they need it?"

"To keep tags on you, I guess. They weren't very bright but clearly someone told them what you could do to them. I guess if they had the timer, they knew where you would be and how long they had to finish," he shrugged, "*whatever* it is they were doing."

"How could they see the spirits? They were mortal."

Naff dropped the timer into his pocket and shrugged. "They had a hard time identifying us, and they seemed unsure about their actual targets," he explained, watching as Michael inspected their identical faces. "It seems they can see us but they can't distinguish—"

He stopped short. Michael had removed the sunglasses from one of the men to expose a set of glimmering metallic eyes, which appeared to be whirring inside the skull.

"Creepy," Naff said with another little shudder.

With his thumb and forefinger, Michael reached into an eye socket and plucked out the metallic orb, leaving a black hole embedded with a fine silver lining inside the skull. He rolled the eye on his palm like a marble. It had stopped whirring, but it still glimmered like polished steel when it caught the light.

"What about these?" he asked, tossing the eye over his shoulder to his friend.

Naff toyed with the catch, bouncing it off his palm with a grimace, as if his friend had just tossed him Chip's balled collection of body hair. He watched it spin uncontrollably out of his hand and onto the sofa. "Never seen them before," he said to the back of Michael's head, hiding his hands sheepishly behind his back. "Could have something to do with our missing souls, though."

Michael stood and straightened with a complementary groan. He looked at his friend and noted his hidden hands with a small flicker of bemusement.

He held a weapon and a vial in front of his friend.

Naff nodded knowingly. "No doubt that's how they collected—"

A cough from the other side of the room alerted them; they turned to see the ghosts of Alan Richards and his wife standing serenely and expectantly. They were both smiling, their arms locked.

"What happens now?" Alan asked them.

"Now you can rest in peace," Michael told him. "Come with me."

"To heaven?"

"To the alleyway."

10

"Hold on," Chip raised a quizzical eyebrow; it looked like a hamster was folding into the fetal position on his forehead. "Didn't the clones have souls?"

Michael continued walking, ignoring the inquisitive imp behind him. The waiting room had filled up somewhat since his last visit. In the corner, a short, stocky reaper who had never introduced himself, or even spoken a word of a greeting, sat with his head down, catching up on some sleep. Beside him, a teenage spirit twiddled his thumbs and took in every inch of the room with wide, awe-filled eyes.

"Clones don't have souls," Naff told Chip.

"But the original one would have," Chip pushed, clearly perturbed by the event.

Michael turned around at this. He grinned at his friend. "Precisely!" he declared triumphantly.

Michael dropped the eyeball taken from the clone onto the reception desk. It bounced with a heavy clunk and then settled.

Hilda stared at Michael and then at the eye. She picked it up with great caution and trepidation and then rolled it around her palm when she decided it wasn't going to bite.

"What is it?" she wanted to know.

"Eye ball."

Hilda dropped the eye like it was made of molten lava.

"Where the hell did you get that from?" she asked, surprisingly disgusted for someone who worked with the dead and looked like she spent her free time cackling over a cauldron.

"Where do you think?"

"Why—"

"I need to speak with Azrael," Michael interrupted.

She snapped her mouth shut and glared at him under thick, arched eyebrows. "I told you no."

"This is important."

Hilda was looking over Michael's shoulder, a hint of perplexity on her haggard face. "Hasn't that naked man been here before?"

"Where is Azrael? I need to speak with him."

"He looks a little lost," she said distantly, her eyes lowered to crotch height as they followed James Waddington on a merry wonder around the room.

Michael shook his head in exasperation. He took the wondering soul by the arm and beckoned for Alan Richards and his wife to follow, taking them all into the processing room and calling for Chip and Naff to stay and wait.

The room sparked into life as Michael entered. An automated voice cackled into existence all around him, issuing instructions as Michael half-heartedly listened.

"Place souls on the marked spheres."

Three spheres lit up on the floor. The three spirits looked mesmerized, their contentedness flicked to reverence. Michael looked annoyed. He gestured for them to step onto the spheres and they did so with a joyful skip in their lifeless legs.

A rainbow of epileptic lights followed; a cacophony of noise. The three souls vanished, as did the marked spheres on which they had stood. The lights overhead dimmed, descending a blanket of darkness over the room. Michael rested against the far wall and allowed his back to gradually slide down until his backside rested on the floor.

He took out the metallic eye and idly flipped it between his fingers as a desk rose from the foundations in the middle of the room, its radiant surface glowing brighter with each incremental ascent.

"Take the ticket for use in the machine," the automated voice said after the desk had finished its climb. A slip of paper poked out of a small computer on the surface of the desk, awaiting collection. "The money will be credited to your account upon receipt."

Michael glanced at the ticket but didn't make a move to collect it.

The automated voice issued a warning after several moments of inactivity. "If you do not take your ticket in the next five seconds, your credits will be cancelled and your account will be suspended."

Michael felt his breath catch in his throat. "What the fuck!" He bolted to his feet quicker than he knew he could and practically dove toward the table, ripping out the ticket like he was snatching food from a lion's mouth.

"Jesus," he mumbled softly, stuffing the ticket into his pocket.

He turned to leave, but the Angel of Death was blocking his path. Michael started in surprise, and then settled, holding his chest. "*JesusFuckingChrist*," he hissed in one long breath.

Azrael beamed at him. "Did you like my impression?" he asked merrily. "It certainly seems to have got you going."

"That was you?" Michael replied, unable to suppress a grin. "The Angel of Death has a sense of humor?"

"Why so glum?"

"*Why so glum?*" he parodied.

Azrael shrugged. "I'm trying to sound informal."

"It really doesn't suit you."

"As you wish," Azrael said with a swift nod. His demeanor instantly changed to something more serious and far more intimidating. "What is wrong?"

Michael skulked forward, stretched an arm to indicate his intentions, and then dropped the eyeball into Azrael's waiting palm.

"I stopped the men," he explained tiredly. "They were clones. They were using this to see the souls. And—" he retrieved the weapon and the vial he had found on the two men, "—this to gather them." He took a step back, sluggishly drooping against the desk and praying it didn't duck back into the foundations, as he wasn't sure he had the energy to remain upright.

"That's all I can do," he said as Azrael examined the objects briefly. "I'm not a detective and I live in a world of few answers and too many questions. This is bigger than those two guys, but I can't find out how big or—"

"Your work here is done," Azrael interjected sharply. He had deposited the objects out of sight and looked ready to leave.

"What?" Michael said, taken aback.

"You are finished."

Michael found the energy to propel himself upright. "That's it?" he asked, incredulous. "What happens now?"

"For you?" Azrael shrugged indifferently. "Nothing. Although what you have done here will be taken into account. It will not be forgotten," he explained with a sense of finality.

"And this werewolf business?"

"It does not concern you."

Azrael turned to leave. Michael hopped forward eagerly.

"No! Stop fucking telling me that!" he spat belligerently. "It *does* concern me. I've spent the last twenty-four hours chasing down two fucking maniacs who have been trying to do my job for me," Michael was so annoyed and caught up in his arguing that he was spraying drops of spittle toward Azrael, who stood with a charmed look on his face.

"You didn't help me and none of your fucking friends helped me." He threw his arm down angrily as he spoke. "I'm sick of not having a clue what's going on, I'm sick of trying and failing to find things out for myself." He was losing his voice, the day and the disbelief taking it out of him. "This is it. You tell me now or I quit. You can take this job and stick it—"

Michael stopped abruptly. He wasn't in the processing room anymore. His grating throat caught a spittle of dried phlegm which he had a hard time trying to force back down as he looked around in horror.

The room was dark, but of a different intensity. Nothing could penetrate the blackness. Michael couldn't see his own hand as he lifted it, trembling slightly, in front of his face. He could see an enormous desk in front of him, though, eclipsing him. The solid structure looked like a fortress and he was an enemy at the meager gates.

Azrael sat behind the desk, his size and his stature fitting perfectly behind it. His eyes bore down on Michael, glittering like fiery orbs in the blackness.

He was in the Angel of Death's office. He had never been there before, but he knew it. He felt it.

"Shit," he said softly. "I didn't mean it."

Azrael ignored the apology. "The weapons and the technology, including the clones, come from a former employee," he explained. "We have been studying him for some time, but he has ways of remaining under our radar. He knows how we operate."

It was hard to feel at ease in such a room, but Michael softened under the realization that he wasn't going to lose his job or his immortality. "Was he a reaper?" he asked.

"No," Azrael said brusquely.

Michael decided not to pursue that line of enquiry; he doubted it would get him anything other than brisk negatives.

"I thought there was no way out of here. How did he just *stop working*?" he asked.

"He found a way."

"Can't you drag him back?"

"He is a very powerful man."

Michael forgot his station again, "You're the fucking Angel of Death," he reminded him. "How powerful can he possibly be?"

Azrael drummed his fingers on the desk, the heavy thuds like shrapnel embedding into wood. "Above ground he is more powerful than me," he admitted with great reluctance. "He, like you, is also immortal."

Michael looked perplexed. "I don't get it," he admitted.

"And I can't explain it."

"Was there a reason he chose Brittleside? Was I a part of this?"

"Maybe."

"Maybe? What's that supposed to mean?"

Azrael didn't answer, but Michael suspected that he knew. He wanted a feckless reaper, he wanted a population that no one gave a shit about. He didn't want questions, he didn't want resistance. Brittleside was perfect, and that annoyed Michael more than everything that had gone before.

"What happens now? I can help you. I can bring him in."

"Your enthusiasm both surprises me and delights me, Michael, but I fear this is bigger than you."

Michael met with the cold stare of his boss for interminable moments. He was surprised at his own anger, but he had every reason to be angry. He had been dragged around town, he had been made to look like a fool. His peers wouldn't remember the escaped demon, the clones; they wouldn't remember the fact that he had foiled a plot so big that the Angel of Death had gotten involved. They would remember the time he missed a few collections, invited a naked werewolf to run around the waiting room, and sulked to his boss.

"That's it then?"

Azrael grinned; he opened his palms in an expressive manner. "I sense you're happier with this conclusion, though?"

Michael nodded. "Maybe," he said. Because as angry as he was, at least all that anger wasn't now directed at his job or his boss.

He looked around unsurely. "Now, how do I get out of here?"

There was a storm of blackness inside a room that bore One, Two, and the prospect of many more equally combative, submissive, and apathetic vessels. The vats were taken apart by unseen, uncaring hands; stripped with great rapidity before any watching eyes could complain.

The machines and the wires followed. A wind of destruction tore through the room, stripping it of its priceless equipment like a superhuman team of removal men.

The man that had programmed the machine, the closest thing that One and Two had to a father, watched the room from his office, peering through the large glass window with little emotion showing on his weather-beaten face.

The room was black and empty in moments—changed from a cacophony of electronics, noises and awe-inspiring expense, to nothing but a blank space.

Dressed in overalls, a pair of spectacles hooked over his ears and tipped up to rest on top of his head, a placid man casually chewed gum and recited from a clipboard he held in his hands, ticking off as he went.

"Cloning vats destroyed. Souls diverted. Suspicious equipment noted or collected. Money transferred. Privileges revoked—"

The older man watched this indifferent display with a rueful scorn. He didn't say a word; he didn't object. When the checklist was completed and the man disappeared, he slumped down behind his desk and glanced around the empty office. Even the electricity had been temporally cut, the fading light of the day now the only thing keeping the emptied area that had held life, and promise of more, from descending into complete blackness.

He slumped his head into his hands and sighed into his palms, breathing in his own despair. The door to his office opened, and someone entered.

"The file you requested, sir," the incomer spoke and then slowly and silently departed, closing the door gently behind them, guiding the lock into place with the faintest of clicks.

He lifted his head and looked down at the file on his desk: a manila folder which concealed an assortment of pictures and papers, all neatly stacked in one thick ream.

The sight brought a smile to his face. He shifted out of his melancholy with some renewed hope, ambition found in the throes of vengeance. He flipped open the folder, checked the first sheet: a reaping license, photocopied. The second: a work sheet. The third, fourth, fifth, and sixth: a biography. The seventh was a picture; he put the others to one side and held onto the picture. He stared at it intensely, his lips curling into an increasingly sinister grimace.

"You have just made a very powerful enemy," he told the portrait of Michael Holland.

He scrunched the picture into a ball, reveling in its destruction, doing to it what Michael had done to everything he had worked on over the last few years.

One photograph didn't matter—he had plenty, and he wasn't going to forget that face. He threw the scrunched-up ball across the room, watching it bounce off the far wall and land anticlimactically next to the wastepaper bin.

He cursed, spraying a volley of spittle across his own desk, but he was already feeling better. He had a purpose now that he had a mission: he was going to kill Michael Holland.

PART THREE

LOVE LOST

1

A spiral of cigar smoke snaked to the ceiling like a dancing cobra rising from its woven basket. It rose through the thickened air and dispersed against the yellowed paint, where a thin layer of grease had accumulated through years of casual neglect, spreading a cloud along the flattened surface.

The smoker coughed, bringing a troublesome glob to his throat before sending it back down with a squeamish swallow. He placed the cigar into a nearby ashtray; wiped his mouth with the hairy back of a dirty hand.

He held the sports section of a national newspaper in his left hand, folded into a neat handheld scrunch and held off to one side. In his right hand, he retrieved a greasy bacon sandwich from the plate in front of him and took a noisy bite without removing his eyes from the latest failures of the England soccer team.

Michael Holland sat on the other side of the diner, watching the hungry reader through tired eyes. It was early, he had been awake less than thirty minutes and along with his cup of coffee and slice of stale ginger cake, death was being served up for breakfast.

He watched the man take another large bite. A pool of grease infused with tomato sauce leaked out of the bread like blood from a gunshot wound. It ran a rivulet down his stubbled chin, heading toward his flabby neck before being wiped away by a grubby finger.

Michael felt sick. He'd had a few drinks the night before and had only just managed to settle his troublesome stomach. He didn't mind dealing with death so early, but having to watch fat people eat and smoke their way to an early grave was unsettling.

"Is everything okay?"

Michael, slightly startled at the voice, quickly turned. A petite brunette waitress stood over his table, a broad smile on her delicate face.

At the sight of her, Michael's face lit up. There was something so endearing and relaxing in her smile, something so sweet about the pinprick dimples on her cheek and something so mesmerizing in her green eyes, which reflected the light from the bright morning over Michael's shoulder.

He had seen her in the back when he gave his order to a dole-faced woman with a pencil behind her ear and a stick up her ass. He heard her humming softly as she cooked up the breakfast currently clogging the arteries of the man opposite. He caught her smile then, thought he saw something there—her eyes had lingered longer than simple customer curiosity required.

"Everything is fine," Michael replied softly, holding eye contact.

She beamed a wider smile, if that was possible. "If you need anything," she trailed off, hooking a thumb over her shoulder toward the kitchen.

Michael nodded. She left a smile with him and then turned, heading straight back into the kitchen without acknowledging the other customer. Michael felt singled out, sure there was a spark there. He watched her go, watched her walk. She made it to the kitchen and then spun on her heels, placing a supporting hand on the doorway as she shot a look over her shoulder, her eyes instantly meeting his. She smiled again, looking a little sheepish, and then quickly turned away.

Michael turned back to the man eating the bacon sandwich. He was almost finished—not paying attention to his food, too intent on reading his paper. Moistened crumbs stuck to his lips, grease pinned the stubble to his chin. He was taking bigger and bigger bites as he neared the end of the large bread bun, chewing less and less.

Michael shook his head in distaste and turned away. He could see the smiling brunette in the kitchen—her slim body and petite face was in profile as she prepped some vegetables. Her hips moved gently to the swing of a song in her head, and her hand took the rhythm of her hips as it diced melodious pieces of carrot.

There was a time when he wouldn't have faltered at her smile, wouldn't have lingered on her interests or her mild flirting. Those times were gone, had been gone for a while now.

Death hadn't necessarily changed him—he had been reborn with the same sex drive as when he had died—but the events following his death had subdued him somewhat. He wasn't the same man anymore and didn't look at women in the same way.

He pulled out his timer and glanced somberly at the screen. He gave it a gentle, understanding nod and stuffed it back into his pocket. He looked at the fat man again. He was shoveling the last piece of his sandwich into his mouth, cramming every inch of greasy bacon into the cavernous orifice. His cheeks bulged like a hibernating hamster when he finished; there was so much food crammed inside that his greased lips could barely meet.

He chewed. Crumbs spilled out of his mouth, over his clothes, onto the floor and the table. The food went down but seemed to lodge. A look of alarm spread over his face, and for the first time he took his eyes off the newspaper.

Michael stood, prepared. He straightened his jacket, double-checked his watch, leaned against the table, and waited, watching.

The man held a hand to his chest. He looked anxious, worried. He coughed, sputtered. Shrapnel of soaked bread flew across the room. He coughed again, slamming the heel of his hand against his chest.

His face turned red. His eyes bulged. He pushed back in his chair; the legs grated against the floor and screamed a shrieking wail. He lowered his head, punched his chest again, and then, with a dramatic gulp and a relieved sigh, he finally forced the food down his throat.

He looked pleased with himself as he pulled his seat forward again and picked up his newspaper. He looked around to see if anyone had witnessed his struggle. He gave Michael a sly smile, which Michael returned with a sigh and a shake of his head.

He pushed himself off the edge of the table and turned toward the kitchen. The profile of the pretty waitress had gone. In her place, looking horrified and unsure, was the stern-faced waitress who had taken Michael's order.

He trotted up to her. In front of her, flat on the kitchen floor, her head inches from the scuffed shoes of her fellow waitress, was the corpse of the pretty brunette: a pained expression on her face, a hand loosely clasped toward her breast.

"It's okay, I'm fine."

Michael looked up. The waitress was in the kitchen, smiling politely behind her friend, trying to console her.

She saw Michael standing there, returning her smile. "She won't listen to me," she said. "Can you tell her I'll be okay?"

The stern-faced waitress was trembling, her whole body shaking. She was crying, wailing gently in shock and horror. She held her hands to her face to hold back the tears and to suppress her quivering mutterings; her eyes stared horrified at the body beyond her flayed fingers.

"She needs to know I'll be okay," the spirit of the waitress said with concern that came from a contented place.

Michael held out his hand. "She'll be fine," he assured her. She looked at his hand, hesitated, her eyes on her former friend and colleague, and then she took it. The beaming, radiant smile returned to her beautiful face.

"What happens now?" she asked pleasantly as Michael guided her toward the back door.

"It's complicated."

Besides Hilda, the stone-faced bitch in the waiting room, the only women he conversed with were the dead or the soon to be. He didn't mind it. There was a finality to the dead that he respected. He couldn't hurt a dead woman, and he certainly couldn't alter the course of her life for the worse. As a reaper, he was there as their first stop on an unknown journey, an important part of their eternity, but one that couldn't effect their existence ether way.

It hadn't always been that way, even since that fateful night when he gave up his own ticket to that unknown land in exchange for immortality. A girl, a beautiful girl, had changed him. After meeting her, nothing had ever felt the same.

2

The night Michael Holland met the girl who changed his new life, he was hunched solemnly over a pint of cheap cider. He had been sitting in the same spot for a couple hours, his slumped posture cutting a depressed figure on the corner seat of a corner table in a quiet pub.

He had been nursing the same pint for more than an hour. A small fly had flown in at one point, possibly when he was in the bathroom, he wasn't sure and he didn't care.

He brought the glass to his lips and stared at the wallowing fly. It beat a buoyant path on the edge of the flat drink, its wings draped by its side in a soggy crucifix. He grimaced and took a long drink, consuming the cider-drenched bug in the process.

He raised his eyes for the first time in twenty minutes, and what he saw nearly caused him to choke on the fermented fly.

The pub had been all but empty when he had arrived. It was Friday, midafternoon: too early for pub crawlers and weekend drinkers, too late for those stopping by for a lunchtime drink. Other than the bartender—a gruff, abrupt man who spoke in a succession of grunts—there was one customer in the pub: a stereotype of the perpetual elderly drunk who has nothing better to do but while away his final days, slowly drinking strong ale and perusing the betting form.

The elderly man was still there, fading into the shadows at the back—his first pint of ale still clutched in the arthritic fist of his right hand, the heavily scribbled betting form in his left—but there were now two women at the bar. The sight of them had failed to cheer up the grunting bartender, but it had certainly piqued Michael's interests. He straightened, kicked the hump out of his fatigued body, and leaned back, trying to look casual and cool.

The women talked happily to each other. The shorter of the two, with long, curly blonde hair, a tight figure, and large hips, gave her orders to the bartender and leaned on the bar while she waited. The other girl seemed much more timid. She spoke with a soft chime, her voice barely traveling the fifteen or so feet to where Michael sat. She had fiery red hair that cascaded down to the middle of her back, and deep, dark, intelligent eyes.

The red-haired girl was facing Michael as she spoke to her friend. She caught his eye a few times—a sheepish, shy look on her dimpled smile. He noticed a brief, instinctive twitch in her features when she caught him looking at her.

They took their drinks and shuffled away from the bar. Michael heard the softly spoken redhead say something to her friend, acknowledging him with a furtive glance in the process; they exchanged a giggle and then took their seats.

Michael drained the cider in his glass, waited for a few moments—stealing a glance in the process—and then sauntered confidently over to their table.

He had been dead for a year and had spent that time trying to become accustomed to his newfound existence, but he still had the charm he possessed when he was alive. Within minutes, he had them at ease in his presence and before long he had learned everything he wished to know about the beautiful redhead.

Her name was Jessica and she was twenty-two. She was a law student attending college in the area, out for a few drinks with her friend before retiring for an early night. She was soft mannered, intelligent, passionate, and humorous. He fell for her instantly, and he thought he saw something in her eyes that said she felt the same way about him.

They spoke for an hour. He addressed them both at first, not wanting to alienate her friend—a dominant and standoffish girl with suspicious eyes—but after an hour of idle chatter she drew him in and they both forgot about the friend.

After saying a brief farewell, the dejected friend left, firing an insidious glance at Michael before departing in feigned good spirits.

They talked even more when they were alone. He found out she loved classic literature, impressionist art, sixties pop music, modern punk, day-trips to the seaside, holidays in winter. She adored takeaway food and it adored her hips. She loved ice cream but hated any flavors other than vanilla; loved politics but hated politicians. She had a thing for Michael Jackson but also had a secret crush on Elton John.

They talked until the pub filled up. Michael avoided any taxing questions about his life, but his clandestine veil was unwrapped when the skies outside the windows had burned the last ember of sunshine.

"So, why were you looking so depressed earlier?" she asked him.

He feigned bemusement.

"When I came in with Julie," Jessica clarified, indicating her arrival with the friend who had left annoyed and lonely four hours earlier.

He shrugged his shoulders, stared down at the floor. He didn't know what to tell her. He certainly couldn't tell her the truth, but he also didn't want to lie to her, so he opted for something in between.

"It's an anniversary," he said vaguely. "It's complicated, but let's just say that one year ago today, something *life* changing happened," he explained, quickly wondering why he had emphasized the word *life*.

"Do you want to tell me about it?" Jessica asked politely, offering her sympathetic shoulder as she lifted her wine glass to her pursed lips.

Michael grinned and tried to shake the question off. "Not important," he said. "Well, not now anyway. Maybe another time."

That night they said their goodbyes, exchanged numbers and a brief kiss, and parted ways outside the pub.

Michael's mood changed. He was happy; he had a hop in his step as he strode down the street, bypassing the clubbers and revelers drunkenly making their way from club to club.

His timer told him that he was going to have a busy night, two dead within half an hour and one mile of each other, but he didn't care. He would sleep an excited and happy sleep that night.

The corpse looked familiar. He had seen that face before. A spark of recognition fired in his brain and was immediately extinguished by a voice from behind him.

"Hello," it said happily.

Michael turned away from the bloodied, broken body to face a happy, beaming spirit. The spirit didn't look familiar, didn't spark the same recognition. Although he hazarded a guess that if he did know this man, he probably knew him as the mournful, dole-faced person looking shocked and broken on the floor, and not the smiling simpleton in front of him. In Brittleside only the dead smiled.

"Good evening," Michael said with an acknowledging nod. He paused before offering his assistance. He glanced at the corpse again. "Do I know you?" he asked.

The spirit shrugged his ethereal shoulders, the smile still fastened onto his face.

"I'm sure I've seen you somewhere before," Michael persisted.

"Maybe I just have one of them faces."

Michael made a humming noise. *One of those faces*, in this instance, happened to be very ugly, with almost impish features, a thick-set jaw, bulbous nose, long and stubbly chin, and eyes that refused to line up. If *one of those faces* happened to be the grotesque sort fit only for a mother's love and a villainous role in a horror movie, then he definitely had it.

"Maybe."

A group of alcohol-scented revelers spilled out of the nearby clubs and began to crowd around the body. Excited whispers, female screams, male bravado. Michael escorted the spirit away as his body became a sideshow attraction for the drunk and the idiotic. In the distance, the sirens from an ambulance and a police car collided to create an approaching cacophony.

"Seems you pissed someone off," Michael told the spirit. "Technically you're my first suicide, you know."

"I didn't kill myself."

"Oh." Michael paused, looking a touch perplexed. "What were you doing on the roof of a club?"

"I lost my Frisbee."

Michael laughed, the spirit didn't flinch. He stared at him, waiting for his grinning stupidity to shift and break into a vein of sarcasm. It didn't budge. He turned away with a blasé shrug.

"Fair enough."

He thought he recognized the second soul, as well. A female, dead on the street. She had choked on her own vomit after ingesting an assortment of cheap cocaine and cheaper vodka. She was alone when he found her, her spirit was waiting by her body, leaning against a lamppost with the casualness of someone waiting for a bus.

"Who are you?" she demanded to know when he approached her. She looked content, as they all always did, but there was a touch of trepidation in her voice.

"I'm here to pick you up," Michael said. He couldn't help but smile as he re-ran his comment through his head and watched as she peeled her scantily clad figure away from the lamppost.

"Is that a joke?" she asked genuinely.

Michael shook his head. "I'm—"

"You're going to take me to the other side?" she interrupted.

"I think so."

"You *think* so?"

He frowned. The dead usually weren't so quizzical.

"Why weren't you here before?" she wanted to know, growing increasingly impatient and uneasy. "I've been here for ages. Three people went by over there," she nodded to the other side of the road, brightly lit under the fluorescent glow of a streetlight. "Not one of them stopped. Not one of them replied. It's like they couldn't even hear me."

Michael thought about replying but quickly swallowed his words. It didn't matter that they couldn't see or hear her needful spirit; they all had probably seen her corpse and not one of them had stopped to check if she was alive.

"So, where were you?"

He had been caught up in his own idleness, drinking stale coffee at a nearby cafe and absently staring into his own thoughts. Most of those thoughts had been about Jessica; she had dominated his mind since he had met her.

"I'm sorry," he said honestly. "But I'm here now."

Samson had told him that he would develop a second intuition. He said he would know the whens, wheres, and hows of his victims' deaths. He said it would come as a second nature, gradually birthing in him from the moment he took the job a year ago.

But he hadn't felt a thing, and he never knew anything; their deaths came as a complete mystery to him until he read their impending doom on the screen of the timer.

He didn't know if the intuition would come to him and he couldn't ask. Samson had seen him twice since his death, and on neither occasions had he stayed long enough to answer any probing questions. The only other higher authority that he spoke to was a repugnant receptionist who wouldn't stop glaring at him and a psychiatrist who read his mind but offered no solutions to the problems within.

He held out his hand to the woman. She looked into his eyes, then at the proffered appendage. "Where are you taking me?"

Michael smiled. They all asked the same thing and he didn't know what to tell any of them.

"To a better place," he assured her.

3

He was living in a bed-and-breakfast on the outskirts of town. He paid minimal board and was fed, showered, and sheltered by the elderly couple who owned and managed the six-room guesthouse.

Their names were Mary and Joseph, and although unconnected to the biblical pair who begot the son of God, they had been dead just as long and were just as compassionate and kind. They had links to a side of the afterlife that Michael didn't know anything about, they knew things he couldn't even dream of knowing, and, like everyone who knew more than he did, they refused to tell him any of it.

"But there is a God, right?" Michael asked Joseph once. They had been drinking on a deck that overlooked a small backyard. It was Michael's birthday, a birthday for a life he no longer had, and Joseph had bought an expensive single malt whiskey to celebrate and to ease the passing of his first redundant birthday in the afterlife.

Joseph hummed and hawed at the question. He lifted his tumbler to his lips and stared absently at the contents. He stroked the lip of the crystal glass with his forefinger, took a small sip, savored the taste with a sigh, and then lowered the glass with a shrug. "That's a tricky one," he explained eventually.

"You don't know?"

"Definitively?" Joseph turned to Michael, lifted his eyes to the blackened skies where a multitude of stars danced in the darkness. "No. But I know enough to hazard a guess."

"And what is that guess?"

Joseph laughed softly. "That guess is just that," he said vaguely. "It's a guess."

Michael sighed. He had been dead for six months at that point, spent most of that time wondering around losing souls, forgetting his timer and getting frustrated at the lack of help and supervision. Mary and Joseph were his only saving graces, and even they failed to soothe all his woes.

"You see, Michael," Joseph said, throwing a reassuring pat on his shoulder. "Death is a lot like life. No one really knows what's going on and no one can really explain everything that happens, but some people know how to handle the unknown more than others. Does that make sense?"

"But there *are* some people who know everything, right?"

"I suppose there has to be, but I have yet to meet them."

The night when Michael returned home after meeting Jessica and then disposing of the murdered man and the drunken woman, he found Mary and Joseph waiting patiently by the fire in the main room. Mary was sitting with folded legs on the edge of the sofa, a crossword puzzle resting on her thighs. Joseph sat silently in the corner drinking brandy.

Michael sat on the opposite side of the sofa. The elderly couple looked up from their respective activities with welcoming smiles.

"How are things?" Joseph beamed. He rose to his feet, headed straight for a liquor cabinet in the corner, and poured Michael a drink without prompt. He handed it to him and then returned to his seat, offering Michael an air salute with his glass.

"Okay," Michael said before taking his first soothing sip. "Actually, a little better than okay."

Mary put down her puzzle, unfolded her legs. "You look a lot better," she noted with genuine glee.

"I am," Michael sat back and threw his arm over the edge of the sofa, dangling the brandy glass between two fingers. "I met a girl today."

Mary and Joseph exchanged a glance. Michael detected concern in their faces, but they were quick to hide it.

"Congratulations," Mary said genuinely. "What's she like?"

Michael told them and they listened to every word. When he started speaking about Jessica, he found it difficult to stop. He only ceased his glorifying when he realized he was gushing like a teenage girl and, although Mary delighted in his revelry, Joseph was looking a little embarrassed for him.

"I'm thinking of taking her to the movies next week," he said.

There was that look again, flickering between them like an unshared secret. Michael caught it fully this time. "Is everything okay?" he asked.

Joseph leaned forward and put his glass down on a nearby coffee table. "I don't want to lower the mood, but you might want to be careful dating the living."

"It's okay," Michael assured. "I know not to tell her I'm dead. She won't suspect anything."

Mary jumped in at that point. "The problem is, sweetie," she said in her soft, reassuring voice. "If anything were to happen to her, it would be your job to *collect* her."

Michael shook it off with a grin. "She's fine," he said confidently. "Long time before anything like that happens."

"Of course," Mary jumped in jovially. "Just so you know."

Michael nodded and stood. He drained the brandy, put down the empty glass, and wished the pair goodnight before ascending the stairs to his small room at the back of the house.

That night, he thought about what Mary had said and he struggled to get the thought out of his head. Not just for Jessica, but for every girl he met—how was he supposed to find someone if he was always going to outlive them and then be forced to assist with their demise?

He struggled to sleep.

4

He awoke in a sweat, breathless. His heart raced frantically inside his chest. He pushed himself up against the headboard and looked down at his naked body. The few hairs on his chest had matted together with the sweat; a glossy sheen covered his skin like oil. He could feel the sheets sticking to his legs, his stomach, and his groin. He peeled them off and flung them to the floor, savoring the cool air that rushed over his body and turned the moisture into a sticky dryness.

He took in a deep breath and tried to settle the rhythm of his runaway heart.

He'd had a dream, a nightmare. It was fading fast in his conscious but vivid parts of it were still fresh in his mind. Jessica was there, he was sure of it, but it wasn't exactly her, at least not throughout the entirety of the dream. She had transformed into someone else, some*thing* else. Beautiful and elegant at first and then—

He shook his head and struck a palm to his temple. The images had vanished. He struggled to recall, feeling a pinprick headache developing at the base of his skull.

Were they in a car together? Was that it? Happily driving; happy in each other's company, and then something unexpected, something terrible. He remembered seeing blood, seeing Jessica looking annoyed, seeing someone dead.

He shivered at the recall and tried to refresh it regardless, but the more he tried, the quicker it faded.

When his heart had settled, his breath had been restored, the sweat on his body had dried and the chill under his flesh had ceased, he had forgotten every aspect of the dream. It was about Jessica, of that much he was sure, but he couldn't remember anything else.

He had gone to sleep worrying about reaping the corpse of whichever girl he chose to spend his, or rather *her*, life with. That thought had clearly prayed on his subconscious during his sleep, festering inside his mind and throwing an assortment of morbid images and anxious feelings his way.

He dressed, showered, shaved, and made his way downstairs for breakfast, which he usually shared with one or two guests in the spacious dining room.

A sullen-looking business man sat by his lonesome in the corner, thinking deeply into a steaming cup of coffee while absently chewing a slice of toast. On the other side of the room, waiting for Michael with a smile on his face, was Samson. There were two cups of hot coffee on the table in front of him and he was gesturing for Michael to sit down.

"What are you doing here?" Michael sat impatiently. He liked Samson, and he felt a paternal comfort in his presence, but his lack of support and his absence over the last year had annoyed him.

"That's no way to greet the man who mentored you."

Michael looked warily at the sullen man on the other side of the dining room, then back at the smiling face of his supposed mentor.

"You taught me fuck all," he spat with a hushed voice, fearful of alerting the other occupant to their conversation. "You left me in the shit; I barely know what the fuck I'm doing."

Samson shrugged casually. He reached out and took a small jar of marmalade and a slice of toast from a steel toast rack. "Want one?" he asked, pointing to a slice of toasted whole wheat bread.

Michael glared impatiently.

"More for me," Samson said as he slowly spread the marmalade over the toast and then took a bite from the corner, watching Michael silently as he chewed.

"What are you doing here?" Michael wanted to know. "Is this some part of my *mentorship*?" he asked with a mocking emphasis. "Are you finally going to help me?"

Samson slowly shook his head. He swallowed the chewed toast in his mouth and then calmly took another bite.

"What then?"

He lowered the food to the plate, brushed his hands against one another, took a drink of coffee to wash down the morsels and—eventually—spoke.

"I'm here to . . . " he made a humming noise and stroked his chin with the width of his forefinger.

"Well?"

"To warn you, I suppose," he said unsurely.

Michael perked up. He removed the disdain from his face, allowing an interested curiosity to take over.

"Warn me?"

"This girl you're seeing. She is your first *female* since your . . . " Samson looked around the dining room, lowered his voice. "*Departure*. Right?"

He nodded. "So?"

"Have you thought this through?"

"What do you mean *have I thought this through?*" Michael was getting annoyed. He didn't like the fact that Samson had ignored him when he needed him, and he certainly didn't like the fact that when he finally appeared, he did so with a critique of his love life. "What has any of this got to do with you?" he asked with a raised voice. "Who told you anyway?"

Samson shrugged his shoulders. He lowered his head and took another bite of toast.

"Was it Mary and Joseph?"

He grinned wryly at the mention of their name—thinking about something else entirely—but shook his head.

"Then who?"

He put the toast down again, brushed his hands against a piece of napkin. "I know these things," he said, the chewed food slid around in his mouth as he spoke. "That's not important, though." He met with Michael's eyes; Michael thought he saw a glint of sympathy. "How is the intuition coming along?"

Michael shrugged his shoulders. "It isn't," he said blankly.

"Nothing at all?"

"No."

"It's a gradual process you—"

Michael interrupted, "So you've said."

Samson stared at him deeply, his eyes unblinking as they cut through his thoughts and extinguished his anger.

"Okay," he said eventually, with an anticlimactic smile. "I better get going."

"That's it?" Michael snapped with surprise.

Samson shrugged his shoulders. He lolled his tongue around in his mouth, flicked a stray crumb out of a chipped wisdom tooth. "Pretty much," he finalized with a nod.

He rose noisily and Michael stood with him. He wanted to demand answers; he wanted to tell Samson that he had questions that *needed* answers. His anger restrained him. He remained silent.

"It was good seeing you," Samson declared, patting a friendly palm on his shoulder. "I'll be back soon."

Michael nodded and sat down, relieved at the closing statement but concerned with what Samson's definition of *soon* was.

Michael contemplated phoning Jessica all morning. He didn't want to come across too keen but he also didn't want her to think he had forgotten about her or wasn't interested in her.

It had been more than a year since he had phoned anyone to ask them on a date and a few years more since he had done it with someone he really liked.

At noon, he dialed her number into his phone. He bit his lip, waited for it to ring twice, and then hung up. He cursed himself, stamped an annoyed foot on the floor, hit redial, and then hung up after three rings.

"Jesus, Michael! Get your shit together," he warned himself.

He hit redial again and pressed the phone to his ear. Jessica answered on the first ring, leaving no time for early hang-ups. She sounded a little annoyed.

"Jessica, it's Michael," he announced. "From last night?" he added.

Her tone changed in an instant. The annoyance drifted away. She was happy to hear from him and told him so.

"Did you just ring me?" she added.

Michael contemplated the question, telling her, as nonchalantly as he could, "Yeah, bad connection, sorry about that." Keen to divert the subject away from his phone-call jitters, he quickly moved on, "I was wondering if you'd like to go see a movie, maybe get something to eat, a drink—"

"I'd love to," Jessica replied almost immediately.

Michael deflated with relief. "Excellent," he sighed enjoyably.

Michael didn't drive; it seemed unnecessary. He hadn't driven when he was alive and didn't care to take it up now he was dead. His job never left the town, never extended beyond the dozen square miles that encapsulated the hovel he had been required to call home. He also couldn't afford a car or the driving lessons he would require should he ever decide to own one. They arranged to meet at a neutral location between the restaurant and their respective homes—Michael at the B&B on one side of town; Jessica in rented accommodation on the other.

He waited for her outside the restaurant, a small family establishment. The food was strictly Italian but the family was Scottish. As a complement to their British heritage, they served most of their dishes with chips and offered a side dish of deep-fried frozen pizza, a batter-coated behemoth of heart attack proportions.

Jessica arrived by foot and greeted Michael with a smile and kiss on the cheek. Her previously tame red hair had been styled into a cornucopia of twirls and twists, sticking out from all angles and increasing the volume of her head three times over. Michael caught the overpowering whiff of hairspray when she leaned in, but he didn't mind—she looked great.

A thickset Glaswegian with a permanent scowl and a way of chewing his words before spitting them out took their order. She opted for the fresh seafood pasta. Michael chose lasagna and chips—after all, the sea was a two-hour drive away.

"So, you never told me what you do for a living," Jessica said when the first bottle of wine had been brought to the table with a basket of fresh bread.

Michael had been waiting for this, and he was prepared. He had thought about telling her he had a job boring or obscure enough not to warrant further examination, like a trainee accountant. But he doubted he could fake it for very long and it also wouldn't explain why he was living in practical poverty in the back room of a B&B. It had taken very little thought before he arrived at the simple conclusion.

"Nothing at the moment," he told her.

She weighed this up with a simple smile and a tilt of her head. "Not to worry," she declared. "I'm sure something will come up."

She picked out a bread roll and broke it open, nipping a slice of crust from the top before applying generous portions of butter to the warm bread inside.

"What would you like to do?" she wanted to know. "What do you *want* to be?"

Michael stared blankly at her. He wanted to be alive. He wanted to be able to talk to his friends again, to see his family. He wanted to be able to contemplate the possibility of a normal existence and not one that revolved around being stuck at the bottom rung of society, cleaning up the mess with little to no chance of advancement. He wanted to be able to go on a date with a girl without watching everything he did and said.

"A policeman," he said eventually.

"Oh," Jessica nodded her head slowly. She took a bite from the bread roll and stared across at him with a cheeky, apologetic smile as her hamster cheeks bulged with bread. "That's honorable," she said when she had finished chewing, licking away a few stray crumbs from her lips.

Michael nodded distantly. He didn't want to be a policeman. He had never really cared for authority. Authority had a way of breeding feelings of superiority in the socially inferior individuals who possessed it. He didn't know what he wanted to be, not now, not when he was alive, it was just the first thing that came to his head and was better than telling her he was hopeless as well as jobless.

There was only one other couple in the restaurant, sitting in the back. They were eating quietly under the shade of a globe that hung from the ceiling like a tacky disco ball; the boot-shaped land of Italy had been highlighted for those who needed reminding where pasta came from.

In the relative solitude, with the wine flowing and the food eaten, Michael and Jessica conversed boisterously. The topics of their lives and goals left the conversation when the alcohol had relaxed them and they began to joke, laugh, and tease.

They left the restaurant in high spirits. Michael was tipsy, having had the better part of two bottles of wine. He felt a dizzying warmth coursing through his blood stream and kicking out his stride, but Jessica, her slight build susceptible to the poisons of liquor, was on the verge of hysterics. She laughed at everything and stumbled carelessly as she walked.

Michael walked her home, cradling her in the crook of his arm and trying to keep his own feet steady while suffering the weight of hers. On the way home, she told him she really liked him and that she thought he was special, then she suggested that he cut his hair and sort out his life before she promptly vomited in the gutter. Michael didn't mind; he felt just as merry and he enjoyed supporting her as he cradled her to her doorstep. He felt human again.

She stopped at the front door, wobbled, supported herself against the frame, and then threw a finger to her lips, suggesting Michael remain quiet while issuing a rather loud *shh!* She dug around in her handbag, grumbled distastefully when she mistook her wallet for her keys, and then finally produced the dangling set, waving it proudly in front of Michael like a child showing their winner's medal to their parents.

"Do you want to come inside for a night cap?" she slurred with a wheezy smile.

Michael leaned forward and planted a kiss on her forehead. When he pulled back, she still had her eyes closed. She peeled them open slowly, looking a little disappointed at the length and position of the kiss.

"Maybe another time," he said softly.

The remnants of a smile dripped off her face. "Oh," she said sadly.

"I'm tired, we're both drunk," he explained. "I had a great time, though," he quickly added, sensing the swarm of alcoholic depression that cut across her features. "I'd love to do it again sometime. Maybe we can have a nice quiet drink and dinner together," he hinted.

Something sparked on Jessica's face; she looked like she had just found the cure for the common cold. "Here!" she declared, throwing her arm around to indicate the house. "We can have dinner here. I have drinks. *And* food."

"Okay. It's a date."

She leaned forward to kiss him, her eyes closed. Michael was forced backward as she fell into his arms. He placed a kiss on her lips; a spark seemed to connect him with her. He thought he felt something strange, tasted something obscene. Something flashed in his mind with an angry insistence—something quick, something unpleasant. It was her, but it wasn't her. He pushed her gently away from him, her bare shoulders felt unnervingly cold in his hands. He held her there, staring into her face.

She slowly opened her eyes, a smile at first, then perplexity, on her drunken face. "What's wrong?"

Michael felt his body twitch. He snapped out of a momentary fit and returned her bemusement with a warm smile. She looked okay; she smelled okay. He flexed his fingers, still clasped to her shoulders. She was warm, her skin was soft.

"Nothing," he said unsurely.

She shook off the momentary strangeness, too drunk to linger. She fiddled with the lock for an indeterminable moment and stumbled into the house, grinning at Michael before closing the door on him.

He looked at his hands when she departed, turning them this way and that while cursing under his breath.

He heard some commotion on the other side of the door and recognized the obtrusive and quizzical voice of her friend and roommate Julia as she unleashed a barrage of questions. He heard a stumbled, mumbled reply, then listened to a pair of hesitant, cumbersome footsteps ascend the staircase.

He turned around to leave, saw the curtains in the main room flicker. Julia's face popped out and glared at him disapprovingly. He gave her a little wave and then left, a skip in his step as he strolled the darkened streets.

5

He woke up with a breathless start, a dream fresh on his mind.

Jessica was there. They were together, arguing. She wasn't happy, he didn't seem to mind. Then she left him, just turned away and walked out of his life.

He saw himself at that point, watching his own image as if through the eyes of a camera. He saw the misery and helplessness on his own face. The anguish and agony in his tear-drenched eyes.

Jessica was gone, she had left him. He didn't know the details, didn't know why or how, didn't know what he had said, what he had done, or how he had said or done it. She was just gone.

He wondered at his own feelings when he woke. He liked her, but he had only known her for a few weeks. Was his subconscious really that anxious that she was going to get up and leave him? Would he be that traumatized if she did? Clearly she would have her reasons and, as much as he liked her, if those reasons revolved around her not feeling the same way, he wouldn't, surely *couldn't*, be that affected by it.

He dressed lethargically, his mind heavy with thought.

He decided to perk himself up with a hefty breakfast and a few cups of coffee. Joseph was a renowned cook and would put Michael on the breakfast order without a moment's thought.

By the time he made it down the spiraling staircase, bypassing one of the lodgers on the way—a short woman with a mousy smile and wiry blonde hair—Michael had already forgotten about the dream and the emotion it invoked. When he made it to the dining room, he also forgot about his hunger.

Samson sat alone in the room at the head of an empty table, his eyes pinned on the entrance that Michael strode cautiously though. He looked serious. The carefree demeanor was stripped from his wizened face, his knuckles pressed sternly and thoughtfully under his chin.

Michael flopped down opposite and absently picked at a crusted mark on the tabletop—the remnants of a previous breakfast.

"What is it this time?" he queried.

"It's about Jessica," Samson said simply.

"Oh, for fuck's sake," Michael spat tiredly. "Not this again—" he paused, stared darkly at his superior. "How do you know her name?"

Across from him, Samson merely shrugged his shoulders, a gesture that indicated there wasn't much he didn't know.

"What do you have against her?" Michael demanded. "Or is it *us* that you have something against? Is it because she's alive?"

"That's not—"

"I'm going to continue seeing her," Michael interjected.

Samson sighed. He rocked back in his seat. A cup of coffee had grown stale and cold in front of him, a thin spoon jutted out of its scummed surface. He reached out and flicked the spoon, watching it dance its way around the cup.

"What's wrong anyway?" Michael said, thrown by the dejected nature of the typically composed man opposite.

Samson glanced up soulfully. "I don't know how to tell you this . . . " he said deeply.

"Try."

He shook his head, rejecting whatever notion his mind had just offered. "You have feelings for this girl, right?"

"Yes, of course. We get along." Michael offered little, not wanting to commit himself to her before their relationship progressed.

"I think you should call it a day." Samson deflated as he spoke, as though he knew his words weren't going to be well received.

"You have got to be fucking kidding me!" Michael threw his hands down on the table. "What the fuck is this? First you leave me in the shit, drop me in the middle of fucking nowhere, tell me fuck all about what I'm doing here and what this place even *is*, and then this?" He stood defiantly, his calves kicking back his chair, which skidded with screeching fluidity across the floor before toppling over.

"Calm down," Samson offered up his hands. "Calm down."

"*You* fucking calm down," Michael said angrily, throwing his hands. "How dare you come here and try to dictate my fucking love life!"

"It's not like that," Samson tried to explain, growing more animated. "If you would just listen—"

Michael roared, "Get the fuck out of my sight!"

Samson stood slowly. A pleading and sympathetic look in his eyes, but Michael's anger wouldn't allow him to see it. He stared straight through Samson until the older man backed down, strafing around his former protégé and leaving through the kitchen door.

Michael heard Joseph and Mary on the other side, the smell of toast and sizzling bacon broke on a wave of muffled discontent.

He paced around his room with the timer held tightly in his hand. Nothing today, nothing all week. Beyond that, who knew? It felt weighty and cold in his hand, an empty digital screen awaiting news of another demise.

He was angry. In that moment, he hated his job and his responsibilities more than ever. He felt like a retaliatory teenager stuck in the throes of parental oppression. A small part of mature logic niggled at the back of his mind, trying to calm him down and telling him to come to his senses, but he ignored it—forced it away on a torrent of righteous aggression. Samson had ignored him and then betrayed him, and was now trying to end the one good thing that had happened since the curse of immortality had been bestowed.

He threw the timer across the room, reveling in the cathartic anger that surged from his muscle as the device was violently propelled against the wall. The plaster chipped, a bright white dent in the soft blue paint. The timer lumped to the floor without a scratch, its screen still alight and patiently waiting.

Michael ignored it. He grabbed his jacket and left.

When he returned in the evening, he continued to ignore the device, kicking it under the bed where it nestled into an unseen clump of forgotten clothing. The following day, he didn't have breakfast at the B&B, instead choosing to dine on a sandwich and a coffee from a local café. On the second and third night, he continued to ignore the timer. He also ignored Mary and Joseph—the couple that had unconditionally sheltered him for a year—and left the building as early as he could to avoid their attentions.

On the fourth night, he saw Jessica for dinner. On the sixth, he took her bowling. By the eighth day, he was seeing Jessica every night, no longer concerned with his job or with the timer, which gathered dust underneath his bed.

After a few weeks, Michael had almost forgotten about his argument with Samson. He was happy, ecstatic in his new relationship. He had been with Jessica for a month and had slept with her for the first time, then the second, third, fourth. When they started they couldn't stop; he felt alive for the first time since his death.

He saw her every day. She had taken a break from her studies— he suspected it was because of him, because of *them*, but he didn't mind. He wanted what was best for her but the relationship was young and fresh, and seeing her took priority over everything else.

They had been together for a month when Michael took her out for a more impressive meal. He spared no expense and blew a fortnight's pay on an expensive dinner. He didn't have much money, but what he did have he spent, and as he had abandoned his chance of finding more work—if there *was* any, he hadn't seen the timer for many weeks—there was little chance he could recoup that money. Yet when he left the restaurant, broke, penniless, and practically destitute, he was happy, because Jessica was happy.

"You shouldn't have gone to all that trouble," she told him, her head peeking around from the crook of his arm.

"It's our month anniversary," he said proudly.

Jessica smiled timidly and slipped back under his embrace.

A wobbling hen party, an olfactory concoction of cheap perfume, cheap wine, and desperation, waddled by. One of them brushed past Michael; he felt her heavy breasts clap against his left elbow. He turned to look at her as she passed, preparing to offer or receive an apology. She beamed back with an unashamed lick of her glossy lips.

She seemed to be horny; Michael felt a little sick to his stomach. She looked like a morbidly obese siren; her fat folds flopped out of her mini skirt and tank top like bread dough in an overfilled tin. She walked backward while she tried to entice him, and her heels hit a chip in the pavement. She stumbled like a flip-flopping Jabba the Hut before being saved by a heavyset friend.

"Jesus," he muttered under his breath as they gathered themselves and clip-clopped their cheapened heels away from the scene, their scents dissipating and their raucous voices fading.

"Except," she said slowly, ignoring the horny women, "you know that *technically* it isn't."

Michael gave her a questionable frown.

"*Anni*, or *annus* rather, is Latin," she elaborated. "It means 'year.'"

"Oh. So a month . . ."

"Isn't an anniversary."

"Oh."

"Is there a word for it then?"

"I don't think so. I mean, probably, but not one we commonly use."

Michael looked a little dejected. Jessica reached around and pinched the back of his jeans as if to spark some life into him.

"And *versary*?" he wondered.

She shrugged passively. "'Turn,' 'pass,' something like that."

A light rain pattered the skies, dotting the pavement with specks of black. The night was mild but the day had been unbearably warm. The sun-stroked streets, still warm from the heat of the day, sizzled under the dripping drizzle. A dozen drinkers patted nosily up and down, leaving the cafés and heading for the night-clubs. A line of taxis, official and unofficial—husbands, wives, mothers, and fathers hired as drivers for the night—stopped, started, and cruised by on the street.

Michael swerved around a group of teenage drinkers exiting a grotty pub, spilling out in the midst of a heated, but amicable debate. He held Jessica tighter in his arm, keeping her away from the concoction of cheap body spray, excessive hair gel, and obscene conversation as they continued down the path.

"We haven't been to a nightclub," Jessica noted. Her dazzling eyes caught the glint of a neon spectacle above a building on the other side of the road, where a stubby bouncer with a Popeye build prepared for a night of intimidation.

Michael sneered distastefully, and Jessica caught the look.

"Not a fan?" she wondered. "I thought a nightclub would be ideal for charmers like you. Rows and rows of drunken girls, all up for a bit of fun?" she said with a cheeky grin. "By the end of the night, they'll all be drunk, high, desperate, or lonely. They'll practically fall into your arms."

"Nah," Michael said calmly. "I never leave it till the end of the night."

"Never?"

A beaten-up car, with teenagers slotted into the seats like sardines, sped by, spilling an assortment of jeers, obscenities, and bone-crushing music out of the opened windows. Michael grimaced and watched it race down the street. It halted with a clattering *thunk* as it slowly turned the corner before struggling to pick up its pace again as the driver floored the pedal to speed down the opposing street.

"Never," Michael said when the noise of the mobile tin-can had faded.

Jessica did a little two-step and lowered her right hand in a ceremonial bow. "Explain, *master*," she mocked.

Michael laughed at her theatrics. "You can't kiss them at the end of the night."

"Me? I wouldn't kiss them at all," she joked.

"You, me. People in general," he explained. "You don't know where they've been. You certainly don't know where their lips have been. You don't know on who or what they've been suckling."

"*Suckling?*" Jessica recoiled at the choice of word.

Michael grinned. "Well, you know, when the drink is flowing and the night is young, most girls are on the prowl. If *you, me, whoever,* decides to pick them up at the end of the night, that's a good four hours they've had to *circulate*. Is that the salt from a margarita I'm tasting? Or the residual spunk from the bouncer?"

Jessica feigned a gagging noise and looked at him in disgust, shifting out from his grasp slightly.

Michael beamed proudly and threw an arm around her. She ducked out from under him, spun around and stopped in the middle of the street, her hands thrust on her hips, a mock look of quizzical shock on her delicate face.

"Is this why you never kissed me at the beginning of the night, Michael?" she asked sternly. A sly smile tried to twitch its way onto her lips.

Michael held up his hands. "I didn't need to with you."

Jessica threw her hand in an understanding nod and moved forward.

Michael continued, "I was with you all night. Plus, if I'm honest, it was your friend I was after."

Jessica stopped. Her face exploded with feigned indignation, hidden behind a smile. Michael took an instinctive step back, avoiding the inevitable slap.

"How dare you!" she roared, unable to suppress a laugh that twitched epileptically at her mouth. She pushed her hands stubbornly to her hips and moved toward the middle of the road, her head turned away in snobbish refusal. She took a few strides out into the road, watching Michael through squinted eyes. "If that's the way you feel, then I'll just leave—"

Her words were cut short by the screech of car tires and a dull thud as her body clattered into the hood of a passing car. She was propelled into the air and then slammed with force against the car's windshield, splintering a spiderweb fracture in the glass.

The driver slammed on the brakes instantly, but the car didn't screech to a halt until it was a good twenty feet from the impact. Jessica's body bounced and rolled to a halt a further ten feet away.

Michael felt his knees wobble. He sunk to the floor, the pavement crunching painfully against his kneecaps. His ears buzzed and whined. The lights from the pubs, clubs, and streetlights danced dizzily in front of his eyes.

There was a lot of noise. The driver and the passenger screamed aggressively at each other from inside the car, unsure who should react first or how they should react. A woman on the other side of the road had witnessed the collision and stood rooted to the spot, squealing like a newborn child. Up and down the street, revelers diverted their attentions away from their prospective clubs to concentrate on the carnage on the road. Conversations were already flowing, the split-second shock had died away, and those who had witnessed the bloodthirsty moment bragged about their presence while those who didn't pretended otherwise.

Michael heard another noise. A low-strung moan which increased in volume with each painful octave. It took him a few minutes to realize the sound was coming from his own throat, a few more before he had the power to suppress it.

He dragged himself to his feet, forced his eyes to tune into the impact over his shoulder. He looked at Jessica and prayed for some sign of life, but what he saw vanquished any glimmer of hope that his heart had held.

Jessica was a mangled wreck on the ground, a dozen rivulets of blood branching away from her torn body and seeping a path into the gutters. Above the body, with a content stance and a warm smile, was Jessica's spirit. She looked at Michael, smiled happily, and then calmly walked over to him.

He deposited Jessica's soul like he had done with a dozen souls before her and would do with many souls after her. He didn't allow himself any emotion, didn't let a single thought of what might have been, what could have been, and what *should* have been.

Jessica said she was sorry they couldn't go on seeing each other. She said it was unfortunate that nothing could become of their relationship and that maybe they would meet on the other side and could try again. Michael gave a few nods and strained smiles in reply, he held her hand gently and he kissed her on the cheek, but it was all for show. When she was dead to the world, she was dead to him, and he was never going where she was going.

He felt cheap and dirty when he collected the money for her. He felt angry when Seers interrupted and patronized him about his position, felt like ripping the smug head off his spindly shoulders and shoving it up his pompous ass. He felt like telling the gravelly voiced, ass-faced receptionist what he thought of her when she sneered down at him under the rim of her spectacles. But throughout it all, he maintained an expression of nothingness, a feeling of complete dissociation.

His first love in his new world, his first semblance of hope in a place he despised and didn't understand, had died, and with it, a small part of him had also died.

A trio of sympathetic ears and open shoulders were waiting for him when he returned to the bed-and-breakfast. Samson, Joseph, and Mary all eyed him as he strode inside, cutting a melancholic figure as he exited the darkness of the yard and broke the cozy glow of the living room.

He stood in the doorway, didn't look at them, didn't meet their pitying glances. "You knew this was going to happen," he said distantly.

"We didn't know," Joseph said defensively. "It's just—"

"Relationships with the living can be complicated," Mary helped. "These things happen. I'm sorry sweetheart."

"*I* knew," Samson said plainly.

Michael lifted his eyes and stared straight at his supposed mentor.

"I tried to tell you," Samson noted, staring into Michael's tired, blackened eyes.

"You did," Michael said softly with a nod of his head.

"I thought you might have known something," Samson added. "Even without the timer."

The images, the dreams, and the strange feelings all rushed back to Michael. He nodded methodically. "It doesn't matter now," he said, turning away from their condolences. "It's over."

PART FOUR

IT'S A
TERRIBLE LIFE

1

Michael had loved Christmas growing up. He loved the festive joy on the faces of even the sourest of citizens. He adored the wonder and joy in the eyes and antics of every school-free child. He was amused by the zealously religious who patrolled the church, the streets, and the fetes trying to make everyone feel guilty for their sinful ways. He liked the Christmas music, the repetitious monotony of the annual playlists that were typically terrible but sound fantastic during the holidays.

Every town in every Christian country geared up for the festivities. Every smile on every face was festooned with the joys of the season. Carefree adults threw joyful snowballs at the mischievous children frolicking in their driveways or on the streets. The tone deaf took to the streets in numbers to blast out high-pitched anthems for receipt of a handful of coins. Sly flirts seized a year's worth of missed opportunities to pinch a kiss under the mistletoe; lovers took to the comfort of their homes, with their warm fires and their candlelit memories; families gathered around a feast on the dinner table, with Christmas crackers and talk of presents, while uncles and grandparents fell into drunken comas on the sofa.

Everything about the season had inspired joy into the living Michael—even as an adult he had loved it—but the dead Michael hated it. He hated the souls he had fished from drunken bodies decomposing in their own piss on the iced streets. He hated the drug addicts who celebrated the festive season by blowing their veins with an overdose of their drug of choice. He hated, and struggled to forget, the bodies of the kids he had seen in the gutters—struck down by drunk drivers—before escorting their souls to an afterlife that came far too soon. He hated the suicides; the murders from moments of drunken domestic violence; the aged and lonely who froze to death trying to save a few pennies on their heating bills.

Christmas was for spoiled kids and carefree idiots; he knew that now. For everyone else, especially those who had to face the mistakes of others, it was a living hell.

Brittleside buzzed just like every other small town during the festive season. As Michael strode sullenly down the streets, he ducked under a dozen lampposts strewn with tinsel. He passed beneath shop windows splattered with multicolored, dangling lights. He heard Christmas songs from shops, houses, and cars that motored steadily by on a sheet of ice that covered the town like a beige film.

He groaned at every note, grimaced at every light, rolled his eyes at every holiday greeting. The big day was two weeks away and already he was losing his patience with the season. It didn't help that he had spent the past few months hassling Naff to give him information about the werewolf murdering clones, and getting nothing but stonewall silence and ejection in reply. At first he thought his friend was holding out on him, unwilling to tell him anything that his bosses might find out about. He didn't blame him for that. In the afterlife, the walls really did have ears. It was like living in a reality TV show, and sometimes it felt like the audience, whoever they were, was just as hell-bent on blood, bitchiness, and drama. But he soon realized that his friend really was as clueless about the whole situation as he claimed.

"I genuinely don't know anything," he had told him after another exasperated round of questioning, his eyes wide, bright, and desperate. "I work the records at a very basic level. I knew they were werewolves. I know that something untoward was happening and I know that it involved one of us. But that's it. Now, can you please release your grip on my testicles?"

Michael had picked up a body in the morning, his first official death of the holidays. The death was unrelated to the season—an aging body finally succumbing to the rigors of prostate cancer—but the spirit of the dead man swam with all the joys of Christmas.

He had asked if he would get to meet Jesus and if it snowed in heaven before relaying the story of his boyhood Christmases and then humming an infuriating seventies seasonal classic in the waiting room.

Michael needed a drink after that. He cut through the streets on instinct, not looking up for fear of what festive atrocity he would see, and then headed for the Dead Seamstress.

The dead hated Christmas just as much as he did. The interior of the pub didn't change for the season. It was still just as dank, dark, and gloomy as it always was. There wasn't a happy humming soul in sight. When Michael approached the bar to find Scrub glaring at him, he felt the urge to jump over the bar and plant a sloppy kiss on the midget's head.

The urge didn't last long.

Scrub cleared his throat with an emetic warble. "Afternoon, Michael," he said with a nod.

"How's business?"

"Slow."

"Ah, well."

"I like it slow."

"Oh, then, well done."

Michael saw Naff looking forlorn and agitated at the corner table. He was staring miserably into a pint of ale, his leg tapping a nervous rhythm on the floor, his mouth chomping the fingernails of his right hand down to the knuckles. When he noticed Michael staring at him he instinctively moved his hand to his groin.

"Give me a pint of beer, Scrub." Michael fished out a few coins from his pocket and dropped them onto the bar. "Chip been in today?"

"Short guy, hairy, looks like the ass-end of a lame horse?" Scrub said as he dropped down from his stool and patted over to pull a pint.

Scrub was a good foot and a half shorter than Chip, but what his physical stature lacked, his intimidation and ego made up for. He felt like a giant and he looked like one to whoever was unlucky enough to be on the end of one of his beatings.

"That's the one."

"Haven't seen him all day."

He reached up and plonked the pint on the bar. A third of it sloshed onto the tabletop. Scrub glanced at it nonchalantly and then quickly scooped up the money in case Michael changed his mind and demanded a refill.

"Thanks," Michael said meekly.

He carried the drink over to his nervous friend, who was rubbing his temples with a rapidity that suggested it was about to explode.

He was seated for less than thirty seconds—enough time to take one short sip, which, thanks to Scrub's heavy-handedness, meant that only half a pint remained—before Naff gave him a desperate, appealing stare.

"I need your help," he spluttered, the tension evident in his voice. He tapped his fingers on the tabletop, ran a stray thumb over a mysterious crust that had infested the wood. "I have a problem," he said with a lowered voice.

"Like the problem I had a few months ago that you refused to help me with?"

"I told you, I can't—"

"Yes, yes," Michael waved his hand dismissively. "I've heard it before. Anyway, I told you before, I can't help you with that, you need to see a doctor."

"No," Naff said, lifting his eyes up and checking to see if anyone else had heard. "It's not that, and that's fine. I mean, it hasn't cleared—look, that's not the problem."

"Then what is?"

"Santa Claus," he answered simply.

Michael nearly choked on his drink. He lowered his glass to the table, slowly wiped a bead of beer from his chin, and then parroted: "*Santa Claus.*"

"He's going into people's houses, leaving presents for the kids, eating cookies—"

"I know who Santa Claus is."

"This is not the *real* Santa Claus, though," Naff stressed.

In thirty years, Michael had never heard those words, but he wasn't as surprised as he expected. "*Is* there a real Santa Claus?" he asked, wondering why it hadn't come up before.

"No," Naff said, with a face that suggested Michael was an idiot for asking. "Of course not."

Michael was relieved. Vampires, werewolves, clones, demons, and bogeymen he could take. He could even live with the knowledge that tooth fairies existed, but he would have drawn a line in the sand at the notion of Santa Claus, especially after spending thirty years in the afterlife.

"So what the fuck are you talking about?" he asked Naff, who was now absently picking stale, two-year-old nuts out of a bowl in the center of the table and popping the glued clusters into his mouth.

"He's a demon," Naff said solemnly. "A few sandwiches short of a picnic."

Michael nodded absently, his eyes on the nuts with something resembling awe. He had always assumed it was potpourri. He had seen Chip eat some a few months back, but he had also seen Chip eat his own earwax.

"He thinks he's jolly Saint Nick, even has the suit and the beard."

"Is it real?" Michael wondered, intently watching his friend, waiting for the moment he keeled over, clutching his stomach.

"What?"

"The beard, is it real?"

"Does it matter?"

He shrugged his shoulders, "Just curious."

"Yes," Naff told him. "It's real."

"What about the belly?"

A pained look of angst spread over Naff's face. "Can you take this seriously please?"

Michael grinned. "I don't see what the problem is," he stated, sure that he saw something crawling around the bowl after the first layer of glued nuts had been excavated. "Some jolly fat guy wants to give kids presents," he shrugged passively. "Where's the harm in that?"

"He's an emotionally unstable demon," Naff said firmly.

"And?"

"He has powers and he has problems. He could be dangerous."

"*Could* be, but isn't."

"*Could* is enough cause for me to want to stop him. And," he strained over a thought, "there's another thing."

"He didn't get you the pony you asked for?"

Naff shook his head slowly and glared at his friend, before choosing to ignore the comment. "It's my fault he's free," he said sullenly. "I let him out."

"Ah."

"If he causes shit, it's all on me."

"I understand," Michael said. "So you can track down Santa Claus but you can't track down my werewolf killer?"

Naff glared at his friend. "Speaking of which, I helped you with that shit. That's what friends do. Friends do not grab other friends by the balls and demand that they tell them something they don't know. Friends help each other. Friends care about each other."

"Have you met Chip?

Naff shook the comment off. "You know, I wouldn't be surprised if you were the one to cause, my . . . *issue*."

"I tell you this now, mate, you don't get STDs from a little squeeze."

Naff slammed the table, making his friend jump. "It's not an STD!" he yelled, appalled. "I mean, it's just a little infection," he added, softening upon seeing that Scrub was now grinning at him over the bar.

Naff sighed. "Look, can you just drop the werewolf shit and fucking help me?"

"Okay," Michael said. Holding his hands up. "So, how we gonna stop this mean, horrible bastard from bringing joy to the lives of children everywhere?"

"He slips in through a chimney, or, failing that, he gets in through an open window. He leaves the kids' presents all neatly arranged at the bottom of their bed and then he stuffs his face with cookies and whatever sherry or wine he can find in the kitchen."

"You think that's why my mother always left cookies and a glass of sherry on the mantel, to stop him from raiding the fridge?"

"Can you take this seriously please?"

"What about carrots, for his reindeer?"

Naff sighed. "*Well . . .*" he prolonged, unwilling to finish. "*Actually.*"

"Really!" Michael looked both amazed and amused. "He takes carrots, as well?"

"Like I said, he's mad. Maybe—"

"Are you sure he's not the real deal?" Michael asked dryly.

"*Positive,*" Naff spat with a great deal of frustration.

"And why are we stopping him again?" Michael wondered. "He's just trying to help out, right? What harm can he possibly do?"

Naff stared at his friend. He inhaled deeply, held up his fingers. "Firstly," he slowly bent one of his fingers back. Michael sighed, realizing he had triggered a lecture. Naff had a way of slowing everything down when he was annoyed and trying to explain something. Michael figured it was a byproduct of being friends with Chip, who was constantly irritating and never understood anything.

Naff continued at a leisurely pace. "He's a demon. He has powers that no human has and he's using them to sneak into the houses of young children and their parents when they are at their most vulnerable. I'm sure I don't need to tell you how badly things could turn out. Secondly," he peeled another finger back, "he's confined to hell for a reason. It's not my place to say what that reason is, but it's hell, not the Hamptons, so trust me when I say there is a very good reason. Thirdly," another finger, another sigh from his friends. "He's mentally unstable, so there is no telling when he will go off. Maybe he'll get pissed when his elves don't show up. Maybe he'll burn down a house because it doesn't have a chimney. Maybe he'll lose his shit when a kid wakes up and asks for a fucking selfie. Who knows, the point is, he's a fucking loony toon. Finally," no finger went back this time. Michael grinned, knowing he had lost count but not wanting to give him reason to retrace his steps. "*Finally*, it's my fault he's there. If he does something, I'm the one who gets it in the neck. If not and they find out, I could still face suspension."

Michael was silent.

"Are we on the same page?" Naff asked.

Michael nodded. He thought about telling his friend that he had understood before and was just being a nuisance, but he didn't want to be lectured again.

A small creature hopped out from the nut bowl with a peanut stuck to its back. It walked a wavy line across the table, like a drunken man trying to find his way home. Naff squashed the peanut beetle and then flicked the dead bug and tainted nut off the table.

"Hey!" a small sharp voice called angrily from behind him. He turned to see Scrub glaring at him. The miniature man had clambered up onto the bar, his feet in the wastage of a hundred pints of cider and beer, and was pointing an angry finger at Naff. "I saw that!" he bellowed. "Stop making a mess in my bar!"

Naff instinctively glanced around the decrepit room. The floor in the immediate vicinity of the bar was littered with the detritus of a dozen drunken nights: chips, crumbs, food packets. Pieces of food, scraps of torn clothes, shoes, shoelaces, and small coins had wedged themselves into the grimy floors around the tables like lost archaeological treasures.

"Pick it up!" Scrub ordered, his patience rapidly fading.

Naff turned to Michael and mouthed the word: "*Really*?"

Michael gave a shrug that suggested he do what the little mad man said regardless of how hypercritical it was.

He picked up the nut, offered a smile to Scrub—who dropped down from behind the bar and allowed his burning facade to cool—and then dropped it back into the bowl. Chip would probably eat it later.

"So," Michael said, rolling his eyes, thankful that he still had eyes to roll. "How did he get out?"

Naff slumped, even more dejected now that the merry murdering midget had told him off. "He, Jacky Sampson, that's his name—"

"Santa Claus?"

"Yes."

"I thought he was—"

"If you say Saint Nicholas I'll rip your throat out."

"Jesus."

"Sorry, just a little on edge." Naff wiped a bead of anxious sweat from his forehead, rubbed his eyes with the palm of his hand, and pressed a finger to his temple. "He was stuck in purgatory. I was his intermediate."

"Intermediate?"

Naff waved a frustrated hand. "It's like a probation officer; I've told you this before."

"In my defense, you talk a lot of shit and I drink a lot."

"Whatever, look, I let him go. I told them he was fit for release. I mean, I thought he *was*," he explained with great pain. "He seemed fine, but, well, clearly he was just faking it."

"Can't be that insane then."

"We've been through this. He thinks he's fucking Santa Claus."

"Good point."

"He started this escapade the same night I released him, and that was a week ago. We've only just found out it was him. Turns out one of the homes had a nanny-cam set up, and they have stills of him. We were alerted by an insider at the news station. He's stopping it from going public but now my boss is on my ass." He sighed and dropped his head into his arms. "What the fuck am I going to do?"

2

In the depths of the darkest hour, with the world under the somatic touch of the Sandman and the streets sparse with foraging animals, lonely insomniacs, and the humdrum tempo of forlorn cars taking their drivers to red-eyed nightshifts, a fat man in a red suit struggled through an open window.

The only sound was the shuffling of bulging fabric and the drowned noise of heavy snoring that pattered a steady path toward the open window.

A stray foot, clad in a heavy leather boot, stood in something unpleasant. The owner reacted with disgusted recoil, lost his balance, and toppled over, hitting the floor with a heavy thud. Through the sound of his own calamitous clambering, he couldn't hear the snoring, and the sound of his own blood, rushing a surprised path through his ears, cancelled out all other noise. When his ears retuned to the silence, he realized the snoring had stopped.

He waited on the floor silent and unmoving, like an animal caught in the glare of the headlights, hoping that its passivity would save it from being skinned.

The snoring started again, choking and gargling into life before erupting into the steady flow of obstructed breathing.

The man in the red suit breathed again. He stood, straightened his glorious white beard, refitted his right boot, and then got to work.

The house around him was dark, lit only by the moonlight from the window he obstructed, but he sensed that darkness was this house's best medium. He sensed dirt around him, felt the clutter and the must. He could smell a thick, bodily grime—the scent of unwashed bodies that had sat, walked, worked, and lain in an unwashed room.

He retrieved a large sack from outside the window, steadily lifting it in so as not to make another noise. Throwing the sack around a strained shoulder, he stepped steadily forward on the toes of his leather boots.

The house unravelled itself as he stepped out of the light.

There was an ancient kettle on the stove, its rough metallic structure bounced the silver sheen of moonlight in a reflective diamond around the kitchen; a fridge stuck with so many ineligible Post-it notes that it was hard to guess the color of the paint underneath.

From the kitchen floor, he crossed to what he assumed was the living room. The floor underfoot was carpeted but hard. Some of it stuck to the sole of his left boot, and he struggled with it, trying to kick and dislodge, finding freedom after ten seconds of panic and struggle.

There was no fireplace, no stockings hung expectantly, at least not in the living room. He crossed to the hallway, entering a completely dark stretch that rendered him blind. Taking a small flashlight from his pocket, he carefully lit the floor, cautious of holding the beam in front of him and waking any of the faces it fell upon.

The snoring grew louder as he crept; it seemed to be emanating from the furthest of the three doors in front of him. He ignored it and opened the first; it was already ajar, saving him the cringe-worthy task of peeling the handle down and slipping it squeakily open.

He pushed it with the tip of the flashlight and shone a light inside: a bed, some discarded clothes, two pieces of tattered furniture. No stocking. Nothing Christmassy at all. He pulled the door a few inches toward him, leaving it as he had found it.

The next door led to the bathroom, a room he sincerely wished he had avoided. He walked quickly away and came to the final door, where the snoring was unbearable. He didn't need to take his time toying with the handle, as there was little chance that the squeak of an unoiled hinge could be heard above the breathless racket, but he did it anyway.

With the door open, he was hit with a wave of sound and smell. It came at him like a wall and he gagged. He took an instinctive step back, then he planted two fingers over his nose and shone the flashlight inside with his free hand.

A short hump lay tight under a stained duvet that billowed under the heavy snoring. At the side of the bed, a lit joint had been allowed to sit unattended in an ashtray. It had burned to a finish, leaving an ashy deposit all over the bedside table.

He spotted what he sought stuffed into the top drawer of that bedside cabinet, draping down over the handle and brushing the floor: a stocking, bright red under the beam of torchlight.

He took the top two presents from the bag, held his nose, and then entered the room. The wall of noise battered him away, but he powered through like a trooper, dropping the two carefully wrapped presents into the beckoning stocking and then quickly exiting the room.

He shone the flashlight back in to admire his handiwork. The present bulged inside the stocking like a chubby calf. He whispered softly and proudly: "Merry Christmas . . . ," he paused and shone the light over a white tag on the stocking where a name had been emblazoned in thick black letters. "Chip," he finished with a smile.

He closed the door, threw his sack over his shoulder, and headed back into the night.

When Michael woke, he did so to the joyous calls of his typically ill-tempered roommate. Chip was happy; Michael was worried. The last time he had seen something remotely resembling happiness on the face of the grumpy tooth fairy was when he successfully trapped a rat that had been plaguing the apartment for several weeks. His shrieking yells of accomplishment came right before he beheaded the rodent, impaled a thin pencil through his body like a sickening stake, and displayed it on the kitchen windowsill to "warn away the others."

Wondering what macabre horrors awaited him in the other room, Michael staggered out of bed, using the bedside cabinet to hold his balance and keep him from falling flat on his face. The small digital clock on top of the table told him it was just before nine. He hadn't fallen asleep till the early hours of the morning, doing so in a mild drunken stupor that left his mouth feeling like the inside of a kangaroo's asshole.

He had left the pub before midnight. Naff was depressing him, but he had continued his drinking at home. Chip had returned home from work not long after, heading straight to bed and drowning the house with his chorus of snores.

He coughed a clump from his throat, rubbed his tired eyes, and staggered forward, toward the fading cheers of joy.

He found Chip in the hallway, proudly clutching a small tablet computer in his hand, a ball of hastily torn wrapping paper lay discarded at his feet. He waved the device at Michael when he approached, a broad smile on his ugly face.

"Look at this," he exclaimed joyfully. "Tablet computer, see." He flicked a grubby finger on the screen. His brow furrowed, his eyebrows arched into disappointment as he retracted the computer. "Well, it was working before. It doesn't matter," he assured, regaining his excitement. "It's mine!"

"Who did you steal that from?" Michael asked dryly.

Chip looked offended. He hugged the device to his chest. "What makes you say that?" he asked, feigning hurt, not letting on that he had been trying to steal one for months but hadn't found an owner dumb or naive enough.

"Where did you get it?"

Chip grinned like a smug child. "Santa Claus."

"Fuck off."

"It's true!"

Michael raised an eyebrow, put a hand on his hip. "Tell me, who did you steal it from?"

"I didn't—"

He waved his friend short. "I don't really care," he muttered, feeling a tired headache creeping through his skull like a parasitic worm. "Just make sure you give it back when you're done."

He brushed past his friend, leaving the little tooth fairy struck sour and outraged in the hallway.

"I didn't fucking steal it!" he yelled, incensed. Michael waved a dismissive hand over his shoulder and disappeared into the living room, but Chip followed, keen to declare his innocence the one time he really was innocent.

"Why won't you believe me?" he wondered, following his friend around the kitchen as he filled the kettle and plonked it lazily on the stove.

Michael shrugged, leaned back against the counter, and struggled to keep his eyes open.

"You should believe me. You're supposed to be my friend."

"You always say that. You're always lying."

"Not this time! Honestly."

"So you're admitting that you were lying all those other times?" Michael wondered. "Like the time you said you didn't know who stole my phone, or my bike?"

Chip diverted his eyes, looked a little sheepish under the accusing glare of his hungover roommate. "What did you want a fucking bike for anyway?" he mumbled. "Only women and—"

"And what about my wallet?" Michael interrupted. "With the winning betting slip in."

"Ah-ha!" Chip said, raising a finger. "I didn't steal that," he said genuinely. "It was lost."

"By you," Michael said with a knowing nod. "After you stole it."

Chip shrugged. "You can't prove anything."

Michael shook his head and turned his attention to the kettle, which had screeched to deafening heights. He rinsed out a cup with a questionable scummy liquid in the bottom, picked a speck of peeled lip from the rim, and dropped a spoonful of coffee and three sugars inside. When the kettle squealed to a halt, he turned his back on his friend to fill his cup.

"So, who did you steal it from?" He had a steaming cup of coffee in his hands and was already feeling more awake. He trotted to the living room with the incensed tooth fairy biting at his heels.

"I'm telling you the truth. Santa Claus gave me it."

Michael rolled his eyes, weighed up the pleading look in his friend's face, and took a long drink. The hot liquid ran a scolding track down his esophagus and to his stomach, heating everything up in its path and clearing away a thin line of distaste that had woven an intricate web through his insides.

He began to object again, a little unsure this time, but something stopped him. He paused with the mug at his lips; the liquid burned through the ceramic and imprinted a heated blotch onto his dried lips. Memories of the previous night returned to him, including everything that Naff had told him.

"Santa Claus?" he said softly.

Chip nodded, beaming a proud and somewhat smug smile, the debated item still clutched tightly in his hands.

"Seriously?"

"On my mother's grave."

"Do you even have a mother?"

"On *your* mother's grave then."

Michael rubbed his temple with the nibs of fingers that had been heated by the cup; the action restored some vigor as the coffee simultaneously soaked into his central nervous system and awakened his senses.

"He came here? To this house?"

Chip nodded. "I wrote him a letter, put up a little stocking near my bed and," he gestured to the computer, "I guess I wasn't on his naughty list after all."

"You know Santa's not real?"

Chip frowned. "Don't be a fucking numpty, of course I know. Try telling that to the mental fuck going around dressed in red and giving people presents."

"You know about him?" Michael stammered. "Have you spoken to Naff?"

"Not for a couple days."

"Then who told you?"

Chip gave a cheeky wink and tapped the end of his nose with the edge of the computer.

"You better fucking tell me," Michael warned.

"Okay, look. I may have *run into him* the other night," he said vaguely.

"Go on."

Chip flopped down on the sofa, reluctantly placing the computer on the arm of the chair but failing to take his eyes off it for more than a few of seconds at a time. "I was on a job," he began. "Four days ago. Seven- or eight-year-old, first timer. Tried to dislodge a loose tooth and ended up knocking out four of 'em. I only had enough money for three, stopped off for a burger on the way." He ran the tip of his tongue over the edge of his front teeth, recalling the flavor of the tainted meat. "You ever eaten at that Dodgy Darren's burger van?" he wondered. "I'm not so sure if he gave me the shits or—"

"There's a reason he's called Dodgy Darren."

"I thought it was something to do with his eyes."

"His eyes?"

"Well, they're all wonky. They don't seem to wanna go in the same direction. It's off-putting. I can never tell when he's—"

"Get on with it!" Michael snapped, feeling his blood rush tempestuously at the sound of his rambling friend.

"Okay, okay!" Chip said with one arm held aloft. "I didn't wanna leave the kid short so I figured I'd nick some from his parents, none the wiser. His mother was fast asleep; no sign of the father. I heard some rumbling downstairs and figured he was still up and about, probably one nightcap too many."

Chip shifted his position, his eye casually moved to the tablet computer, his mind temporarily forgetting his place in the story. "So, anyway," he said after some deliberation. "I sees an old fatty downstairs, rummaging around in a red suit. At first I figure it's just the dad, probably lost his mind, into some kinky solo sex games, whatever. I ignored him, started doing some rummaging of my own. I found the money, but all the while I sees this fat jolly guy stuffing presents into a stocking with a constant smile on his face and a little song on his lips. I followed him into the kitchen, sees him pick out a few cookies and pour himself a glass of sherry.

"Now, I've seen Santa Claus stories. I work with kids; I know how this shit works. Jolly Saint Nick, Rudolph, an' all that. This guy looked like the real deal. Real beard; real belly, as far as I could tell. The suit looked impressive as well. Heavy-duty, not some flimsy costume shit. So . . ." he shrugged nonchalantly. "I figured if he came for the kid, then maybe he would come for me."

"Really?"

Chip nodded. "Yes," he said. "Also," he added as an after-thought, "Naff texted me two days ago."

Michael slowly shook his head, watching as his friend's attention quickly diverted back to the tablet computer. After a few moments, he held it aloft, a look of pure serenity on his face, a life-affirming smile on his lips.

"It can stream porn!"

3

Michael and Chip met with an expectant and haggard Naff in the Dead Seamstress. Chip's face was still ablaze with joy. He walked with a skip in his step—which resembled the stammering motor-izing of a recluse hunchback—and a high-pitched, ear-popping whistle on his lips.

When he and Michael finally made it to the Dead Seamstress, Michael was preparing the final postscripts to his murder/suicide plot.

"Well?" Naff said, looking agitated. His right foot was propped up on the toes, the heel jangled with an uncontrollable twitch. "What is it? What did you want to tell me?"

Naff looked at Michael and clearly feared the worst. Michael must've looked like he had bad news; he was sure his face was gaunt, pained. He probably looked like he had recently suffered. Naff then turned to Chip and saw bright, uninhibited glee on his little face.

"Oh God," Naff said with a sudden immovable lump in his throat. "It's bad, isn't it? Did someone die?"

Michael furrowed his brow and breathed out a deep and relieved sigh, happy that the journey was over. "Chip, you fill him in," he said, gesturing to Naff.

Chip sat down happily, engaging Naff in an immediate and long-winded conversation. Michael ordered himself a double whiskey from the bar, drank it down with one quick gulp, and then ordered three cokes.

"Long day?" Scrub said as Michael slammed the empty tumbler onto the bar.

Michael shook his head. "You ever heard of a tablet computer?" he asked the bartender.

Scrub twisted up his face, making himself look like a hairy, confused baby.

"Well," Michael said distantly, "until this morning, neither had I."

When Michael made it back to the table, Chip was still in full flow. He put the glasses on the grimy top and slid in beside his pungent friend.

"... HD and 3D videos, anything from hardcore to anal," Chip was saying excitedly.

"It only has porn?" Naff replied, baffled.

Chip looked at him like he was made of cheese and smoking a pipe. "I mean, it has other stuff too, I guess," he said absently, "if you're into *that sort of thing.*"

Naff shook his head as if to clear the cobwebs his friend's absurdity had woven. "Is that it?" he said to Michael. "Is this what you brought me here to tell me?"

Michael looked at Chip and shook his head in disappointment. "I meant fill him in on the Santa Claus thing," he instructed.

"I have all the porn in the world at my fingertips and you're more interested in a fat man in a suit?"

"You saw him?" Naff said with a start, dismissing Chip's comment.

"He gave Chip the computer."

Naff glared at Chip. "*You* saw him."

Chip put down the computer with a thud, and Michael ventured a look at the screen. He immediately wished he hadn't. "What do you mean *me*?" he replied with the same emphasis.

"How did you see him?" Naff said, softening his tone, not wanting to get into a shouting match with someone who could shout with the stamina and pointlessness of a stubborn politician.

Chip picked up the computer; the sounds of exertion and screaming could be heard above the rumblings in the pub. "I wrote him a letter," he said with a degree of finality.

Naff looked frustrated. "And?"

"*And* what?"

Naff simultaneously groaned and sighed at his miniature friend. "Well, did you address it to the fat man at the fucking north pole or what?"

"Hey, don't get snappy with me!"

"How did you get in touch with him?"

Chip fell silent for a moment, staring at his friend. "Maybe I don't want to tell you. Maybe you need to ask me nicely."

"You've gotta be fucking kidding me."

Chip turned his head away and folded his arms across his chest—a pout on his grubby lips.

"For fuck's sake," Naff mumbled under his breath. "Okay, I'm sorry, but this is very important to me. Tell me, how did you get in touch?"

"Buy me a pint and I'll tell you."

"Chip!" Michael and Naff chorused with a great deal of annoyance.

"Okay, okay," Chip said, holding up his hands. "I just wrote him a letter. Nothing special. 'To Santa,' that was it. No address, nothing."

"Really?" Naff said with a scrunched, disbelieving expression. "How the hell did he get that?"

Chip offered a nonchalant shrug in reply.

"He could be a postman," Michael offered.

"You think Santa would moonlight as a postman?"

"He's not really Santa, remember."

"Yes, great, well done," Naff said unenthusiastically. "Thanks for reminding me."

Michael sipped the foam from the top of his beer; a bitter, acrid wash of soapy bubbles coated his mouth. Scrub had been washing out the barrels again. "Ideal job for a man masquerading as Santa Claus when you think about it," he said, sticking his tongue out at intervals. "Not much difference really. He gets to carry a sack, deliver parcels."

"Drive a giant sleigh pulled by a dozen reindeer?"

"Admittedly, that's where the similarities end."

He took another sip of the bitter beer, refreshing the acrid taste in his mouth, before pushing the pint along the table to Chip, who didn't ask questions and barely acknowledged the gesture. In a matter of moments, the glass was half empty and Chip was grinning satisfactorily.

Naff looked tortured. His face twisted into a complex assortment of pain and thought as he tried to work out a solution to a problem that his previously lax inattentiveness had created. He rested his elbows on the table, sunk his head in his hands.

He groaned and murmured disconsolately to himself. After a while, he lifted his head and stared at his friend with defeated and red eyes. "Okay," he said reluctantly, "I guess it's a possibility, and as we have nothing else to go on—"

Chip interjected without looking up from the computer screen, where a tangle of tanned flesh romped to his delight. "We could send him another letter," he said simply.

Both Naff and Michael turned to him. "What?" Naff said, more shocked than anything.

Chip gave them a casual shrug, still not averting his eyes from the onscreen orgy. "It worked once, why not again?"

For the first time that day, a smile crept onto Naff's face. He turned toward Michael who was staring at the tooth fairy, contemplating killing the sinister little demon who had taken over the body of his roommate.

"What do you think?" Naff asked him.

Michael turned to him, a strained look of bemusement on his face. He lowered his voice, *"I think something's wrong with Chip,"* he said with an assured nod.

4

The Records Department was the red tape of the afterlife. In an organized and structured world, where everyone and everything had a place, these employees maintained order and made sure that everyone and everything was where it should be.

The headquarters of the department rested on a plane between this world and the next, accessed by any of its tens of thousands of worldwide employees through personal portals around the globe. A world on its own; a busy, functioning heart through which the lifeblood of the afterlife pumped. Without the department, there would be no death and there would certainly be no afterlife; the dead would be stuck in a constant state of limbo.

It was rumored that the heads of the department were the top angels and demons themselves, but nobody really knew. The leaders, if any—as the department breathed and beat to the pulse of its many lower-level workers and didn't need a head to function—were a secretive, unseen group.

Naff had worked at the department for longer than he cared to remember. He could no longer recall his birth, his death, or any of his life outside of the one he had grown so accustomed to. None of it mattered anyway—whether he had a worthwhile mortal existence, whether he was a scoundrel, or whether he had never lived at all. The only thing that mattered was his current existence, a life devoted to the department and an endless track of data.

He was paid well for his services. His salary earned him more money than Michael and Chip combined and had allowed him to buy a comfortably sized detached house in a quiet*ish* suburb on the edge of town. It was still Brittleside so it was still rife with squalor, and, a mere stone's throw from Naff's front door—over the neatly trimmed hedges of his pedantic neighbor and beyond the potholed road boarded by rows of overgrown weeds and broken glass—was one of the worst estates in the town. But Naff liked Brittleside; he had been there a long time and, although he couldn't recall it being anything other than a dumping ground for the worst portraits of human existence, something about the town endeared him.

Michael always felt like he was dirtying Naff's house whenever he entered. He always took his shoes off at the front door despite being told not to, yet he still trod on the fluffy cream carpets with great care, worried that the cheapness of his unwashed socks would somehow transfer a film of dirt onto the floor.

He always refused to sit on the soft, upholstered three-piece sofa lest he transfer the dirt from his clothes. He chose instead to sit, precariously, on the edge of a wooden chair brought in from the kitchen.

Chip, on the other hand, bounded into the house like he owned it. He never took his shoes off, barely acknowledged the trail of mud he so often left behind, and threw himself onto the sofa like an athlete attacking the high jump.

Naff did tell Chip to remove his shoes, but he rarely listened. This time, as Michael carefully placed his coat over the edge of the hardback chair and sat—with a careful and awkward consideration—Naff didn't mind the trail of mud left behind by the impish tooth fairy soiling his expensive sofa. The homeowner stood in the middle of the living room next to a marble-style fireplace.

"We need to lure him here," he suggested with a thoughtful finger on the tip of his chin. "We write a letter, give him my address, ask for something we know he'll feel obliged to deliver." He tapped his chin as he spoke, his eyes wondering ponderously away from the faces in front of him. "We wait for him and then—" he lifted his hands and widened his eyes. "Bam! Gotcha."

"We jump him and kick the shit out of him," Chip said with an agreeable nod.

"What? No," Naff said, disapprovingly. "We talk to him, see if we can—"

"Talk to him and then kick the shit out of him?"

Naff shook his head solemnly. He turned to Michael, who returned his bemused expression with a shrug.

"No fighting," Naff insisted. "We let him come to us and we keep things civil."

Chip looked disheartened, but he quickly perked up.

"So we hide in the dark, wait for him to approach, and then jump out?" Chip exclaimed excitedly.

"I guess . . ."

Chip buzzed with childish glee, his little body practically trembling under the veil of his own pent-up excitement. His mind seemed elsewhere as he spoke: "And then we say something cool, something like, 'The only presents you're getting are—,' no wait. *Oh, oh,* I got it, 'They'll be no chimneys where you're going.'"

"What? No, I don't think—"

Chip held up an apologetic hand. "You're right," he said softly. "It's terrible. Don't worry, I'll think of something better."

Naff stared with open-mouthed disbelief at his friend, lost for words and detoured from his own train of thought. Chip turned his own thoughtful eyes to the carpet, his mouth forming silent words as he tried to come up with a better punch line.

"What do we do when we have him?" Michael wondered as he shifted uncomfortably on the seat. "We can't just ask him to nicely follow us back to hell, can we?"

Naff tapped his forefinger against his lip thoughtfully. "I can take his powers away first, that would help."

"No shit."

"But I can only do that if he willingly gives them to me."

"Ah, no problem there then." Michael said with a sarcastic nod. "You guys sure do like your red tape." He said, adding, "Unless it involves werewolf-killing super-demons," under his breath.

"Without his powers, he's harmless, we can overpower him," Naff said.

Michael nodded again, "Good luck with that."

"But first," Naff drifted into the kitchen. His friends listened as he opened and shut drawers that rolled on hinges and thudded against frames. He rummaged around inside a few, spilling and shifting cutlery and papers. Eventually he returned to the living room with a pen and a notepad, which he offered to Chip.

The tooth fairy looked at the pad with caution, as though seeing one for the first time.

"You need to write the letter," Naff explained after a few seconds of awkward staring. "It'll be better coming from you."

Chip raised a thick eyebrow suspiciously. "And why do you say that?" he quizzed.

Naff hesitated, so Michael explained for him, "Because you write like a child."

"Ah," Chip acknowledged with a nod of his head. "Gotcha." He took the pad and pen and awaited their instructions.

A spitting spool of undelivered letters—a myriad of bills and season's greetings awaiting undesignated recipients—raced along a succession of conveyor belts that overlapped one another like a high-speed spaghetti junction and dropped with a fling and a flutter into large bins.

Among the clattering calamity of ferocious machinations, a handful of dole-faced workers moved like automatons, picking out armfuls of the dropped letters and transferring them, with skillful rapidity, to their chosen slots, which beckoned like a wall of birdless pigeon holes behind them.

A heavyset worker moved quicker than the others, his hands barely visible as he tore through the mountain of letters before they had a chance to accumulate. His large white beard flicked and waved under his chin, gracefully shifting with the movements of his overfed body.

He blocked out the chaos, blocked out the mayhem. He was in his own world, a highly efficient machine.

The bearded fat man with the blank expression and the motor-ized hands halted his speedy work. The flicker of a smile twitched at the wrinkled corner of his eye, pulled his skin momentarily taut, and then departed just as quickly as it had appeared.

The address on the letter in his right hand had been scribbled by the hand of a very special, very young child. The handwriting was a mess, scribbled erratically by an incapable hand. The words weren't uniform, some were heavily pressed in and some barely visible. They bounced around the page as if they had a mind of their own. The spelling was atrocious; every word had been spelled incorrectly.

The smile threatened to return, but he quickly banished it.

He looked around at his fellow workers, an army of boys in blue who worked like systematic machines, flipping and sorting the letters without a flicker of emotion. He looked back at the let-ter, happy in the knowledge that he wasn't being watched.

These letters were his favorite. He felt like he was doing an honorable job by responding to them; these were the children who needed him the most. He was excited about the prospect of open-ing it, of finding the required present and then taking it to the child in need, but that had to wait.

He eagerly ripped open the letter and stuffed the torn envelope into his pocket. He read it with an unrestrained smile on his face, a face that had now come to life and shone with an empathetic and wise glow.

He was almost giddy at reading the callous writing. This child was clearly troubled, clearly in desperate need of his services. They wanted a toy, a popular military action figure currently doing the rounds on the playgrounds and in numerous advertisements tar-geted at children.

Every misspelled word was clearly a pained struggle for the child. He was either very young or had severe learning difficulties, yet he had made the effort to write the letter himself instead of turning to an adult or a computer for help. He read the name at the bottom with a warmth in his large heart, like a parent seeing their child's first scribble.

"Naff," he read softly to himself. Odd name for an odd kid, but he would do his best to give him exactly what he wanted. He placed the letter back in his pocket and continued with his robotic job. The smile, and the warm expression, banished from his face.

5

The chunky man in the cushioned red suit whistled as he walked from one house to the next. Trade was picking up, Christmas was nearing. On the first few nights of the season, he had visited a few children in houses pockmarked all over town, but now there were dozens to see, a ton of presents to deliver.

Strangely enough, for him at least, there had also been a handful of adults. Christmas was for children, yet over the last few days, he had delivered three bottles of whiskey, a crate of beer, and what he hoped was a lifelike, simulated friend, but suspected was a sex doll. He didn't mind, of course—adults needed cheering up just as much as children, and who was he to judge who received presents and who didn't?

Well, okay. But he preferred not to.

He visited two neighboring houses, squashed together in the center of a terraced street. The sleeping boys seemed to be of the same age and had probably sent their letters out together. One got a brand new video game system; the other got a selection of games to play on it. He enjoyed that, the togetherness that the boys clearly shared. There was a good chance they would come to blows in the future over their split-share presents, but he thought it honorable and in the spirit of the season that they would split their presents instead of greedily asking for a bundle each.

He was in good spirits when he left their houses and quickly made his way to the next. His sack was still brimming, the night had just begun.

He was at the next house before the children in the previous ones had passed a second of slumber, shifting the several hundred yards with an effortless thought of his magical mind. He only wished that his powers extended to stopping or slowing time, thus giving him the ability to traverse the country in one season and bring goodwill and joy to children all over the world and not just the town of Brittleside, but it didn't matter. He knew that there were thousands of others just like him. He hadn't seen them—they, like him, were a secretive bunch—but he was confident in their abilities nevertheless.

The next house was bigger than the last, the occupants a little more well-off than he had imagined. He sidled to the backyard via a darkened path that carved between the detached house and the one next to it. He slowly opened a tall iron gate that blocked his path. He could walk through whatever structure he wanted—one of the perks of the job, but the presents wouldn't follow him. He also enjoyed the thrill of doing it the old-fashioned way. Next to the joy he knew he was giving to the children, and the free booze and cakes—another perk of the job, everyone remembered to leave out cookies and sherry for Santa, and if not, they often left it in the fridge or cupboards for him to find at leisure—the creeping and sneaking was the best part of the job.

One of the windows at the back of the house was wide open, inviting him inside. A little odd, he thought to himself, but convenient. It would save him the trouble of trying the doors and windows or reverting to his powers.

He clambered through into a room of pitch black. He hadn't been in the best of shape or practice this season, but over the last few days his guile and agility had returned and he was able to make it through without tripping over and falling on his ass. He did knock over something that sounded fragile, the realization of which came when he heard it shatter into a dozen pieces on the floor, but you couldn't make an omelette without breaking a few expensive vases.

He pulled in the bag from outside and walked slowly forward, cringing as his feet crunched the broken pottery pieces.

The lights snapped on, the room suddenly lit with a bright glare that the man in the red suit tried to shield with a hand thrown to his eyes. He dropped his sack, and stumbled backward.

In front of him, standing in a line of three and looking like an abstract Evolution of Man, were three adult males.

The man in the red suit stared at them. He put on his best wizened smile, took a step toward them, and retrieved his sack, dragging it by his side.

Chip was the first to speak. He folded his arms, put on a menacing expression, and delivered his best action-movie line. "You got something in that sack for me, big man?"

Santa Claus paused mid-reply, swallowing his words and flashing Chip a perplexed stare. Naff and Michael also turned to their little friend, bafflement and disappointment on their faces.

Chip weighed his comment in his head, met each of the disappointed stares, and then turned a shade of red. He hung his head, "That came out wrong," he admitted. "Just forget I said anything."

The jolly man in red looked at each of them in turn, spending significantly more time on Chip. An expression of perplexity, without the slightest hint of trepidation, creased his features. "What is this?" he asked.

Chip was the first to reply. "This is where the road ends for you, where *your* road ends," he chewed the sentence like a small stick of toffee. "This is where, ah for fuck's sake."

Michael turned to his friend. "Give it a rest, Chip."

"*Fuck you,*" Chip spat back.

"This has to stop," Michael told Santa Claus, stepping forward. "You can't keep breaking into people's houses, it's not right." His voice was warm and innocuous.

The big man looked bemused. "But I bring joy to children all over town. There's something in this sack of mine to please everyone."

Michael and Naff turned instinctively toward their smaller friend. He didn't meet their gazes; he didn't speak.

"You're causing chaos. Parents know Santa Claus doesn't exist. How do you think they're going to feel when they wake up in the morning to discover Jolly Saint Nick is alive, well, and has been rummaging through their fridge looking for a midnight snack?"

Santa Claus looked confused. "But I do exist."

Michael realized this wasn't going to be as easy as he thought. "It's stealing. It's breaking and entering. More importantly, it's fucking weird."

"But I bring joy. What's not right about that?"

"Jacky, look," Naff offered, moving closer. "You need to stop this."

"Who's Jacky?"

"You are. Don't you remember? Your name is Jacky Sampson. You're on probation."

Santa Claus retained a blank expression.

"I'm your intermediary, Naff. No? Nothing? Look," Naff said, waving a hand. "The point is: you're *not* Santa Claus. You're a mentally ill demon escaped from hell."

He glared back momentarily, then he turned to Michael, aiming a swift and indicative nod in Naff's direction. "Is your friend a little . . ." he twirled his finger around his temple.

"Asks the fat guy in the Santa costume," Chip noted, returning to the conversation.

"This is not a costume. I *am* Santa."

"Of course you are, mate, and I'm Gandhi."

"You look familiar," the man in red noted. "Didn't I bring you a present?"

Chip was overcome with a childish sense of bashfulness. "Maybe."

"That's right," the fat man waddled forward, pointing a knowing finger. "You're Chip." He dug a hand into his pocket and brought out a list, a myriad of heavy-handed names and information formed a visible impression on the back of the sheet. "Some multimedia device it seems," he recalled with the know-how of a grandfather seeing his first Xbox. "Some state-of-the-art computer—"

"My wank box," Chip cut in knowingly. "Yes, that was me, and for that, I thank you."

The jolly man looked a little less jolly. "Your *what?*"

"But the point remains," Chip continued. "This is wrong and downright freaky, and you have to stop. I mean I know you gave me a present an' all, but I have to stick by my friends on this one." He coughed nonchalantly. "Unless you have something else in that sack for me?"

"Well, no," Santa replied, even more bemused. "You only get one,"

"Okay," Chip said resolutely. "Then this is wrong, you should stop."

Santa's eyes lingered on the little man for a moment and then shifted to Michael. A desperation had crept onto his jolly face. "I don't understand," he swapped his stare between Michael and Naff, ignoring Chip.

Naff calmly said, "You're not well."

"But I feel fine."

"You have . . . problems," Naff said, hoping that those problems wouldn't present themselves anytime soon. Not only was this sham Saint Nick twice his size, but with the powers he possessed he didn't even need to touch Naff to crumble him into an undead ball.

"I mean, I'm a little stiffer in the joints than I used to be but—"

"You *think* you're Santa Claus," Naff cut in.

"I'm not *the* Santa Claus," the man in red scoffed with a satirical grin creeping onto his face.

Michael and Naff looked at each other, suddenly wondering if they had made a mistake, if the demon wasn't really delusional after all. Maybe he did just want to bring joy to the children and sex perverts of Brittleside.

"You don't think you're Santa Claus?" Naff asked suspiciously, not failing to note the red suit and the large toy-filled sack.

Santa laughed derisively at the outlandish question. "Of course not," he smirked.

"Oh, well—"

"I'm not the *only* Santa."

"What?"

"Well, think about it," Santa said seriously. "How can one man travel the world delivering presents? Hell, I only deliver to one town and even *that* takes me all season."

"You've lost me."

"There are thousands of us," Santa said with a booming smile.

Naff nodded. "Ah. Right."

"Sounds familiar," Michael muttered softly.

"Can we lock this guy up now?" Chip asked.

Santa seemed taken aback by the comment. The smile dripped off his face, replaced by a sudden suction of depression that distorted his features like a melancholic stroke.

"You're going to lock me up?"

Naff sighed, shaking his head at the tooth fairy next to him. "We just need to take you . . . ," he paused, ". . . *somewhere*," he said, maintaining a smile. "Just to sort a few things out."

"Prison?"

"No. No," Naff was quick to assure.

"Hell," Chip added helpfully.

"*For fuck's sake, Chip!*"

"You're taking me to hell?" the big man looked hurt. His heavy frame sagged under the weight of his own depression. "Oh. Okay."

He staggered over to the couch and slumped down with a heavy sigh. His broad back arched painfully; his head aimed at his big boots.

"I'm sorry," Naff offered.

The big man sucked in a large lungful of air and pushed it out in a long-winded sigh. "You do what you have to do. If you want me to go with you, I'll go."

"I can't take you back with your powers," Naff told him. "You have to relinquish them."

Santa gave another long and tireless sigh and slowly rose to his feet, standing right in front of Chip and eclipsing him with the shadow of his stomach. He held out his hands, his arms out-stretched, and turned his head away dismally. When a number of moments passed without his hands being cuffed or touched, he lowered them slightly and turned back to Naff. The studious office worker had sat down and was filling out a form, using a thick *TV Guide* to rest on.

"What are you doing?" Saint Nick asked.

Naff didn't seem to hear. His bookish eyes scanned the paper, scribbling quickly and intermittently on its surface. He turned over a sheet, folded it to the back and then tapped the end of the ballpoint pen against his teeth. "How big would you say you are?" he wondered with his eyebrows arched inquisitively.

Santa seemed taken aback. "I have no idea."

"Two hundred and eighty pounds, easily," Chip said.

"I don't think so," Santa replied, looking a little hurt and suck-ing his stomach in.

"Maybe two hundred and ninety, three hundred and ten," Chip pushed, gauging the stomach just above his head. "Three hundred and twenty at a push. No more than three hundred and thirty-five."

"What's going on?" Michael interrupted.

"Three hundred and fifty, put down three hundred and fifty."

"I'm taking away his powers," Naff answered matter-of-factly, jotting down a rough estimate on the form, deciding to go for one of the few numbers that Chip hadn't mentioned.

"Seriously?" Michael said with a touch of awe. "This is how you do it?"

Naff ignored his friend and continued scribbling.

"This is your job?" Michael said when Naff had finished and stood, more of a statement than a question. "You truly lead a sad existence, mate."

"Somebody has to do it," Naff said out of the corner of his mouth. He handed the man in red the forms and a pen and pointed to a marked spot at the bottom of the first sheet.

"Well, yeah, but surely there are better ways than this."

Santa reluctantly scribbled his signature, a cursive and flamboyant script. Naff took it from his large hands with a bright smile, a smile that soon faded upon seeing the scribble.

"This says Santa Claus," he noted.

"That's my name."

"But—" he paused, looked from the big man to the form and then back again. He shook his head. "Never mind, it'll do. I'll be right back." He disappeared out into the hallway and up the stairs, leaving an awkward tension in his wake as the three men stood around, unsure what to do with themselves.

Michael stuffed his hands in his pockets; Santa feigned interest in the cards on the mantelpiece, squinting to see them from a distance of six and a half feet. Chip craned his head upward to stare at Santa's beard.

"Where do you get your presents from?" the little one asked after a few moments of thought.

Santa looked down at the questionable thing peering up at him. "Excuse me?"

"Surely you can't go spending thousands of dollars on toys just to give them away. You get nothing from the kids in return."

"I get satisfaction of knowing—"

"Nothing," Chip reiterated. "It's hardly a self-sustaining business, is it? And on top of that, you have travel costs, suit hire, food expenses. Wrapping paper isn't cheap these days."

"I don't . . ." he struggled to finish his own response.

"I mean, you could make them, but then there's a limit, right?"

"Right?"

"Well, yeah, you can't go around reproducing brand-name products can you? You can get away with it a few times but eventually they'll catch you and fine you. It just takes a few loud-mouthed runts to mouth off and you're fucked. You can't afford a fine; you barely make any money as it is."

"Right." Santa nodded.

Michael watched, though he had no idea where Chip was going, he prayed that he would stop before it required any input from him.

"You steal it, don't you?" Chip accused.

When it came to criminality, Chip was usually on the ball. He had a built in radar that allowed him to detect cons, mostly so he could join in with them.

"No," Santa snapped. "Of course not. They leave it out for me. Along with the sherry and the pies."

"They leave *money* out for you?"

"Well, it's more of a treasure hunt really. Sometimes it's in their coat pockets, sometimes it's on the mantelpiece."

Chip looked to Michael, clearly taken aback, although Michael suspected it was because Santa had managed to get away with something he never could. Michael shrugged. He was a mentally ill demon who thought he was Santa Claus and was using his powers to break into homes. A little thievery was the least of their worries.

"Done," Naff strode back into the room.

"That's it?" Michael asked his friend, who was grinning with a sense of achievement.

"All gone," Naff said. He nodded at the man in red, gesturing for him to try his powers. He lifted an arm tentatively, staring at the crimson cotton that dangled from his wrist. He swiped it this way and that, slowly at first. Nothing happened. He attacked the air with more aggression, tried snapping his fingers together, to no avail. He lowered his arm, sunk his head depressingly into his chest, and sighed into his long white beard.

"Gone," he said.

Naff looked proud of himself. Santa returned to the couch, flopping onto the material like an angst-ridden teenager after losing his first girlfriend.

Chip was the first to react. He held up a hand to his friends, mouthed, *"I've got this,"* in a confident tone, and then plonked himself on the sofa next to the sullen Santa.

Michael and Naff breathed a sharp breath of consternation as Chip prepared himself. They exchanged pained expressions as their minds capitulated to the inevitable trauma they were about to witness.

Chip put an arm around the big man's shoulders, having to straighten and stretch to manage the feat. He cleared his throat, threw a reliable wink at his friends, and then began, "Look on the bright side: your job is done. No more trekking from house to house lugging all that shit around. And no more kids."

"But I like kids."

Chip weighed a thought and offered an alternative. "Well, at least you'll get away from the British winter. The dark nights. The downpours. The freezing winds."

Santa turned to look at the little man, shaking his arm from his shoulder. "I don't understand."

"Well, it'll be boiling where you're going."

He stared at the grinning, grubby face for an interminable time, a blank expression on his own, once-jolly, facade. He shook his head slowly and turned back to face his own shoes. "I just wanted to bring joy to the children," he said solemnly.

Chip sighed and shifted away. "*Again* with the children."

"A lot of them don't have anything else. Christmas is the one time they can share in the joy that *all* children should experience."

"On the plus side," Naff helped, "I'm sure you already brought joy to a lot of children this year."

"It's not enough. What about the others? How will they feel?" He looked up at Naff with pleading eyes. "Their friends and class-mates were visited by Santa, but he rejected them? It's hardly con-ducive to the season of joy and togetherness, is it?"

"Fuck 'em," Michael offered blandly. "The parents will buy them all the shit they need. I'm sorry, but as much as it pains me to say it, I'm with Chip on this one."

Chip glared at Michael suspiciously, refusing to break his skeptical stare even when Michael flashed him an agreeable nod.

"And let's not forget," Michael said. "If you hadn't stolen from them in the first place, maybe the parents would have bought them those presents anyway."

"I didn't steal anyway," Santa insisted. "And even if I did—"

"You definitely did."

"—*Even* if I did, those parents wouldn't have used the money for presents, trust me. I saw the houses; I saw the neglect. And so, what if they would have done? I gave them so much more. What do you think a kid would prefer, knowing that a present came from their parents, who only buy them stuff to shut them up, or from an omniscient being who loves them unconditionally and gives them hope that a better world exists beyond this one?"

"Well, when you put it like that," Michael said.

Naff and Chip looked a little less convinced and a lot more confused.

"What's this about stealing money?" Naff asked.

"What the hell does omniscient mean?" Chip asked.

"Some of these kids have nothing," Santa continued. "Christ-mas is their time to feel on par with the kids all over the world who *do* have something."

"It means fat, doesn't it?" Chip mumbled, to no one in particular.

"This is Britain, not Africa, these kids have plenty," Michael said. "There's only so much crap you can buy them."

Santa opened his mouth to discard the comment, but he quickly swallowed his words and lowered his head again. "What's the point?" he breathed.

"There's the spirit," Chip exclaimed.

"I'm with the big guy on this," Naff suddenly offered, catching the attention of the room and bringing a glint of hope to Santa's eyes.

"Really?" Michael said in disbelief.

Naff shrugged at his friend. "What can I say? He's right. To be honest, I quite like Christmas."

"You traitor," Michael uttered.

"It's happy, it's joyful," Naff declared. "Don't try to drag down the spirit of the season just because of your own shitty views."

"*Bu—but.* You've gotta be fucking kidding me."

"No," he replied defiantly. "I think what he did, or *tried* to do, was honorable. If it wasn't for," he paused with a sheepish smile. "Well, you know."

"The fact that he's an insane kleptomaniac from hell?"

"Yes. That."

"Then let me finish," Santa stood, his pleading eyes beamed at Naff. "Please. For the sake of the children. Let me finish what I started."

Michael groaned heavily. "This is turning into a fucking Hallmark special."

Santa ignored the belligerent reaper and petitioned Naff. "There are only a few houses left," he pulled a list from his pocket and thrust it at his ally. "Let me finish and then I'll happily go wherever you want me to go."

Naff studied the list thoughtfully. His eyes shifted from the uncrossed names to the desperate, beady eyes bearing down from the bearded demon.

"You don't have your powers," Naff noted. "I can't give them back to you, and this lot . . ." he gestured to the list, "will take you more than one night on your own."

The hope in the demon's eyes faded.

"But we'll help you," Naff said with a cheering smile. "We'll help you finish."

"Thank you. Thank you so—"

"We?" Michael interjected.

"Yes," Naff nodded. "We're *all* going to do it. That way we can get it done tonight."

"You must be *fucking*—"

"You owe me," Naff cut in sharply.

Michael snapped back with an open mouth, but his words caught in his throat. He cast a forlorn look to the floor. "Fine."

6

"Just so you know in advance," Chip explained to the demon by his side. "I think this is a stupid idea."

The 221 bus plodded along at a stuttering pace with a succession of flicking streetlights lighting its way. The driver, a chunky man in his twilight years, watched his passengers through the rearview mirror with an expression of bewilderment permanently embedded on his wrinkled face.

Sampson, still dressed in his Santa suit, was watching a youngster at the back of the bus, a boy of no more than thirteen who dressed like someone much older, his trousers and hoody far too big for him, a mass of dangling chains around his neck. He had initially scowled at Chip and Sampson, as he no doubt did every adult he saw, but he now viewed them with an air of childish curiosity, or so Sampson liked to think.

He had never experienced life as a human child, but he had encountered plenty of children. They possessed an innocence he adored, a sense of the fantastical and the impossible that stayed with them and refused to leave, even when faced with glaring evidence to the contrary.

That level of belief and innocence remained in every child until adolescence. The world had a way of beating it out of the unfortunate ones and those forced to grow up too young, but he was a firm believer that the faith in the impossible still lingered and could be restored.

"I mean, you can't even do the door thing."

"The door thing?" Sampson asked distantly.

"Walking through them," Chip clarified simply. "Not anymore at least."

"Well, if you hadn't taken away my powers . . ."

"Not my field of expertise, mate, although quite frankly I wouldn't feel comfortable sitting on the bus next to a demon a few loaves short of a bakery."

"What's that supposed to mean?" Sampson wondered, pulling his attention away from the curious youngster at the back of the bus.

"You're insane," Chip translated.

"I make it my duty to bring joy and hope to children all over the world, and you're trying to stop me. Maybe you and your friends are the insane ones."

"Nah, mate. It's definitely you."

Sampson, looking a little offended, turned back toward the boy at the back, watching him slyly through a reflection in the opposing window.

"Naff can't do the door thing either," Chip noted to himself. "Seems the two least interested in helping your fat ass out are the two who have to do the most."

Sampson didn't reply; he had barely heard. The Christmas spirit had now gone from the face of the youth. His eyes were fixed on the large sack in front of Sampson. Sampson assumed the kid wasn't pondering whether there would be a present in there for him, but rather what he could get at the pawnshop for the contents.

The bus stuttered to a stop. They remained seated but the youth stood. Despite being on a bus, he glanced around himself, almost as a criminal instinct, and then plodded forward with his eyes on the bag. Samson was too dejected to stop him, but Chip called to him without even looking up.

"Touch that bag and I'll break your fucking arms," he said brusquely with a great deal of believability.

The boy was already reaching out, but he withdrew his arms as though his hand had brushed hot coals. He quickened his steps and rushed off the bus without turning back. Sampson watched him skulk away—his hood up, his hands in his pockets, his back hunched—and felt sorry for him.

"And *you* wanna give these delinquents toys," Chip said.

Michael hated giving gifts at Christmas. He had enjoyed it as a child, and as an adult in the living world, he hadn't objected, but in the afterlife, he hated it. He hated the greed and the selfishness on display in the mouths and minds of every child in the Western world. He hated the inept inattentiveness on behalf of the parents, who put their financial futures, and thus the futures of their children, into jeopardy by blowing their household budgets on stacks of worthless pomp and plastic, half of which would be forgotten about until the following Christmas when it would be discarded in anticipation of even more worthless stacks of shit that could sit unattended and unloved for another year.

He remembered enjoying the feeling of waking up on Christmas morning and diving into a pile of presents. As an adult, with the benefit of hindsight, he could appreciate the warmth and pleasantry of being with family during those moments, with the parents in pure devoted mind-sets, the world frozen in motion for a week or more, and the dreams and ideas of the child allowed to flourish, but he knew that, as that child, the only thing he cared about was unwrapping and playing with those presents. There is no sentimentality with the young.

"Cheer the fuck up," Naff told him as he drove them both across town.

Michael groaned in reply and turned his head to glare disinterestedly out of the window. They had already been to two of the houses on their list. In Michael's eyes, that was just another two kids who would wake up tomorrow morning to one extra piece of mass-produced crap—a sugar-coated start to a day that would probably end up with them crying and screaming at their parents, the result of an exhaustive mix of emotions and an overload of sugar.

"I don't recall you ever being this annoyed about Christmas," Naff noted. "You usually just hole up and get drunk for a few days."

"I don't recall ever being asked to be fucking Santa Claus before," Michael replied.

"Touché."

The next stop on the list was an end-terraced house in one of the estates on the edge of town. The street was dead as they pulled up. Further down the road, a domestic dispute raged behind closed doors—the calls and clatters of drunken violence broke into the night like a distant whistle. A few lights in a few windows flickered on and off—televisions and computers playing to those overexcited and unable to sleep or those already asleep and unable to move.

Michael recognized the street. Just two weeks earlier, he had picked up a job from one of the houses. A young man, no more than twenty. He was living alone and had evidently tired of his monotonous and pointless existence. He tried to kill himself with a bottle of whiskey and what he thought were painkillers he had stolen from his grandmother. The tablets turned out to be iron supplements for his grandmother's anaemia. Instead of a blissful slide into the abyss, he had suffered a painful and seemingly endless battle with his own internal organs, which had eventually given out on him a few hours after the whiskey had worn off.

Recollection of the misery he had encountered on his last visit only furthered his bad mood. Grabbing the sack from the trunk, he sauntered toward the house with a lazy and reluctant swagger.

"Cheer up," Naff said as he tottered behind Michael, who was slumping down the side of the house like a creeping stalker. "It's Christmas."

Michael ignored his cheery friend. At the back of the house, he heaved the bag off his shoulder and walked through the door. In the darkness and silence beyond he slowly and carefully unlocked myriad deadbolts, hoping to open the door and let Naff and the presents inside. A noise behind him awoke his attention and he froze.

During his first year on the job, he had taken to walking through whatever door he pleased, enjoying the freedom that the ability allowed. That habit stopped after an unfortunate experience in a locked, and assumed empty, toilet stall where a half-naked man had been vigorously masturbating to the lingerie section of a clothes catalog. The experience was traumatic for him, but it seemed to spur the man on.

He needed the ability—people had an unfortunate way of dying behind locked doors—but no longer desired to use it for anything unnecessary.

A small voice, almost a whimper, filtered through the silence.

"Christmas soon," the voice was saying in a softened, reassuring whisper. "Don't worry."

The voice of an unseen child whispering into the darkness is innately creepy and would have sent chills through Michael's body when he was alive, but now, in the world he had been forced to adopt, the ghostly voice suggested the possibility of unfinished work.

He followed the sound of the voice to the living room. A spill of moonlight cut through the closed curtains at the front of the room and shed a glow onto a small patch at the back, behind a dining room table and tucked away into the corner. A small boy sat on the floor, hunched over a large dog; its ears pricked to the air, its chest gently rising and falling.

The boy was stroking the dog with great care and affection, soothing the fading beast with every gentle repetition—whispering meaningless absurdities into its ear as he did so.

He had been around death enough to recognize the presence of impending doom that hangs in the air like a weighted inevitability. The dog was dying and probably wouldn't see morning. He felt a twinge of sympathy in his heart. There were no tears on the boy's small face, no quivering in his voice.

He quietly walked back to the kitchen. The key wasn't in the back door. Nor was it on the nearby ledge or the counter. He searched around for it quietly—not wanting to alert the boy or the dog in the other room—and then headed outside.

"Problem?" Naff asked.

Michael threw a finger to his lips. "Be quiet," he said hastily, hooking a thumb over his shoulder. "There's a kid awake in there."

"Too excited to sleep?" Naff asked in a sufficiently lowered tone.

"His dog's dying, looks like he's comforting it."

Naff grinned. "Sounds like a surprisingly unselfish thing to—"

"Shut it," Michael warned, pointing a threatening finger.

He took the intended present from the top of the bag and scanned the house and the door. There was a cat flap at the foot of the door; the rubberized door gently lolled in the breeze, but the present, a boxed toy of some sort, was too big to fit through.

"I'm going to have to open it."

"You can't—"

Michael cut the protestations short. "If I don't, then he doesn't get it," he said sternly. "Unless you have any other suggestions."

He waited in the silence. A breeze kicked up behind them and billowed out Michael's coat. The noise of the distant argument, now settling down into sporadic screams, passed on the wind.

Naff didn't say anything.

Michael opened the present as carefully as he could, taking great care not to make a noise. Even if the kid didn't hear, there was a good chance the dog would.

"I can't believe I'm standing out here in the freezing fucking cold opening a fucking G.I. Joe for some spoiled little shit," he remarked under his breath.

Naff sighed.

"I mean, seriously," he continued as he picked apart the paper. "What does it fucking matter? One more present, one more piece of shit for the pile," he groaned. "Why did we listen to the fat fuck in the suit?"

"Maybe he has a point," Naff said. He stuffed his hands inside his pockets to brace against the cold. "I don't care what you think, this is kinda admirable: giving these kids some extra joy, some extra love."

Michael groaned another disagreeing reply and ripped the final shred of paper from the toy. He began another tirade, another complaint against the season, but stopped short when he saw what was in the box. His words ruptured in his throat.

"What is it?" Naff wondered, sensing the shock on his friend's face.

"It's a dog's toy," Michael said softly. He held up the box. Inside was a small chew toy in the shape of a slipper. "I don't—" he paused, looked instinctively back at the house.

"I don't get it. What am I missing?" Naff asked.

Michael didn't answer him. He gently opened the box and removed the toy before slipping it through the cat flap and retrieving it on the other side. He took it to the living room. A shade of darkness covered his face as he crossed the threshold and listened to the boy, still whispering in the corner of the room.

"Santa's gonna bring us something special," he was saying happily. "We can play one last time."

Michael slipped the toy inside a stocking that dangled temptingly from the fireplace. It was marked with the child's name but had been filled with a wealth of toys for both man and beast.

He checked on them before he left. The dog seemed to see him standing there, its black eyes glistening against the reflective light of the moon. Its ears were pinned to the air for any sound Michael might make, but it was reluctant to move. It didn't even lift its head. The boy didn't notice Michael at all; he was using the dog as a pillow, his head resting on its rising and falling chest as his hand continued to stroke it.

"What was all that about?" Naff asked when Michael joined him outside.

"Nothing," Michael said, attempting to restrain his emotion.

"You look different," Naff noticed, hopping around him like an excited and quizzical child. "Something happened in there, didn't it!" he exclaimed. "Ah, what was it? What was it? Tell me. Did someone finally pull that stick out of your ass?" he asked, practically skipping with joy.

"Fuck off, Naff."

"This is bloody heavy," Chip complained. He slugged a wrapped box through the living room to a fireplace, where a selection of presents had been laid out between three bulging stockings.

Santa watched the tooth fairy struggle with the box, nearly trapping his fingers between its edge and the soft carpet as he plonked it down with little care or attention before cracking himself upward with a jolt and holding his back with a pained expression.

"I think that one's a train set," the fat man noted. He glanced around at the room and smiled. It was alight with tiny, multicolored bulbs and bristling tinsel, all neatly and carefully placed—covering the frames of paintings and pictures and dangling from light fixtures. An advent calendar was open by the stairs, and all but a few of its chocolate-filled doors stood open.

"You like this, eh?" Chip said, watching the fat man's expression.

Santa nodded, feeling massively cheered up after the depressing incident with the youth on the bus. "Very much so."

A hushed sound caught both of their attentions and they turned toward the stairs just in time to see a little head pop out and then disappear. The sound of hasty footsteps on creaky steps followed and Santa ushered for Chip to hurry up. Before he heeded the advice, he heard the gleeful chants of a little boy who had made it to the top of the stairs and was calling to his parents.

"Mommy! Daddy! Mommy! Daddy!" came the joyous screams. "Santa is downstairs! Santa is downstairs!"

"Ah, sweet," Chip said, despite himself.

The kid continued, "And he's brought his ugly little elf with him!"

"The little fucking shit . . ."

"Come on," Santa beckoned with an open arm, "the night is young."

Michael gazed up at the dazzling house in awe, his jaw hung open like a hungry toddler. "Jesus Christ," he muttered to himself. "It's lit up like. . ."

"Christmas?" Naff offered.

"Yeah," Michael said noncommittally, ducking his eyes from the house—whose every inch had been covered with glittering, multicolored lights—and feigning an unimpressed look.

Naff waited by the front door with a big grin on his face. He was enjoying their adventure, especially now with the Christmas spectacle draped over the house before them and the battle of wills that ensued on his friend's face.

"After you," he nodded at the front door.

Michael gave him a vexed stare as he passed through the front door. Inside, it was just as colorful and spectacular as it was outside. The walls were strewn with an assortment of glittering tinsel and flashing pinpoint lights. An army of ornaments—Santa, Rudolph, snowmen—had been lined up on the windowsills, coffee table, and mantel piece. Stick-on snowflakes adhered to the insides of the windows, advent calendars waited by the front door, and stockings hung from the mantel.

Michael quickly and silently unlocked the door before walking deeper into the room. At the back of the room, a large Christmas tree stood defiantly. Its plastic bristles scratched the ceiling; its arms reached every piece of furniture within a two-foot perimeter.

He stood in front of it, gazing up. On the top of the tree, sitting before a crown of branches that picked at the textured ceiling, looking comfortable and majestic, was a handcrafted wooden angel. A great deal of detail and care had been taken over every minute feature, every fold of her skirt, every sparkle in her eye.

Naff brushed up beside him with the sack trailing at his heels.

"I don't think you hate Christmas after all," he noted happily. He moved to put an arm around his friend's shoulder, but then thought better of it and feigned a stretch and a yawn.

"I loved it as a kid," Michael noted, smiling at the glittering angel on the top of the decorated tree. "Everything about it. I think that's my problem; that's why I hate it now."

Naff gave him a puzzled expression. "You don't like to be reminded of your childhood?"

"What?" Michael flashed him a bemused look. "No, no. Far from it," he uttered, turning back to the tree as its succession of flickering lights bathed the room in a sea of temporary blue. "I miss being a kid," he explained softly.

"Ah."

"The innocence. The joy. There are other things I miss, of course. You can't enjoy some of the best things in life until you're older, but as a kid . . ." he shrugged. "I guess things just felt . . . *better*." He smiled and turned to Naff, who didn't seem to be taking in the information. "You know?"

"Not really."

"You were never a kid?"

"If I was, I can't remember. To be honest, I mean, I like them an' all, but they seem like a completely different breed to me."

"Kids?"

"Yep."

Michael watched the tree as a dazzling and epileptic wash of colors swam over its plastic leaves. "I'm with you on that one," he agreed. "But still, it's different when you are one."

The two stood in relative silence, watching the lights in the room flicker from one neon spectrum to another. A gentle buzz from the electric lights and the purr of a muted snore from upstairs were the only sounds to come between them until Naff somberly noted: "This world isn't all that bad, you know. The afterlife, *this* life."

"What?"

"Well, that's what this is all about, isn't it? You loved Christmas when you were alive and hate it now. It reminds you of what you've lost."

Michael glared at him. He pondered dismissing his part-time pseudo psychology but shrugged it off and offered a simple nod. "I guess so."

"We can live forever," Naff continued "We can see the dawn of new civilizations. We can witness and survive catastrophic natural events, wars, and human crises."

Michael sighed. "But we can't stop a random demon from trying to kill us with a pair of dimwitted clones. And we know nothing of heaven, hell, or anything else for that matter."

Naff didn't seem affected by his friend's words. "It's a great opportunity; a great life."

Michael watched the heightened features on his friend's face as they flickered with a fusion of delight and coercion. "I was just beginning to enjoy myself here," he said softly. "Don't fucking spoil it."

7

They met back at Naff's house. On the journey home, Michael didn't stop smiling and he didn't mind Naff noticing, nor did he mind the smart-ass comments that filled up their journey for its entirety. He felt good—certainly a lot better than when they had started on their quest. The alcohol had helped. Despite being a few days away from Christmas Eve, the final house had left out a bottle of port and a couple glasses on the dining room table, and the thirsty friends agreed it had *probably* been left for them and wasted no time in drinking it—snacking on a few cookies from the kitchen and tempting candy canes from the tree.

They arrived back just as Chip and Sampson were turning onto the street. They were equally joyous. Sampson walked tall and proud, the look of dismay had been stripped from his face and filled with one of pride and happiness. Chip was equally happy; he knew there was nothing separating him from spending the next few days with his wank machine.

Naff poured the drinks and shared some slices of suspicious-looking ginger cake. He was proud of his work, happy to do a good deed for the people of the town and for the demon he had been hired to look after. He was always happy when his work had been completed sufficiently and expertly.

While Naff, Michael, and Sampson drank and shared in the revelry of the season, swapping jokes and stories, Chip sat hunched up in the corner with a broad smile on his ugly face as the computer screen flashed a fleshy light onto his glossy features.

"So," Naff said, having drained his drink following a toast, put down the glass and rubbed his hands. "Same time next year?"

Michael glared at him, his mouth full of brandy. He swallowed and snapped open his lips to scratch back a heated reply, but Naff halted him with a raised palm. "I was kidding, for fuck's sake."

Michael managed a restrained smile.

Naff turned to Sampson. "Are you ready to go then? It's time."

The demon nodded contently. He finished his drink and put down the glass without letting an inch of that contentedness slip from his chubby, reddened face.

He moved to Michael and offered him a hand. "Thank you," he said. "I'll never forget what you and your friends have done for me."

Michael nodded back, keeping his distance in case the big man decided to go in for the hug. "Even if we did send you to hell in the end?"

Sampson shrugged apathetically. "You were just doing your job."

"Fair enough."

"You've made many children happy tonight," he said, turning to Naff. He shook his hand firmly, clasping it in both of his colossal palms. "You're a good man."

Naff tried to look modest, but his pride burst through in a red bubble.

He moved to Chip and stood over him, his ominous shape casting a shadow over the little man hunched up on the couch. Chip looked up after several moments and seemed surprised to see the wannabe Santa Claus standing there.

"Hello," he said meekly.

"I'm going," Sampson stated.

"Oh," that was all Chip was prepared to say before he returned his attention to his porn, but a forewarning look from Michael and Naff forced him to do otherwise. He groaned like a reluctant child and rose to his feet.

"Good-bye," he offered. "Have fun, keep safe an' all that."

Santa grinned wryly and turned to move, but Chip, in one final moment of curiosity, stopped him.

"Do you still think you're Santa then?" the little man wondered. "I mean, after all this. And now that you're going back to hell, you must realize that you're a demon. You can't really still believe you're *him*, can you?"

"Maybe . . ." Santa began, looking at Chip, "maybe the real Santa *is* a demon. Maybe the reason no one believes in him anymore is because he was resigned to the bowels of hell, away from his beloved children and his true home. Maybe the real Santa just found a way to escape those clutches and to get back to his rightful position as the bringer of joy and mirth to the world. I mean . . ." he paused, beamed a mystical smile, "no *human* could possibly do what Santa has to do, could they? He would have to be a demon, wouldn't he?"

Chip's mouth dropped open as if the hinges of his jaw had snapped. He glared at the fat man in front of him. He watched him disappear, fading into nothingness right in front of him, then he turned his awe toward his friends.

"It really was him!" Chip declared loudly.

A brief second passed before Michael burst into a fit of hysterics. Chip shot him a look of bemusement before turning to Naff, who was shaking his head in disbelief.

Naff said, "You truly are a fucking numpty, aren't you?"

PART FIVE

THE BASTARD

1

Michael practically fell into the chair, his body and his breath uttering a simultaneous groan as he sat; a noise muffled by the sinking percussion of the soft leather seat.

His eyes immediately fell to his feet, his mind elsewhere from the outset.

"*Well*, you're looking cheery today." The warming tone of a pleasant professional—typically, it was comforting, but now it felt like nothing could comfort him.

His clothes stank—the stench of dirt and body odor from many sleepless nights and insomniac wanders—but a scent of something pleasant now mingled with his own dreadful stench: a warmth of cinnamon or frankincense, a comforting, bubbly scent that spewed forth from an oil burner somewhere in the room. He breathed it in slowly, quickly forgetting the stench that had lingered on his person for the last few weeks.

"Are you just going to sit there?"

His head felt like it was made of lead. He felt a strained complaint in his neck muscles as he gradually, and with great difficultly, lifted it to face the woman seated opposite.

Her expression took on a somber tone at the sight of him, a concerned, sympathetic twinge that bled into her comforting features. "What's wrong?"

Michael sighed deeply, an action that seemed to repel the energy from his toes to his head. "It's a long story."

She nodded knowingly and pressed a button on her desk. "Rearrange my next appointment," she said into a small intercom.

"Yes, doctor," came a statically charged reply.

The smile returned—an expectant and compassionate smile. "We have as long as it takes," Doctor Khan told Michael softly. "Go ahead."

"It started typically enough, just another day; another call, like any other . . ."

Michael had his feet up, his chin touching his chest, his mind on nothing in particular. It was Friday, just past midnight, and he was weighing up his options: to have another drink with Chip or go to bed. The former was a questionable concoction of fruity substances that he had allowed his friend to pour and mix but refused, for the sake of his own sanity, to watch or ask any questions about.

Next to Michael, Chip was half-conscious, seemingly poisoned by his own concoction as he sat, slouched in on himself, murmuring incomprehensibly.

Michael was in the process of nudging his friend awake when his timer buzzed. His heart sank. Most of the time, he knew when death was coming. He could sense it and plan for it. But sometimes, when other forces were involved, it was as much of a surprise to him as it was to them.

He didn't have far to go. It was a five-minute walk from his house, an alleyway nestled between buildings of empty squalor. He figured it would be another overdose, more life ejected from society with a soiled shot of euphoric venom, or the suicidal throes of a desperate drunk downing his last drink.

He smelled her before he saw her. She had only been dead for ten or fifteen minutes—the time it had taken him to drag his intoxicated self off the sofa and plunge into the cold night—yet there was already a sickly smell wafting from her corpse. A trail of blood led from the gray of the alleyway entrance into the impenetrable blackness at its center, and he followed the coppery scent to find the reason for the stench.

Her body had been ripped open like a toy doll given to a rabid dog. Half of her insides were splashed on the cold, unforgiving concrete. The darkened pavement was decorated with an assortment of discarded organs and viscous pools of blood, like the cast-offs at an abattoir.

He felt his stomach kick; the contents of Chip's questionable cocktails fought a path to his throat. He held them back, forced them down with a stringent swallow. Then a light from across the street burst into life with a flickering stutter and illuminated her face in all its deathly glory.

Her face had been skinned, flaps of flesh remained, dangling like slack strings of sloppy spaghetti, but most had been peeled and removed. Her eyes stared emptily out from a face that had been worn to a mass of muscle and bone. The skin of her neck remained, but had nothing to attach to.

She was standing over her body, watching Michael as he watched what used to be her.

"I was pretty," she said softly. "Wasn't I?"

He nodded a reply, pulling his eyes away from the scene as best he could. As usual, the spirit didn't look depressed or angry. She was content. There was no change there, but considering what lay at his feet, it disturbed Michael to know that she wasn't angry.

He held out his hand, she moved forward and took it. They didn't say another word to each other, but every time Michael looked into her smiling face, he saw the image of her flesh-stripped corpse, an image he couldn't get out of his head all night. Despite Chip's best chemical efforts and his own state of fatigue before leaving the house, that night he struggled to sleep.

It was the first time in a long time Michael had felt such an attachment to the deceased. He had seen plenty of murder victims before, but this was different. It wasn't a crime of passion or a bungled robbery or mugging—this was brutal and sick, an act committed to fulfill some deep-seated inner desire. At least, that's what Michael thought, and those thoughts were confirmed just a few days later.

The second victim was a few years older. She was in her late twenties and had probably lived a fuller life than the previous girl, but not by much and that still wasn't any consolation to Michael. She had a couple of kids but had hit on hard times: drink, drugs, petty theft. He thought she might have resorted to prostitution, but whatever the reason was, she was wandering the streets at night with barely enough material on her skimpy frame to shield her from the bracing cold.

That morning, the papers had reported that the first girl had been strangled before she'd been mutilated, and it appeared this girl had suffered the same fate—the ligature marks around her neck proved that. The killer had also removed her eyes, carved them out of her skull with a rash rapidity that had scarred the dead tissue on her cheeks and forehead.

For Michael, the only thing worse than seeing the dead lying there like that was seeing their clueless spirit hovering over their corpses. That contented, simpleton look—he knew it didn't suit the dead at the best of times, but it certainly didn't suit the victims of a savage murder.

The second victim didn't say a word. She simply walked over to Michael when she saw him, drawn to him like they all were. Her eyes and his face asked and answered all the necessary questions.

Those two murders were enough to capture the attention of the press. There headlines covered every local and national newspaper. They seemed torn between "The Brittleside Ripper" and "The Brittleside Butcher," but Michael didn't like either. He had seen the bodies close-up; *Ripper* and *Butcher* didn't cut it. It was primal savagery, it was inhumane.

He voiced his disagreement to Chip, who had a suggestion of his own: "The Brittleside Bastard." It wasn't quite as poetic or fit for the press, but it was a better fit nonetheless. Whoever could commit those murders was an abomination; a beast not borne of man.

Michael stayed awake for a few days after that. Two murders in as many weeks. He was scared to sleep in case he had to rush to another hapless soul cut down by the Bastard. He was late for the third victim. He had fallen asleep trying to stay awake, ironic, but inevitable.

There was already a scene when he arrived. Despite the ungodly hours, despite the shit-forsaken backstreet of a God-forsaken town, a flock of car-crash spectators still managed to flock there. The police were struggling to hold them back with miles of tape and shows of intimidation.

Beyond the throng of idiots and coppers, a forensic tent had been placed over the body and a line of men and women in white suits came and went through a foldaway entrance.

Michael walked straight through the crowd, barely noticed, as usual. It was like a mosh pit in there. He could feel the anxiety and desperation among the people as they shoved, barged, and edged their way forward, trying to steal a look or convince one of the two unfortunate cops on guard to let them in. One of the desperate spectators offered to flash the makeshift guard her tits if he would let her beyond the line so she could snap some pictures for her blog. It made Michael sick to his stomach, but it didn't surprise him. These were his people, this was his town. He knew what to expect.

It seemed like every other person in the crowd was holding up a camera or a phone, snapping pictures and taking videos, trying to edge as close as they could to catch a stray splatter of blood or a pound of flesh.

They let Michael through without even realizing they'd done so. He ducked under the line and headed for the tent. The soul was waiting outside; watching the crowds as they unknowingly flashed their cameras in and around her.

A couple of detectives were chatting behind her. One was drinking coffee and munching on something wrapped in pastry that showered his jacket as he chewed. He looked half-asleep and was mumbling as he spoke. "We'll never catch him," Michael heard him say. "But who gives a fuck? He's doing our job for us: getting the scum off the streets."

They both laughed at that and Michael felt even sicker. She was standing right in front of them and could hear every word, although he doubted that she cared or even understood.

Michael would have agreed with them in the past. He had always said that there was a place for everyone in this world and that for most of Brittleside, that place was six feet underground. They were generally horrible people and had little to contribute to society, such as the tit-flashing woman who was, at that point, resorting to promises of blow jobs to get her way. But no one, not even *her*, deserved to die like that. He knew that, he could respect that, and he had never thought anything to the contrary.

He took the soul away from the detectives. She asked him if he was her guardian angel, as they all did. Most of the time, he wanted to tell them that he was, to make them feel more comfortable, especially those who pass in such a horrible way, but what could he say after that? "Yes, I'm your guardian angel but I was on a coffee break when that guy butchered you. Sorry, but what're ya gonna do, eh?"

Maybe people need guardian angels, Michael thought. It would stop them from doing stupid shit and fucking up their lives to the extent where they end up as bitch to a butcher on the streets of Brittleside. But then, he'd seen the sort of people employed in this world, *his* world. He'd seen who they employed as tooth fairies—if anything should call for a small, dainty, and timid female it's a tooth fairy, but instead they employed Chip and his cronies. The most disturbing thing about it is that Chip had the best personal hygiene of the lot of them. He was the good-looking one in the office. So maybe not, he thought. Maybe guardian angels would be a terrible idea. But whatever happened, humans needed some guidance in life, especially those who didn't get that guidance from their parents.

Michael slumped further back in his seat, tired from his own ranting.

Doctor Khan watched him momentarily and then asked, "Is that something you want to talk about?"

Michael raised a sneering eyebrow at her. "Is *what* something I want to talk about?"

"Parents and guidance. Your own parents perhaps?"

Michael grinned. "You can read minds, Doctor," he reminded her. "Why don't you look into mine and see if that's what I want to talk about?"

Doctor Khan peered deeply into his eyes. She shifted uncomfortably on her chair and then quickly changed the subject. "Don't you consider yourself human anymore?" she asked.

"Excuse me? Is that what you found in there?"

She smiled and then allowed the smile to fade into a serious look. "You referred to people as *humans.*"

"Well, that's what they are."

"You didn't seem to include yourself in that description."

Michael gave this a brief thought. "I still think of myself as human. But, well, I guess I don't group myself with those who are alive. I haven't been that way for too long. In fact, I've been dead longer than I was ever alive." He raised his eyebrows, "Scary thought."

"Do you see the *living you,* the *memories* of the living you that is, as a different entity to the *you* as you are now?"

"That's a mouthful, eh?" he joked with a wry smile. "I'm not sure that *this* me would have liked *that* me. I was cocky, arrogant.

I thought I knew it all and I thought I could take on the world."
He made a *harrumph* noise and sunk further in on himself. "Ironically enough, I thought I would live forever. I never even made it to thirty."

"Yet you *will* live forever."

Michael shook his head, disagreeing. "This is not living; picking up the scraps of society: the druggies, the prostitutes, the idiots, and the detritus of some morbid fucking serial killer."

"It can't all be that bad. You have friends here, right?"

Michael shrugged indifferently. "I guess. They make a bad situation slightly less worse, but if you're swimming in the Thames, it doesn't matter if you're wearing a suit of silk or not, you're still wading through shit."

"Hmm."

"Anyway," Michael said, straightening up. "Back to the Bastard of Brittleside."

"You took to calling him that after all?"

Michael shrugged casually. "What can I say? A lot of things coming from Chip have a habit of sticking to you." He smiled and continued with his story.

2

For two or three weeks, Chip's daily routine consisted of smoking bucket loads of dope and lying on the sofa watching an obscure channel that showed nothing but crime shows. *Columbo*, *Monk*, *Ironside*, *CSI*; new, old, British, American, he watched them all. On one of the few occasions he changed channels, he did so because he couldn't stand to watch a repeat of the same episode four times in two days, and he ended up watching an obscure Brazilian crime show with French subtitles.

Inevitably, he became an expert in the Bastard and was equally absorbed in his activities as those of the fictitious detectives he had whittled away his days watching.

Michael didn't think the police would bother to catch the killer. They didn't care, so he decided to try to hunt him down himself, to stop him from butchering any more women. He didn't always have control in his job, he didn't always have things his own way. The incident with the werewolves had proved that. This time, he was determined to stay in control. He was determined to get to the bottom of the issue, stopping more young women from meeting their demise in the worst possible way and proving a point to his bosses, his peers, and himself in the process.

Naturally, he turned to Chip for help, but he quickly regretted it.

Chip had a number of theories and pinned down a long list of potential and obscure suspects, which included Michael. He said there was a chance, however minimal—and that point he stressed—that he was doing it to drum up business for himself. After he accused Michael of the ultimate act of savagery, he was apologetic, but did hasten to add, "But a good detective goes with his instinct and that instinct is telling me it was you."

That instinct also fingered the head of the police, who apparently had a guilty expression when speaking to the press; the postman, because there is always something suspicious about someone willing to get up at four in the morning; and the skinny hippy who worked at the newsstand and had refused to let Chip in the shop because it took him two weeks to get rid of the smell the last time he happened by. He was perpetually stoned and confused, but he was also eager and refused to accept no for an answer, so Michael let him help to find the killer.

The only information they had to go on was what they learned from the press and what they had seen themselves. The girls were all between eighteen and twenty-four years old and all of them had fallen on hard times. Two were prostitutes, and the third, the final girl, was a homeless smackhead. The cliché of the modern-day psychotic serial killer is to pick on the young and the desperate, those considered the dregs of society, the eradication of which would serve some higher psychotic purpose, but *everyone* was like that in Brittleside. You would have been hard-pressed to find a young girl who wasn't broke, addicted, and desperate. If they were not single mothers living off the benefit system and gorging themselves on the seed of strangers and battery-acid cider at a buck a bottle, then they were homeless and literally feeding from the gutter.

Michael had always wondered if he just thought in black and white, and if that attitude was to blame. But it was hard to find a gray area; it was hard to be neutral in a town constantly at war.

The police resorted to house-to-house inquiries, a brave thing to do in Brittleside. As far as the amateur detectives could gather, no information had emerged from those enquiries. There were leaked reports that the girls had parts of their bodies removed, different ones for each murder. Michael knew that had been the case with the first two victims, but he hadn't seen the third; he hadn't ventured inside the forensic tent. It was also public knowledge—thanks to the diligent journalists who saw the savage butchery as a way to further their careers and their fame—that the girls were all killed by a quick and efficient hand. The witness who discovered the final body testified to seeing the victim alive and the murder scene empty just fifteen minutes before stumbling onto the scene of carnage.

A relatively barren spell of three weeks followed the third murder. The town throbbed with an excited pulse as a population of fifty thousand excited and nervous locals awaited the next victim. The streets were typically empty at night, but now they were busier than ever. Have-a-go heroes were waiting on every corner, hoping to catch the killer and earn their fifteen minutes of fame.

With the increasing numbers of men walking the streets at night, the prostitutes saw their chance to earn a few extra dollars. It was like holiday season in Blackpool to them; they were staying out all hours, covering all areas of the streets to drum up as much extra business as possible. In a town with a predominately unemployed population, where the only people working were those brought in to arrest, save, or extinguish, no one had anywhere to be in the morning, so the town thrived at night. It was like a carnival—when the sun went down, the people came out and the mayhem began.

It looked like the killer wouldn't strike again, certainly not in Brittleside. But Michael knew that when he did, he would do so in daylight.

Michael opened the window as he drank his first cup of tea and it felt glorious. The sun was out, breaking through a thick cloud and pouring in through a slit in the top of the glass, just enough to bathe his face in a mild glow. Rain had fallen during the night, and the smell of wet pavement drying in the heat lifted up through the open window. Somewhere a fire burned, it could have been a house on fire or a psycho burning his collection of bodies, not unlikely, but whatever it was, it smelled great.

Michael had been drinking the night before. He expected a hangover. He expected to feel like a zombie, unwilling to get out of bed and face the day. But for whatever reason, he felt great. He felt fresh, alive.

He decided to go for a walk and even managed to throw a smile at some of the depressed faces he passed on the way. There was a throng of noises coming from the center of town, a line of people popping curious heads out of their windows or standing in open doorways in their dressing gowns, a cigarette in one hand, a coffee in the other, a look of tired interest on their grumpy faces.

He followed the noise and the crowd to the town square. He didn't see what they were looking at, but it had captivated them and seemingly forced their bodies into a wall. He saw lights up ahead and heard fading sirens. Someone was shouting orders.

When he saw them, his heart dropped. Another young girl, another pretty face. Victims number four and five, squashed together in a lustfully morbid embrace, naked, bloodied, and stuck out in the open for all to see. A shop worker setting up her stall had seen them, and her shouting had alerted the nearby houses that kick-started a domino effect which had sucked in a large chunk of the town. The police and the ambulances arrived on the scene just twenty minutes or so after the bodies had been discovered, but that was more than enough time for everyone else to get their fill.

The pictures were all over the internet in moments. Two girls, killed in two separate locations, stripped, dragged to the center of the town, and displayed in violently suggestive poses for the entire town—and moments later, the world—to see. The police set up a forensic tent and cordoned off the area but their efforts were futile.

Michael found the souls sitting sullenly on the curb by the bustling roadside. He sat down beside them and they both smiled at him. He told them he was there to help, that he would take them where they belonged, but that he first needed their help to catch the man who had killed them.

A blonde, the younger and prettier of the two, answered for them both while the other looked away absently, watching the crowd as it began to reluctantly disperse.

"We didn't see him," she said.

"You must have seen something?"

She merely shook her head. He was deflated. His morning had been ruined and his hopes of catching the killer had been dashed. Being able to converse with the dead was the only advantage he had over the inept cops, and if it proved futile, then his chances of catching the killer were just as lowly as theirs.

"There was *one* thing," she told him, lifting his spirits.

"Yes?"

"A smell." She looked into the middle distance as she spoke. She twisted her face. "It was like . . ." she pondered on this but failed to find the finality.

The second girl snapped out of her trance. "Menthol," she offered. "Like a hot menthol."

"Hot menthol?"

"Like a hot, *sweet* menthol."

"Hot, sweet menthol?"

They both nodded and flashed their simpleton smiles. It wasn't much to go on, but Michael knew that it was probably more than the police had.

"And you didn't see him?"

"He came into my home," the blonde told him. "I had only been up an hour or so, just finished breakfast. I didn't see him, didn't know. He took me from behind. The rest . . ." she trailed off.

Michael looked to the second girl, she grinned back.

"And you?"

"I was sleeping."

"He killed you when you were sleeping?"

She nodded slowly, and then turned away.

3

Cop movies and television dramas operate on the same principles whenever there is a serial killer on the loose. There always seems to be an unkempt, stressed-out insomniac copper assigned to the case who devotes his entire existence to tracking down a psycho killer and becomes an equally obsessive psychotic in the process. It's a tired formula, but one Michael began to sympathize with, because he became that obsessive and slightly psychotic detective as he hunted down the Bastard.

He thought about little else, and, as those movies and TV shows would testify, it got in the way of everything he did and everything he was. A week or so after the double murder, he went to retrieve another young dead girl. The news came as a surprise to him, flashing on his timer when he was deep in drink and thought. He rushed out, hoping to catch sight of the killer lingering on the scene.

It was after dark, the carnival atmosphere of the previous weeks had died away, and the streets were painted the typically forlorn colors of degradation and despair. The depressed and the destitute were the only ones tripping and stuttering their way through the streets or slumped and cold in alleys and doorways.

The victim was young and female. Not the picture of beauty. At one point in her life, she could have passed for respectable, but those years were long behind her. Michael's hopes of running into the killer vanished when he realized there wasn't one. She was a victim, but only of her own vices.

A tourniquet hung loosely from her arm, the marks of its tight indentation still painting a red ring around her pale and painfully thin wrist. He checked his timer and it confirmed the suspicions he had. Her death had been in the pipeline for a while. He had missed it. He had been so wrapped up in everything else, so set on finding the killer, that he failed to remember people were still dying by their own hands and by the hands of fate.

"You look disappointed to see me," she said when she saw Michael approach. She was waiting patiently by her empty corpse, her eyes smiling softly into his.

"I am," he told her honestly. "I was hoping you'd been murdered."

A couple of days later, Michael woke to some commotion. He had been sleeping little and often, getting to bed around three or four in the morning and sleeping intermittently until lunch time. He listened to the noise outside his door. Chip was shouting at someone, sounding like he does right before he loses an argument and resorts to dirty and brutal fighting. He checked his clock, it was barely nine, and the light breaking through a gap in his tightly squeezed curtains was hot and stung his eyes.

The noise culminated with a shriek, an appalled and agonized scream of surprise. Then the front door slammed shut and Chip crossed the corridor to Michael's room with a whistle on his lips and a skip in his step. Expecting the worst, Michael groaned and turned over, hoping to pretend he was sleeping. But Chip was a tooth fairy, he knew how to spot whether someone was asleep or only pretending. He also had a trick he deployed to be doubly sure, which involved punching the person in the leg and chanting, "I know you're awake. I know you're awake." Until they definitely were awake.

"Package for you," Chip yelled, tossing said package at Michael as he spoke.

Michael turned to face his friend. He was picking apart a stack of letters in his hand, scrunching some of them up and sticking others in his pocket. A number of them were smeared with blood, but it was early and he didn't want to question why.

Michael sat up with a groan; he never received packages. He certainly had enough junk mail sent his way—leaflets from stationary stores begging for repeat business when he was sure he'd never ordered from them; pamphlets on how God would be his savior if only he could be bothered to recognize his existence; and a shit-ton of sales spam trying to sell him crap he already had and still didn't want—but rarely did he get anything worthwhile.

Inside was a letter and a small box wrapped with numerous layers of paper and tied with a bow. The letter was written on a small square of paper. The writing inside was neat and precise, drawn by a methodical and calculated hand.

It said:

Dear Reaper Man,

Hello Mr. Reaper Man, collector of the souls; the killer of the copied sons and wasters of this world. A plump and fluffy little bird said that you were after me. Is that so?

I do pray that you will be more fun than those gluttonous fools currently probing the town with their idle questions. I know of your credentials; I doubt your capabilities. Tell me, Mr. Reaper Man, why does a lowly cast-off like yourself think he can catch me? Why do you even try? Surely, you, more than anyone, know how worthless and pointless these women are. You spend your days scraping them from the gutter, picking up the one worthwhile piece of their existence that remains and transporting it away from their drug-ravaged, bloated corpses.

Do you want to help me—is that it? Well, you flatter me Mr. Reaper Man, but I fear it would be a rather belligerent partnership and would simply never work. I'm sure my partner in crime would agree with me. After all, three's a crowd . . .

I'm honored that you are following me. I heard you had become quite a fan. I am going to kill the next one just for you. If you don't appreciate the act, I hope you at least acknowledge the effort.

I'll be seeing you.

Your friend,

P.S. Where is it you take these souls exactly? Do you even know? Answers on a postcard please.

P.P.S. I almost forgot. I've enclosed a small present to show my appreciation of your devoted support. Enjoy!

Michael was awestruck, breathless. It hadn't crossed his mind that he was dealing with a supernatural being, but there was no doubt. He knew what Michael did, and he seemed to know exactly who he was as well.

When Michael finished reading the letter, shock etched visibly on his face, he noticed Chip was staring at him. He passed his friend the letter without saying anything. After a few minutes, his little face lit up.

"It's him," he said, practically yelling.

Michael nodded solemnly and climbed out of bed with the package in his hands. Chip followed behind. He could hear his excited footsteps skipping along at a hasty pace; could feel them brushing the backs of his heels with every other step. In the kitchen, he carefully removed the bow, stripped back all the layers of paper, and prepared himself to open the box. He got the corner cranked open when Chip interrupted him.

"What if it's a bomb?" Chip wondered. "Rigged to blow when you open it."

"We are immortal."

"It still fucking hurts. I know hemorrhoids aren't going to kill me, but that doesn't mean I'm gonna start popping them like balloons just for the hell of it, does it?"

They both looked down into the hole they had created. They could see the blackened contents inside.

Michael shrugged, "Ah well, I guess we'll find out soon enough."

He peeled it back with even greater care. A sickening smell cut through the air and he knew it wasn't a bomb. He used a pair of kitchen tongs to pick it out, holding it at arm's length before dropping it onto a nearby plate. Chip stared at it like he would a naked supermodel coated in chocolate.

They didn't know what it was, but they knew it was human and had, at one point, been inside a body that was now rotting in a morgue or decaying under six feet of soil.

The victims all had had parts of their bodies removed. Michael theorized that the offal on his kitchen table had been preserved, as there hadn't been a murder in nearly two weeks and it looked and smelled much fresher than that, as the cloying taste at the back of his throat attested.

After many minutes of probing, questioning, and reading online reports about the crimes, with Michael using Chip's tablet computer and regretting doing so with every swipe and every click, they deduced it had come from one of the girls in the most recent double murder. One had been missing a kidney, the other a liver.

"I'm sure it's one or the other," Chip said.

Michael wasn't concerned with which organ it was. What concerned him was that it had been sent to him and not to the police. It mattered that he knew who he was, where he lived, and what he did for a living.

"He also knows about us," Chip pointed out. "About what we did last year."

Michael frowned at him in reply. He was still tired and feeling a little sick to his stomach. The offending human detritus presently resting in a pool of expanding black liquid didn't bother him all that much, but the note, and the suggestion that he was now a player in a game orchestrated by a sick serial killer who knew more about him than he knew about them, did.

"The werewolf business," Chip elaborated. He produced the letter and pointed to the opening paragraph. "Killer of copied sons," he said slowly. "The two clones?"

For a man who often missed so much, Chip had noticed something Michael had ignored.

"But who knows about that?"

"No one living," Chip said. "And maybe only a handful of the dead. It's not just one person either," he pointed to the note again, "it says he has a partner. So, there are at least two people out there who know about what happened, people who know about you, and seem to have something against you."

"Why? Why me?"

Chip shrugged. "Maybe they've met you."

Doctor Khan was intrigued. She looked a little upset when Michael stopped talking and took to staring absently at a framed poster on the other side of the room: a man, dwarfed by his desert surroundings, stood before a colossal sand dune entwined with a pencil-thin path that spiraled to its summit.

A few moments of silence passed before Michael said, "That's new."

The doctor shifted on her seat and checked her notes. She had barely written anything down that Michael had told her. She knew about the murders and had followed them eagerly, as had everyone else. It had been a nationwide, and eventually worldwide, story. She was intrigued to know Michael's version of events—from the horse's mouth, so to speak.

"I put it up two days ago," she said without removing her gaze from his.

"Whatever happened to soothing art or analytical posters? When did this nonsense with motivational posters begin?"

"You don't like motivational posters?"

"I'm not sure of their purpose."

The doctor stared at him blankly for an interminable time. "They're supposed to motivate," she said eventually.

"But *do* they? Who could possibly get motivated by a poster?"

"Some people—"

"Okay, I'll rephrase, who, *in a psychiatrist's office,* could possibly be motivated by a poster? If they worked, then pharmaceutical companies would be dead and the people putting clichéd art into cardboard frames and selling them for twenty bucks a pop would be billionaires."

"It's just a little extra motivation."

Michael didn't look convinced. "Do they work for you?" he asked, staring at the doctor with unblinking eyes.

She flashed an uncommitted expression and then shook her head.

He slumped back in his chair, folded his hands between his tightly closed thighs, and sunk his head forward.

The doctor noted the dismayed expression. "Is there something else you want to talk about?" she asked.

"Something else?" Michael said, glancing sideways at her. "Other than what? Moronic posters or sadistic serial killers?"

"Well, both."

He turned back in on himself and shook his head. "There's a whole list of things," he told her. "I hate my life—*my death*—whatever the fuck this is. I hate my job. I hate my house. I hate this town."

"Is there *anything* you like?"

He gave this some thought before he answered. "There's a few things I tolerate. I wouldn't go as far as to say I *liked* them."

She made a note, the first since he had skulked through her door. "Do you want to elaborate?" she wondered.

He sighed and arched his back upward. It clicked; he groaned. "No," he said abruptly. "Another time. Maybe. Let's get back to the story."

4

Michael and Chip went to see Naff. They realized that this was one of those rare times when it paid to have a friend who worked in the Records Department and was, by nature, a know-it-all. Or at least that's what they thought.

"I have no idea," he told them. "Hell, if not for the letter, and the fact that it's actually legible, I would have put my money on it being Chip."

He agreed that the killer was probably a demon but added, rather reluctantly, that their exploits with the werewolf hunters were not as confidential as they first thought. Naff had boasted of his involvement by sending out mass emails and bragging to everyone he knew.

"I file papers all day," he told them. "I sit at a desk staring at words, doing sums, stamping, authorizing, checking. This was the first time I've had something to brag about in ages, so . . . I may have overdone it."

Some hope came in the form of one of Naff's coworkers. His name was Idlewild, or so he wanted everyone to believe. His actual name was Herman. He was a highly strung geek who refused to make eye contact when he spoke, instead choosing to dart his bespectacled eyes around the room like he was on the lookout for wannabe attackers.

He was as obsessed with his work as Naff, but, unlike Naff, he took it home with him. According to Naff, his obsession made him an expert on everything.

He lived in a squalid flat above a fish-and-chip shop in the center of town. The air was rank with the stench of fried fish. A line of obese, sweaty, and hungry customers were filing out the door when they arrived. Michael had no idea why the queue was so big; he'd eaten there before—the fish was beaten to the texture of polystyrene and coated with so much batter that there was an inch of uncooked dough between the soggy fish and the burned shell; the chips were semi-cooked and tasted more like fish than the fish. He could only assume the owners were giving out free cake.

The three friends had to wade through the crowd to get to Herman's door. The stench of greasy fast food followed them inside the building, up the stairs, and into the flat, where it was joined by the rank stench of unwashed clothes, stale food, and body odor left to ferment in a sealed room for months on end.

There were books and papers everywhere, piled in random places on the floor. The only furniture was a dirty coffee table that sat on a dark-brown rug in front of a dusty sofa. Through an open door on the other side of the room, they could see his bedroom: a single shoddy mattress on the floor, a scattering of dirty clothes all around it. He remained at the office whenever he could, so absorbed in his work that he often refused to leave and either worked all day and all night or just pottered away on his computer, sleeping at his desk.

Chip seemed to admire the place; he had a thing for filth. He didn't trust cleanliness and said it had an ulterior motive. He was uncomfortable around anything that was too clean. He also hated being told, by Michael, to clean up or to stop leaving his bodily bits lying around like some malting leper, so for him, Herman—a man who undoubtedly shared his disinterest for cleanliness—was the ideal roommate.

Herman didn't seem to know what to do with his new house-guests when they arrived. He looked Naff, Chip, and Michael over in turn and then concentrated on Michael, looking him up and down with his hands in his pockets. He wore big black-rimmed spectacles that kept sliding down his nose.

"Naff said you have a letter from the killer," he said, watching Michael's pockets with a glint in his eye.

Michael noted a gleam of sweat on his acne-riddled face. He couldn't have been more of the stereotypical geek if he'd have greeted them in a Star Trek outfit speaking Klingon.

He showed him the letter and his glossy face lit up. He waffled to himself for a bit before anyone could pick out what he was saying.

"I knew it," he was repeating.

He waved the letter. Michael shrugged.

"Sit down," he said, flicking his sliding glasses back to the bridge of his noise. "I'll explain."

Chip practically dove onto the couch. Before his ass cheeks even touched the cushions he was glancing around for a snack and the TV remote.

"I'd rather not," Michael told him. He wasn't sure what horrible diseases or insects were lurking inside the dusty confines of the tattered upholstery.

Herman shrugged, shook it off, and then launched into a monologue about the killer.

"I think I know who it is," he began. "I had my suspicions from the start but I couldn't be sure. For all I knew—and indeed, as I first suspected—the killer was human. Just another sexual deviant getting his kicks from murdering women, but the pieces continued to fit and now, with this letter . . ." he gestured to the paper clenched in his sweaty palm, "it confirms it."

"Confirms what?"

"Abaddon."

"Excuse me?"

He was doing laps around the couch as he spoke, growing increasingly excited. "An ancient, powerful demon. Older than the human race, older than time itself. I've studied him before, in his other *incarnations*." His sweaty fingers highlighted the word with air quotes.

"*Another* demon," Michael said with a sigh.

"Ah," he thrust one of those sweaty fingers at me. "He is not just *any* demon. He is not resigned to hell. He lives *here* on earth, and he has done so since the dawn of time."

"So what? We find him and send him back to hell?"

He shook his head. "You can't send him back to hell. He's not an entity in himself; he's more like a spirit. He has no substantial form of his own, but rather he possesses others. He chooses who he likes and stays with them, and when they grow old or worthless, he moves on. But, there is always a rest period."

"A rest period?"

"A period of inactivity, when he is between existences. He is neither spirit nor possessor, he is just a spectator, watching and waiting for his next victim." He spoke with a jittering excitement; seemingly unable to linger on one thought for fear that the next one would slip. His feeble body trembled with a shifting agitation.

"He thrives in small locations. Small cities or towns, where the fears of the whole combine into one hysterical consciousness. He chooses his victims for the same reason: he picks the innocent and the helpless, often the women, instilling fear into the minds of other women and a sense of guilt into the men."

He stopped his restless shifting, and stood in front of Michael again with a quivering excitement shaking through his malnourished body. He had finished his lecture and seemingly wanted praise.

"How do you know all this?" Michael asked.

He swiveled his head around and extended an arm. No doubt he was gesturing toward the piles of books scattered around, but it was hard to look beyond the filth.

"There's little I don't know," he said with an air of a man who hadn't been able to control his excitement and had let it spill into an ego that far outweighed his personality.

"Why me?" Michael asked. "Why write to me? Why involve me at all? Who am I to him?"

"My guess? Someone else is involved. I don't think Abaddon would willingly choose Brittleside or you. I mean, why would he care about something so pointlessly hostile, so disgusting, so grimy, so down on its luck and—"

"Are you taking about the town or Michael?" Naff jumped in, a smile on his face.

Herman looked a little confused, apparently missing the joke. "The town," he said. "As for you, no offense, but you're not his type," he told Michael. "I mean, a fairly substandard reaper working the worst beat, with little respect from his peers?" He finished with a shake of his head.

Michael glared at Naff; Herman caught the look and was quick to say, "He didn't tell me. I work in Records, remember?"

"Okay, then," Michael said, telling Naff he was forgiven.

"It might not be because of that," Herman offered. "Maybe Abaddon finds you fascinating."

Chip laughed. It was quick and abrupt but it was definitely a laugh. Michael turned to stare at him, but he'd already sheepishly diverted his eyes.

"Okay, so someone might be involved, someone might not be, what does that mean to me?"

"It means someone may be using him to get to you. Someone may have awoken him. They may be directing him. Do you have any enemies?"

Chip sorted. "How long have you got?"

Michael turned slowly to Chip and then to Herman. He nodded and shrugged, in agreement with his impish friend.

"Okay, well it's beside the point anyway. They are using him for a reason. He's powerful, maybe more than they are."

"And how do I stop him?" Michael asked the oily oracle.

It was his turn to laugh—a mocking laugh. He knocked up his glasses from the bottom of his nose when he'd finished. "You can't stop him."

"I have to."

He shook his head and gave an apathetic shrug. "Just wait. He'll stop when he's had his fill."

Michael felt anger rising inside of him. That was the attitude he hated. The blasé bloodlust that personified this town and made it the thing he despised. Women were dying, and he was treating it like a game.

"I need to know how to stop him. There must be a way."

"*How to stop him?*" another derisive laugh. Michael was barely holding onto his nerves. "You mean do what so many have failed to do?"

Michael felt his fists clench. The anger and frustration was visible on his face as he struggled to restrain his desire to shake and strangle the nonchalant smugness out of the man opposite. He spoke to him through gritted teeth, "Just fucking help me."

Sensing Michael's anger and frustration, Herman wiped the smugness off his face. "Look," he said calmly. "I've been reading about this guy for a while now, hell, I've been waiting for his return for a long time. From what history has told us, what little we have gathered from the times he was *caught—*"

"He was caught?"

"Well, yes." There was a cheeky smile on the corner of his mouth. "Everyone makes mistakes, even *he,*" he spoke like he was praising an idol. "He has a certain type. Usually the artistic, creative type. Maybe he sees himself as an artist, maybe they're more accessible, who knows." He scuttled to the other side of the room and pulled a book out from underneath a chair. The chair toppled over lopsidedly, barely balancing on a shortened leg.

He opened it to a worn, well-read page and ushered Michael near. He hovered over Herman's shoulder, trying to stay away from his warm and musty scent.

The book was written in English, but in a cursive and historical style that the reaper struggled to grasp. The words were accompanied by a portrait of a stern-looking young man with boyish, almost feminine blue eyes and a pointy chin.

Parallel to the picture, where a flamboyant and oversized letter began an undecipherable paragraph, Herman pointed with a grubby forefinger. "In the fourteenth century, he inhabited the body of a painter. A prodigy. A genius by all accounts. He butchered his mother and his three sisters on the same night, reveling in the agony of the father who returned home to find his family obliterated; his wife and daughters dead, his only son insane."

"Jesus," Michael uttered, struggling to believe that the dainty person in the picture (who looked like he would struggle to hurt a fly) could commit such atrocities, possessed or not.

"He was captured in the act and hanged a few weeks later, but not before we had established who he was."

"We?" Michael asked him.

The cheeky grin had returned. "We have been here for a *very* long time, you know." Michael could smell his breath when he spoke. He took a step back, trying to hide his distaste with an averted glance.

He looked at Naff, who gave a gentle and knowing nod.

"In 1620 and in 1750," he continued with a grubby finger scrolling across the page. "Two more painters, thirteen more victims."

Michael nodded, keeping his distance. Apparently Herman wasn't as averse to the rotten fish-and-chip shop as he was. There was also a good chance—evident by the rancid air that seemed to be clinging to the pores on Michael's face—that he hadn't brushed or rinsed the fetid orifice that had fed on those battered monstrosities for weeks.

"In 1813: a young poet, seven victims," Herman slammed the book shut with a thud, and a cloud of dust sprayed into his face, but he didn't seem to notice. He dropped the book onto the coffee table where it was enveloped by a wall of dust that rose from the unwashed surface like a rogue wave.

He turned to Michael, smiling. "He enjoys the act of murder but he prefers the vicarious suffering that their death brings. In London, Jack the Ripper thrived on the fear of a city. In San Francisco, the Zodiac tormented and teased the police. This time it seems that you're his reason and *this* is his town."

"Great," he said meekly.

"Just remember," Herman said, "our technology has improved since those years, as has our understanding of what he is and what he is capable of. My guess is that he has partnered with someone else as a way of learning this new world and stopping it from getting the better of him, wouldn't be for the first time. Alternatively . . ." Herman trailed off.

"Yes?" Michael pushed.

Herman shook his head. "Let's forget about the alternative scenario. It's highly unlikely."

Michael stood to leave, keen to get as far away from this emetic hermit as possible. "If the last thirty years have taught me anything, highly unlikely is an inevitability."

5

The grimy-faced geek with the encyclopedic knowledge had told Michael more than he had expected to hear, but nothing he could really use. If anything, he was in a worse position because he knew that the Bastard was killing to get at *him*, to make him suffer. And he *was* suffering. He was struggling to sleep; struggling to eat.

The killer sent Michael another message, this one less subtle than the psycho prose with the human offal. He struck again, and this time it was right on Michael's front doorstep.

The alley that led to his front door was a haven for beggars and addicts. There was an overhang on the roof and the alley was narrow, so all but a thin strip in the center was sheltered. It was an ideal, albeit small, place for them to find shelter for the night. On any given night at least two of them would curl up there, and more than once Michael had tripped over them on his way to, or away from, the apartment.

He had been up all night, drinking horrible coffee mixed with cheap rum. He tried to sleep, but his mind refused to shut down. The caffeine helped his body sync with his mind; the rum took away the bitter taste and sedated him to neutrality.

There was a commotion outside the door. Through the kitchen window, which looked onto the street ahead, a stream of pedestrians and cars passed by, heading for the alleyway and the back of the house. Before Michael could awaken himself to the situation and sneak a peek at what was going on, someone knocked on the door.

Chip had been watching from his bedroom window and bolted to the door while Michael was still on the couch. He heard two suspicious policemen introduce themselves. Their initial suspicions, evident in their overheard introductions, grew rapidly when they saw Chip and drank in his treacherous, appalling, and criminal facade.

They said there had been a murder in the alley. Michael's heart sank.

"A murder?" he heard Chip exclaim excitedly. "Is the body still there? Can I see it?"

They dismissed his comment. Michael peeked his head into the hallway and watched from the living room as one of the cops took out a notepad and scribbled something on the top. Chip had been promoted to lead suspect.

"Can we ask where you were last night?"

He was quick to answer, "No. Can I ask where *you* were?" he wondered in a suspicious tone.

"That's not relevant to—"

"Oh. It's *very* relevant. There's a murderer on the loose, you know."

Michael interrupted before the inevitable chaos ensued. He nudged his friend out of the way and could feel him trying to claw him aside as he faced the two officers.

"We were here all night," Michael explained, smiling warmly at them.

That was all they needed to know. A spark glimmered in both of their eyes and, as if caught in a trance, they turned and walked away without saying another word.

Chip managed to squeeze his way past. He popped his head out of the doorway and traced suspicious eyes over the retreating coppers before relenting with a reluctant sigh.

He turned to the person who had taken their place, waiting patiently with her hands folded across her groin. "And who the fuck are you?" he asked the grinning specter.

She looked from Michael to Chip and then back again. She shrugged.

"She's the victim," Michael said, stepping out to greet her.

He didn't linger to catch a look at the body. Chip tried, but the nearby officers refused to let him step out of the front door.

"What about him!" Chip screamed, pointing a finger at Michael as he strode through the cordon without anyone batting an eyelid.

Michael didn't want to see any more of the killer's work. He'd seen enough. He also knew that this one was different; this one was worse, because this one was for him.

The letter that arrived the following day confirmed his thoughts:

Dear Mr. Reaper Man,

I hoped you liked my gift; I hope you liked the way I cut and opened both her wrists. I said it would be for you, I said she was yours. She reached for you in death, Mr. Reaper Man.

I know what you're thinking. I should have come in, had a cup of coffee, maybe some cake and a chat, but I was in a rush; I had things to do. Maybe another time. Because, of course, there will be another time.

How is your search going, by the way? I'm guessing you haven't found me yet. Be sure to yell when you do.

"So what now?" I hear you ask. Well, I think it has to be something special, doesn't it? Something to top this. You can leave me to my thoughts for now, but rest assured that the next time you hear from me, it will be spectacular.

Your friend

There was no package this time, there was no need for one; he had left the entire package at Michael's front door. The alleyway was bad enough without the liquid remains of death coating the pavement and clogging the gutters, leaving an unmistakable stench that would stay for many years and linger even longer in Michael's memory.

He was at breaking point. Chip, looking rather sheepish, offered some help.

The body outside had been hauled away in a large van that had spent the morning parked right in front of the kitchen window, it's deathly motif staring hauntingly at the occupants from above the kitchen sink where a pile of dishes waited for someone brave and willing.

"Look," Chip said. "I have a suspect. I didn't want to tell you before but—"

"It's not me again, is it?"

"No, you don't know him. He's weird, *very* weird."

"You sure I don't know him?"

"Positive."

"Because that sounds like a lot of my friends."

"Can I finish please?"

Michael held up his hands defensively. Chip continued, "I've seen him a few times on my route; he was still popping out teeth in his twenties." He walked to the kitchen while he talked, spying on the lingering car-crash spectators as they slowly and begrudgingly filed back to their mundane lives.

"He's a loner; a weirdo. He spends most of his time in his room. It has that, *'lived-in'* stink. He lives with his mother but she's old and demented. He could be running a brothel up there and she'd be none the wiser, I don't think she even goes up, I'm not sure she *can*. She has a bed downstairs in the dining room and—"

"How the hell do you know all this?"

He lifted his shoulders into a sheepish shrug. "I *know* things."

"You've been spying on him?" Michael accused.

"You would if you'd seen what I've seen!" Chip insisted, getting heated. "It's *him*, it's gotta be him."

Him turned out to be Harry Goldstein, a twenty-nine-year-old man with the pale, insipid features of a depressed vampire and the scowling personality of a rotten fish.

The two friends followed him on his weekly trip to collect his benefits—a journey that Chip had been tracking for a few weeks, hoping to catch the pale murderer in the act.

Goldstein walked with his head down, a skulking skip in his step. He looked timid, almost unsure of the open air, yet when an elderly stranger greeted him with a generic salute and gesture, he nearly bit the poor man's head off.

"Stay away from me, you foul-smelling drunk!" he yelled. "Take your monotonous salutations elsewhere."

"See," Chip whispered as they crept down the path. "I told you he was weird. He talks just like in the letters."

Michael had been dubious of Chip's beliefs at first. He has a habit of being so completely wrong on so many occasions that he had every right to doubt him, but there was promise in what he said.

Michael could get a lot of information from people. It made his job easier and it also gave him something to do when he was bored. There were a few exceptions, and the undead and the volatile were always amongst them. The fact that he couldn't get anything from Harry suggested he could have been either.

Harry had the mannerisms of a recluse and the personality of a psychotic chauvinist. He was a combination of two worlds that rarely collided. He sneered and ogled a number of women—old and young—who passed him on the street and even stopped one of them to ask her a question, the answer to which was a look of disgust and a quickened step in the opposite direction.

"It's him," Chip affirmed.

Harry bounded into the dole office after wolf-whistling at a confused octogenarian in a parked car. Michael could only shrug and nod in agreement.

They went to the house that Harry shared with his mother while he was occupied. The back door led into the kitchen, and when Michael slipped through, he found her hunched over a counter, her hands trembling as she tried to pour a spoonful of sugar into a cup, shaking it onto the counter instead. It took her a few attempts before she managed to get a sufficient amount of sugar into the cup, at which point she had to re-boil the kettle since the water had turned tepid.

The door rattled behind Michael. Chip was waiting on the other side and he'd evidently grown impatient. Michael remained still, waiting for the old lady to turn around and attempt to beat him to death with the misshapen cane she used to support her frail frame. She didn't budge and merely continued to watch the kettle boil.

He slipped off a deadbolt at the top of the door and unhooked another at the bottom. Chip was ready to complain when he opened the door to let him in, but he paused at the sight of the old lady. He gently closed the door behind him, before attempting to tiptoe across the kitchen floor with the stealth and finesse of someone much more stealthy and finessy than he. He knocked over a rack of pans and then stumbled headfirst into an open drawer of cutlery.

The old lady didn't fail to notice that. She swiveled around with a creaky pirouette and squinted at him through filmy cataracts.

She looked at his slumped figure, her eyes trying to find a glimmer of focus. "Chester?" she asked.

Chip looked up at his friend unsurely; he received a shrug in reply.

"Woof, woof!" Chip snapped in his best canine voice, which was surprisingly quite believable.

The old woman seemed taken aback by this. Her wizened face creased, she leaned forward, shuffled closer. "Chester?"

Stuck to the fridge with an assortment of tatty fridge magnets, Michael saw a picture of an overfed tabby cat whose fancy collar was emblazoned with the word: Chester.

"It's a cat," he whispered. "*Cat!*" he hissed again.

Chip turned back to the woman and gave her his best cat impression. Apparently Chip had never encountered a cat in his life. Michael sighed, ready for the worst. The woman moved closer to Chip.

Michael took the initiative and made a cat noise, trying his utmost to throw his voice. It seemed to work because she stopped still; a tear crept into her eye.

"You're alive!" she exclaimed, both surprised and delighted. "You've come back!"

"*Ah, for fuck's sake,*" Michael mumbled. "Just go," he whispered to Chip, wafting his arms at him.

Chip scampered away and Michael shifted by as inconspicuously as he could. The old lady looked at him and acknowledged the passing blur, but didn't say anything. They were in the living room—on the way up the stairs to search for dead bodies and murder weapons—when a noise on the other sound of the room alerted them. They turned to see Harry standing in the doorway, staring right at them.

"Oh my God," he started when he saw Michael, nearly jumping out of his skin. His eyes darted around the room and then fixed back on the reaper. "*You!*" he said distantly.

"Me?"

"Is this it? Am I dead? Did you come for me?"

"You know who I am?"

Harry nodded, his face bright with disappointment and a quickening realization.

"I told you it was him," Chip said confidently. "Come on then, let's kill him and get this over with."

Harry was mumbling to himself, looking distraught. "I knew this was a bad idea," he muttered. Behind them, the old lady had dragged herself to where Chip had been lying. She mumbled soothing reassurances to the dead and invisible cat. Then, with a deft swiftness, she raised her cane and brought it crashing down onto the floor. A scowl filled her face; her words were fused with venom.

"Get out of my house demon cat!" she yelled repeatedly as she dealt a number of swift blows to a stainless steel pot that sat toppled on the floor.

"Your mother is just as bat-shit crazy as you, I see," Chip said.

Harry noted her briefly but didn't dwell. He shifted over to the sofa and slumped down with an exhaustive sigh before burying his head in his hands.

"He's not going to cry, is he?" Chip whispered.

"She's not my mother," Harry said into his hands.

Chip gave Michael an inquisitive shrug.

"I mean, she is *his* mother, but I'm not really *him*. *Me*, I mean. Look . . ." Harry lifted his head to look at the two intruders. His eyes were puffy and on the verge of tears. "I'm not him."

Chip turned to Michael and twirled a forefinger around his temple when he thought the sulking Harry wasn't looking.

"And I'm not insane!" Harry snapped.

Chip pretended to be scratching his ear.

"I'm not even human!" Harry pleaded.

"We know," Michael said with a nod, feeling little sympathy for him. "We know what you are, we know what you did."

He looked distraught at the statement. "You know . . . *what I did*?" He sunk his head into his hands again; a gasping cry escaped his lips. "It was an accident," he cried. "Please don't send me back, please—"

"An accident?" Michael snapped, incredulous. "You killed five fucking women! How is that a fucking accident?"

Michael's anger was at a boiling point. Harry looked startled, but his sobbing halted and he gazed at the reaper with hazy and perplexed eyes. "Killed? I didn't kill—"

"We know what you did." Michael moved toward him. Harry stood up quickly and took a step back.

"You've got me mistaken," he begged. "I didn't kill anyone. Please . . ." He raised his hands in front of his face and prepared to suffer a beating. Michael paused and looked down at his pleading, pathetic face. It certainly wasn't what he expected from the demon who had sent him the letters, a demon who had racked up scores of brutal killings throughout the centuries.

"Explain yourself," Michael said.

Harry peeked out above his fingers and then slowly withdrew them from his face. "Okay, look . . ." he began with a deflated sigh. "I'll tell you." He sighed deeply and removed his gaze from Michael's. "I'm a sex demon."

"You think a lot of yourself," Chip noted.

"No, I mean *literally*."

"You're a succubus?" Michael asked.

"You rape men?" Chip chimed with a look of disgust.

"No. Well," Harry paused, his eyes trailed off momentarily, and he pulled them back. "Not intentionally. I'm an incubus, I *was* an incubus."

"Is that a yes or a no?" Chip wondered.

Michael stepped in, "But you're possessing this guy? I didn't think your kind did that."

"We don't."

Michael folded his arms across his chest. "If this is your way of explaining, you're not doing a very good job."

Harry sighed again. They all paused briefly as the old woman ventured out of the kitchen with a cup of tea trembling in her frail hand. She walked a couple yards behind them without seeing any of them—her eyes on the cup as it sloshed its contents all down her stained nightgown and onto the floor. By the time she had crossed the living room and stuttered into the adjoining dining room, the cup was all but empty.

"She'll be back to make herself another one soon," Harry said when he saw Michael looking. "She can go back and forth for most of the day, terrible I guess, but very funny."

"Why doesn't she just drink it in the kitchen?"

Harry shrugged, a smirk still on his face.

"Okay. Now, explain," Michael demanded. He may have not been the killer, but there was something about him that Michael found innately evil and devious, a sort of sweaty, perverted sadism that seemed to ooze out of his soul.

Harry nodded and sat himself down on the sofa again. "Look, I'm fairly inexperienced in the role. I don't get out much, so to speak." He looked away as he spoke, his eyes on the old woman still staggering to her bed, muttering to herself as she splashed the remaining droplets of her tea on her billowing nightdress.

"I was losing what little respect I had from my colleagues so I decided to up my game, to sleep around a bit more. It started well. There was a drunk girl who'd fallen asleep against the back wall of a club. She was a little messy and I don't think I was her first that night, but you know what they say, any port in a storm."

"That's disgusting."

"It may be, but it's also my job. The next one was younger, cleaner." There was a perverted smile on his face as he recalled his conquests. "She was a pretty little thing, didn't—"

"Can you get to the point please?" Michael asked, hearing a disagreeable groan from Chip.

"Okay. Things went a little tits-up on number five. I was on a roll, but there's only so much I can take. I was tired, I was distracted. I entered the dreams of an elderly woman and found myself in her bedroom. I quickly got down to business. She was a little hairier than I thought and far tighter than I would have ever given her credit for—"

"Oh come on, drop the details, *please.*"

"Well, as it turned out, to cut a long story short . . ." he stammered, hesitating. "The elderly woman was sleeping in a bed downstairs." He turned away as he spoke, sickened and embarrassed by his recollections. "I had just fucked her thirty-year-old son."

Michael groaned loudly, Chip burst into laughter.

"It was an easy mistake to make," the incubus begged them to believe. "It was a long night; I was tired, running on fumes. I overshot my mark and then . . ." he trailed off.

"Hit the wrong hole?" Chip offered.

Harry's face turned red, but Chip was in heaven.

"I don't get it," Michael said, waiting for the laughter to die down. "How did you end up inside him?"

That was enough to start Chip off again.

"How did you come to *possess him*?" Michael rephrased.

Harry shot a distasteful glance at Chip, who was moments away from exploding. "I was embarrassed. I couldn't go and face my friends and colleagues after that. I'd be ridiculed for eternity. It's not the done thing. So . . ." he shrugged nonchalantly, "I figured I'd just, sorta, well, *stay.*"

"You possessed him to avoid embarrassment?"

"You don't know what it's like, it's horrible down there!" he snapped defensively. Chip wailed another round of breathless hysterics, gasping for air. "I couldn't face that. It's not like he had much of a life anyway. He spent all his time in his room for God's sake. He doesn't have any friends, doesn't have a job, has never had a girlfriend and is still a vir—" He stopped, swallowed his words. Chip finished his sentence for him:

"He was until you came along!"

"You see," Harry said with a stern expression and a nod toward the laughing ball of hair. "This is what I'd get for the rest of eternity, only ten times worse."

"Okay, okay." Michael agreed, "Fair enough."

"This is not permanent and I have every intention of going back . . . I just need a lifetime or two to let the air clear."

The twinge of a smile rested on Michael's face as he recalled the story. He sounded a soft, suppressed laugh. "Strange experience, to say the least," he said.

Doctor Khan was also smiling.

Michael straightened up, groaned as his back clicked and spasmed. "I think my time's nearly up," he noted with a glance at the clock on the wall. He had talked away the afternoon; the light cutting through the thin slats in the blind was tinged orange.

"We have time," she told him.

"You're usually trying to get rid of me."

She shrugged. "What can I say? I'm intrigued. Did you ever ask your boss about all of this? I can't help but think that you and your *sidekick* were a little up against it."

"It didn't feel like that at the time. But no, I didn't. I couldn't take any more vague statements or blank stares. I knew he wouldn't help me, and I knew I probably couldn't get a hold of him even if I wanted to. In my experience, you don't talk to Azrael unless he wants to talk to you. And he didn't show up so. . ." he shrugged. "I took that to mean I was alone."

"Which, in this case, you relished, right?"

Michael didn't reply. He merely shrugged. "And anyway, I had Chip. So I wasn't really alone."

"So. I think you need to finish the story."

"For your sake or for mine?"

"For both our sakes," she told him.

He nodded, grinned, and then lowered his head.

"Because if you don't, I'll kill you."

He laughed and then straightened his face. "The humor stops there, though," he warned the doctor without meeting her gaze "It's all depressing from here on out."

6

The Dead Seamstress was a depressing pub, a hole in the ground where the vermin gathered to while away the days and avoid regular society. Michael liked it. In his eyes, there was nothing wrong with hunkering into a hole and drinking your sorrows away with the other moles. But after the chaos of the previous days—after he had struggled to sleep properly, to think straight—he needed something different.

He took his friends to a new club on the outskirts of town. The glitzy establishment looked out of place in a town like Brittleside. But it had only been open for a couple weeks so they figured they would enjoy the polished and fresh feel before the windows were boarded up and the bar had been burned down, built up, robbed, and restocked enough times for the owners to submit and sell.

It was as fresh and clean inside as it was outside. A succession of small spotlights were embedded in the ceiling, rows and rows of pinpoint fluorescence that lit up the building with a sparkle. A large dance floor, noticeably devoid of wrappers and spent chewing gum, was lit from above with red, blue, and green bulbs, providing an array of colors for the polished floor to reflect.

There were only a couple customers in when they arrived. One, a timid-looking hipster in brightly colored clothes, was sitting before a stage, which was being prepared by a smiling bald man in a casual suit. The other, a woman, sat at the bar and watched Michael, Chip, and Naff as they approached.

The bartender was happy and his enthusiasm and politeness took Michael by surprise. He was used to his bartenders being a little more sullen, a lot more aggressive. The woman by the bar watched Michael as he contended with the newfound pleasantry. She was pretty, fairly young. Her hair was a deep, dark red. Her eyes the brightest green.

When the drinks had been poured, the money exchanged, and menial conversation finished, Michael introduced himself. Her name was Isabella and her smile increased even further when she told him so.

"I haven't seen you around here before," Michael said.

"You come here often?" she said with a chuckle. Her right hand rested on the bar, her fingers lightly clasped around a wine glass, yet while he remained standing in front of her, she never turned to take a drink, never removed her gaze from his.

Chip and Naff had drifted off. They were arguing on the other side of the bar, their voices ripe and punishing in the silence. Isabella never once looked over Michael's shoulder to witness the source of the distracting tones, and he knew that because he never moved his eyes away from hers.

She was from the city and was visiting a friend in town. She asked Michael if he was staying at the club for a few more drinks. His intention had been to swallow a quick succession of the expensive beers and then head back home, nicely sozzled, to continue his inebriation with a bottle of cheap whiskey, but he told her he would be there for most of the night. If she was going to be there then he had every intention of staying.

"You'll see me later then," she told him with a glint in her eye. She stood and walked away, taking her wine glass with her and flashing a smile at the bartender. Michael watched her go, waited for her to disappear around the bar into an unseen room, and then he joined his bickering friends in front of the stage. At that point, his sorrows didn't need drowning; she had already cheered him up, and the prospect of seeing her again was enough to further lift his spirits.

The club began to fill as the night wore on; a group of chattering women with shortened skirts and wailing laughter, teenage boys on the pull, two elderly men comforting themselves with a corner table and pints of foamy bitter, and a young couple, the man devotedly staring at the woman, the woman staring everywhere but at him.

Isabella didn't make an appearance. Michael watched and waited, but after an hour and a half, she didn't show. He was losing patience and drifting back to his melancholic state when the stage, empty and lifeless until that point, flickered into life. The happy-faced man who had been setting up the equipment earlier was now standing among it, a microphone stand before him, a guitar, a drum kit, and a number of amplifiers behind.

In an enthusiastic voice, he yelled a greeting to the crowd and received very little in response. Most of them hadn't known he was there and nearly dropped their drinks when he called to them through the booming microphone.

He repeated himself a couple times, received a meager reaction in response, and then gave up. He introduced a band that waddled onto the stage with a timidity that suggested they had been forced to play by their parents.

There were three of them in total, two carrying guitars, the third cradling drumsticks. They took up their respective positions without even acknowledging the crowd, their chins against their chests the entire time. The crowd had been paying attention until that point, but diverted their interests when the musicians skulked onto the stage.

Then the singer came on. He too was carrying a guitar, a striking blue instrument printed and adorned with an array of stickers and emblems. He leapt to the front with a great, unrelenting energy and quickly attracted everyone's attention. He grabbed the microphone, and in a few energetic warbles, he had generated the excitement that the announcer could have only hoped for.

The band played for half an hour. They were good; they were all capable and talented, but the singer blew the others away. He danced around the stage like Jagger in his youth and could play the guitar like the best of them. Michael used to adore music and while he hadn't quite rediscovered that love in the afterlife, he still enjoyed himself and completely forgot about the Bastard.

The singer finished with an exhaustive guitar solo and bowed to a raucous reception from a crowd that had thickened to a couple dozen. His talents, and those of his band mates, deserved much larger audiences, but he seemed to enjoy himself. He exited the stage with just as much energy as when he had entered; his band mates skulked off without an ounce of enjoyment.

Isabella was next on stage. She strutted on with a wave to the crowd, flashing a cheeky wink at Michael. She had an acoustic guitar and was accompanied by a friend. They broke into a number of country and western songs. She had a nice voice, but didn't seem as comfortable on stage as her friend, who oozed confidence.

Michael broke off halfway through their set to go to the bar and saw the previous band lingering there. The singer, looking just as slick and confident even without his guitar, was watching him as he approached.

His band mates were loitering further away, collecting near the other end of the bar in a hunchbacked, depressed cluster. They didn't acknowledge Michael, but the singer opened up as he arrived, a wide, welcoming smile on his face. Michael didn't make a habit of talking to strangers, not living ones anyway, but something about the musician drew him in—before he knew it, Michael had bought him a drink and invited him to his table.

His name was Sammy. He lived in the city and was staying at a friend's house in town. He liked it in Brittleside. "There's something raw and glorious about humans on the edge," was how he put it. "The city is rife with pricks and pomps, those who have it all and those who want it all; those who aspire to be assholes and those who *are* assholes."

He spoke with an intelligent fluidity and passion, regardless of the subject. He was often animated, he rarely stood still, throwing his arms and head this way and that when he spoke, reacting to every other syllable with bodily exclamations. When he wasn't talking, his mouth still worked, sucking noisily on candy or twiddling a toothpick between his front teeth.

When Isabella finished her set, she joined them—with her friend, Janie, tugging behind. Her friend took an instant liking to Sammy, flirting openly from the first moment her heavy brown eyes fell upon him. Chip and Naff had already said their goodbyes, heading home to settle a FIFA-based argument that had been ongoing since they arrived.

It was the most fun Michael had had in a long time. The bands finished on the stage and someone turned the music on full blast to compensate. With Isabella by his side, leaning in close so their conversation overpowered the sound of generic rock playing at a thousand decibels, he was in heaven. He hadn't been with a girl for a long time, hadn't even been interested in doing so, but with Isabella he found himself wondering just why he had let the experience pass him by.

They talked and talked. She was funny and interesting. She was amazing. She was everything he had ever wanted in a woman.

Sammy and Janie were involved in similar shouting conversation, but Sammy didn't seem as interested. Every time Michael looked over at him, he was staring back, bored by the gorgeous girl sitting dotingly by his side.

"You not interested in Janie?" Michael asked him after Sammy had followed him to the bathroom.

He tilted his head back and laughed boorishly.

"She's cute," Michael pushed.

Sammy shrugged his shoulders nonchalantly. "She may be cute, my friend, but she is also a fucking idiot."

It was harsh but Michael knew it was also true.

"Did you know she has six cats and four of them are called Freddy?"

Michael didn't know that. "Why Freddy?" he wondered.

Sammy laughed again. There was something odd about his laugh, Michael thought, a glimmer of insanity spewed with an infectious wail. It was hard for him not to join in and even harder not to look at his flicking eyes or maddening expression while he performed it.

"When I asked her why the name was so important to her, she gave me a blank look and said it was important because it was the name of four of her cats."

They both laughed.

"It's like talking to a brick wall," Sammy said.

"But she *is* very pretty."

Sammy gave another nonchalant shrug, genuinely uninterested in the aesthetic qualities of his date. He seemed more interested in spending time with Michael and groaned a note of displeasure whenever they were at the bar and Michael refused to linger. At one point, he even suggested that they leave the two women and and head to a nightclub to "find a bit of rough."

"You mean a homeless crackhead?" Michael had asked.

"They'd be more interesting," Sammy argued, his eyes sparkling in the reflective fluorescent light from behind the bar.

"Really?"

Sammy directed Michael's attention to the main room. Janie and Isabella, seated across from each other, were engaged in tipsy conversation. Janie was facing them but looking away. She knew they were watching and was toying with a strand of hair and pouting unnaturally as she pretended to listen to Isabella. She lifted her eyes toward them to make sure they were still watching, and when she saw that they were, she flinched, darted her gaze away, and then broke into a loud blast of hysteric laughter in an attempt to hide the awkwardness.

"She's a fucking idiot," Sammy said plainly, looking away from the giggling woman. "I'd prefer the crackhead, the down and out. Someone torn down by the extremes of life and the human condition. Someone who will take things to the extreme because they no longer fear death, humiliation, or the impending misery that bad choices with bad people may bring."

Michael was drunk and too eager to get back to Isabella to pay attention to what he was saying. "You're crazy," he told him.

As the night wore on and the drunken customers stumbled out into the cold streets, the music was turned down in increments until it became nothing more than background noise, joining the pattering of the rain that beat a jarring staccato on the windows. The announcer, looking tired and withdrawn but still retaining a sense of enthusiasm, announced last orders on the stage and thanked everyone for a wonderful night.

Michael's voice was creaking and groaning with every word he spoke. Isabella's had taken on a smoky quality.

"Looks like we're the last ones left," Sammy noted, looking around.

A pair of middle-aged women had been the last to leave, their voices audible above the remnants of music as they joked and laughed from the back of the room. At one point, one of them had tried to flirt with Sammy, collaring him when he was at the bar and doing everything in her power short of flopping out her tits on the varnished surface and asking him to suck them. Unsurprisingly she repulsed him.

His repulsion for Janie also increased as the night wore on. When the music softened and silence crept through the speakers, he didn't talk to her. He barely acknowledged her.

"You two had a good time?" he asked Michael and Isabella, his eyes flicking between them.

Michael felt a little embarrassed at the question and Sammy noticed, shooting him a cheeky grin.

Sammy took Michael to the side before they left, ushering him away from the girls.

"Listen," he said, checking to make sure they couldn't hear, "Janie wants to go back to my place. I didn't drink much; I can drive her. You want to invite Isabella back, as well?"

"To yours?"

He grinned proudly. "I live alone, plenty of room, no one to wake up. Come on, we can have some fun with them."

Michael was tired. He could feel the sedating effects of the alcohol hovering over him like a specter of doom. "Not tonight," he croaked.

Sammy shook his head with slow exaggeration. "Tut tut tut, Mr. Charmer," he said with a grin. "I thought you were a night owl. An animal."

"Well, I'm not," Michael told him, running pressured fingers up and down his larynx in an attempt to soothe the croak.

Sammy threw up his arms jokingly and then slapped his thighs. "Ah well, I guess they're all mine then, eh?" he flashed a knowing wink.

Michael's face turned in an instant.

"Just kidding," Sammy said with a grin. "I'll give them a lift back, though, since it's pissing it down. I'll give the little idiot the bad news on the way. Tell her I'm washing my hair or having a wank or something, anything's preferable to *that* really," his eyes flickered with disgust when he looked at her.

He turned back to Michael, put his right hand on his shoulder, and dug around his pocket with his left. "Here," he said, handing him a candy. "Suck on that, it'll sort your throat out a treat." Sammy left him with a wink and departed to talk to Janie, helping her put on her coat and feigning a gracious and friendly demeanor.

The candy did help Michael's throat somewhat. It also took away the taste of alcohol that was souring on his tongue.

"I'm going to walk back," he told Isabella, happy that his voice didn't quite grate so much anymore. "I don't live too far from here. Sammy will take you and Janie home."

"I can walk with you," she assured. "Janie's place is only a few minutes away, on Sycamore Street."

"It's pissing rain. And I'm going the other way."

"So, I don't—"

He cut her short with a kiss. She pulled back with a wide grin on her face, her eyes still closed, her tongue circling her lips and licking the sugary taste from them.

"I'll see you another time then?" she asked hopefully.

Michael nodded. He gave her his number and took hers; there was no way he was letting her go without the assurance he would see her again. As a group, they walked outside into the pouring rain and then Michael watched them depart. They climbed into Sammy's car; he'd had a couple of pints but looked fresher and more alive than at any point during the night.

Isabella climbed into the backseat. A drunk and excited Janie slipped into the front. Isabella waved at Michael and blew him a kiss. The car pulled away into the rain-drenched night and despite the cold and the rain, Michael felt a deep, lingering warmth as he watched. There was nothing better than the feeling of a new relationship, knowing that it was the start of something exciting, something life changing. He had found himself a happy, beautiful girl and even though it was still too early to tell, she could make him a happy man. If nothing else, she would give him a few amazing weeks.

Or at least, that's what he thought. Because Michael would never see that face again. At least, not when it was happy, not when it was smiling, not when it was at its most beautiful.

7

Michael enjoyed the walk home. In Brittleside, the rain had a way of washing away the human debris that usually littered the streets. There were no beggars wrapped in blankets of cardboard and newspaper. No scantily clad, malnourished women offering sexual favors for the price of a fix. Even the muggers and the criminals stayed out of the rain.

A warm, alcoholic buzz followed him on the journey through the belting rain, tinged with the warmth of finding a beautiful girl. There was a certain joy to the start of a relationship, when all the hope is bound up into one little ball of energy. So many possibilities, so much excitement. It doesn't always last. Relationships sour, people are innately intolerant of monogamy and yearn to start the cycle all over again, but sometimes it works and it sticks.

Naff was fast asleep on the sofa when Michael returned. Chip had taken advantage of the fact. Michael walked in to find him straddling Naff's shoulders with a malignant grin on his face and a permanent marker in his hand. Naff boasted a dozen new and obscene tattoos, including an intricately drawn penis on the center of his forehead.

"Dirty stopper-outer," Chip said, pointing the pen at Michael.

"What?"

He threw himself off Naff and bounced onto the floor. The tattooed man stirred, mumbled something, and then turned over. "So, did you and the singing girl, you know . . ." he did something with his fingers that made Michael gag.

"No."

"Oh. You and the pretty boy, then?"

"Fuck off, Chip."

He stopped Michael before he could retire to bed. His face had been the picture of pleasantry—it usually was when he had been wallowing in the impending misery of one of his friends—but that happiness was eradicated in a moment. "What's that smell?" he asked.

Michael lifted his nostrils to the air, tried to suck it in. "I told you to open the window after you—"

"Not that," he waved the response away with a flick of his wrist. He ducked closer, standing on his tiptoes to get as close to Michael's mouth as possible. He pulled back sharply, a look of indignant horror on his putrid little face. "Menthol," he said accusingly.

"What?"

"What are you eating?" he demanded to know.

Michael popped the candy out onto his hand and offered it to his friend. "Take it," he said. "It served its purpose."

Chip sniffed it, taking a few seconds to gather the scent in his grubby nostrils. "Menthol," he said without lifting his head. "And something like . . . cinnamon. Right?" he asked, his eyes meeting Michael's.

"I guess so."

"Hot, sweet menthol," he stated simply.

Michael nodded. It didn't sink in. He was tired, inebriated. He wanted to go to bed.

"Hot. Sweet. Menthol," Chip repeated slowly.

"For fuck's sake, Chip, I'm going to bed."

Chip grabbed him by the wrist and pulled him back. "Listen, you fucking muppet," he spat. "Remember what the two dead girls said? About the killer? That he smelled of—"

"Hot sweet menthol," Michael said with a sinking realization. He looked down at the candy as his thoughts began to slowly gather themselves. "I got this from Sammy."

In that moment, his desire for sleep vanished. His heart sank; his blood pressure sparked. A shot of adrenaline jump-started his fatigued mind.

"Sammy," Chip said. "The musician? The *artist*?"

Michael turned and ran back into the night; the rain heavy on his face once more, only this time it didn't feel good, it didn't feel warm. The streets looked just as dark and depressing as they always did as he cut a breathless path through them, twisting and turning as fast as his tired legs would carry him.

He couldn't believe he had been so stupid. Not only had the killer been right in front of him, taunting him, but he had led Isabella into his arms. He had denied her the opportunity to walk home. He had told her to get into the car with Sammy. With the killer.

His lungs were raw by the time he made it to Sycamore Street. He stopped at the entrance and looked down the street. A long line of terraced houses lined either side of the road with an unbroken line of cars parked outside each one. A few stuttering streetlights provided illumination, but from the foot of the street, in the flickering light, every car looked the same.

He bounded over to each of the cars, stopping and checking all of them in turn. Sammy had driven away in a red Nissan. He hadn't noticed the make or year and had no reason to pay attention to the license plate, but that was enough to go on.

He halted in front of a Nissan, its true color blackened by the night. He rested his palms heavily on the hood. A river of water poured down from the windscreen and spiraled around his fingertips, soaking the cuffs of his jacket.

He had noticed one thing about Sammy's car: a small ornamental dog that dangled from the rearview mirror. He peered in through the windshield of the dark-colored Nissan, edging his way as close as he needed to be to see through the blackness. A weathered cardboard Christmas tree hung from the mirror, emanating dregs of holiday cheer through its scented pores, but there was no dog, no ornament.

He should have gone with him, he knew that. He could have been there to help them—to stop *him*. Two girls were going to die because of him, because he was too drunk, too carefree, too blind. In the past, alive, he wouldn't have given it a second thought. It wouldn't have mattered how drunk he was or how drunk his date was. He thought he was a better person. He thought he was doing the right thing. And maybe he was, but she could be dead because of that.

Another Nissan. It could have been black, gray, or any darkened color. He peered through the windshield again and slammed his fists against the hood when he failed to see an ornament.

The rain poured down heavily. He was soaked through; clothes sticking to his skin like plastic wrap. There was a breaking frustration deep inside of him, a frustration at the knowledge that he had done something so innately stupid, so potentially damaging, yet had no power to correct it. It was a crushing feeling. Despite the flood of emotions battling for prestige in his mind, he still found space for a big chunk of self-loathing.

He crossed the street. A curtain flickered in the house opposite; a nosy old lady popped her head out through a gap, saw him looking, and then quickly retreated.

He wiped his mouth, flicked the excess water away. Another Nissan. This one had an ornament. He held his breath, leaned forward.

"Fucking dice!" He screamed into the night.

More curtains flicked open, more curious heads popped out. Michael was becoming a spectacle for the curious neighbors, drawing their idle attentions away from nighttime television and casual drunkenness.

He was running out of time. The longer he took, the longer Sammy had to kill them, to do as he pleased with them. Every second that slipped from Michael's grasp was a second Sammy could be using to torture those two innocent women.

Michael's body was on fire but he picked up his pace. He began to jog down the path, checking the cars as he passed.

Another Nissan to his left. He tucked his head in toward the driver's side window. There was the dog, lit by a stuttering fluorescence from a streetlight a few meters behind. Michael turned his attention to the adjacent house. The lights were on downstairs, an orange glow emanated from outside the main window and from the cracks in the front door. The neighboring houses were dark, lost to the night, so this had to be the one—even sadistic killers needed light.

He ducked in through the side. He didn't take care to soften the sound of his footsteps. He was in a rush. No time to spare. And it didn't matter regardless—the rain drowned out any sound he made.

A back door led into a darkened kitchen, where the stale smell of mold and must rotted in the air. The door was shut but unlocked, barged open in a hurry by someone moving quickly or someone with his hands full.

Michael held his breath, conscious of the sound of his flustered breathing despite the roaring thumps of rain pelting onto the blackened streets. He cracked the door open gently and stuck his head through the gap. At the other end of the kitchen stood an open doorway leading into a lit hallway; both the kitchen and the hallway were empty.

He pushed open the door further; it resisted noisily. It hit something small in the way and dragged it along the linoleum. Michael paused and cringed, thinking that the game was up and he was about to be ambushed.

He waited in the silence and then stuck his head through the gap again, craning to catch a better glimpse of the hallway. He could see into the living room, lit with a ferocity that looked even brighter from his darkened perspective.

A shaded figure was lying down on a sofa; another was lying on the floor in front of them. Michael's heart sank at the sight, but there was still a chance they were alive. He couldn't see any immediate signs of blood or any more signs of a deadly struggle. There was a good chance they were just unconscious, or even drugged.

He pushed the door open all the way and crept forward.

In the hallway, with the living room only a few meters away, he could see that Isabella was the one lying on the sofa. She didn't look like she was sleeping but she didn't look dead. Janie was on the floor in front of her, equally ambiguous, her posture slightly more sprawled. Even he couldn't tell if they were alive or dead from where he stood, but he couldn't see any lingering souls waiting with a smile of expectation, and that was usually a sign of life.

There was a staircase next to where Michael was standing. A light had been turned on and he could just about hear the sound of a TV or a radio. He assumed Sammy, Abaddon, or whatever he was, was up there and guessed that his approach would be a groaning, thumping one—aided by the age of the house—that he would be able to hear in the deathly silence. He also knew that Sammy wasn't working alone. He had said so himself. But he had no idea who else was involved, if they were in the house, and if they were currently upstairs or down. He had to take a chance, he had to assume they were upstairs, because beyond standing where he was for God knows how long and hoping that something would happen in his favor and that the two girls wouldn't die, he didn't have any other choice but to proceed.

Michael made it to the living room, one eye still on the staircase, before he realized his mistake: Sammy wasn't upstairs, he hadn't been oblivious to his arrival, and he had led him directly to where he was currently standing.

The floorboard behind him creaked. He awoke to the realization that someone was standing over him and then his world turned black.

Michael woke in a well-lit room. The light shot through his eyes and it felt like his brain was going to explode. He instinctively tried to clasp his hands to his head but they were restrained against a coarse material. Through the blinding pain, he saw Sammy standing over him, glaring with his glittering eyes, his hands tucked calmly behind his back, as he studied his suffering.

"It's alive," he exclaimed joyfully with a broad, beaming smile.

Michael had enjoyed that smile. He had found it fresh and alive. He had spent most of the night thinking just how commendable it was for him to look so alive and happy despite struggling through life as a talented musician working out of the gutter, playing to poorly populated rooms of drunken philistines. Now he hated it. He felt an instinctive sneer creep into the corner of his mouth; it made his skin crawl.

"I'm glad you could join the party." Sammy slowly walked around Michael. He tried to turn, to watch his captor, but his restraints stopped him from doing so.

"I thought I'd killed you," Sammy said from behind him. "I hit you very fucking hard. But, then . . ." he popped his head over Michael's shoulder, his grinning face an inch away. "I remembered! You're the grim fucking reaper! You can't die."

Michael's mouth wasn't restrained and Sammy's face was close enough for him to tear into with his teeth, but his reactions were too slow and Sammy had turned away again before the thought formed.

"Kinda baffling that you even *can* be knocked out," Sammy said in contemplation. He was in front of Michael again, his arms still folded casually behind his back, his eyes bearing down at his victim. "Not that I'm complaining, of course."

"Where's Isabella?" Michael grunted.

An excited energy pulsed through Sammy as it had done earlier in the night, but now it was stronger. He was almost dancing on the spot.

He dove toward Michael and clasped his hands on the arms of the chair. Michael flinched, ashamed for doing so. The chair groaned as he spun it around, making Michael nauseous in the process.

"*Et violà!*" Sammy exclaimed with a theatrical throw of his hands.

Isabella was lying on her back on the couch, her arms straight and neat by her side. There was little sign of life, but Michael knew that she was alive. She was clinging on. Maybe only barely, but it was something.

"What are you going to do?" Michael begged for an answer. He could hear the desperation in his own voice. It made him cringe.

There was a window a few feet ahead of him. The curtains, a sickly and tacky mix of floral hell, had been drawn but there was a portion of visible glass in the middle where the ugly fabric struggled to meet. With the light in the room and the darkness outside, Michael could see his own torrid reflection, with Sammy's grinning, delighted face bouncing joyfully above his.

The window painted the perfect portrait of his misery. He looked like death: distraught, tired, beaten, and haggard; Sammy was the harbinger of his death, looming over him with a sickly-sweet smile on his proud face. Michael had had plenty of low points in the last few decades, but at that point, looking at his own face and seeing how helpless he was, he felt lower, angrier, and sicker than ever.

"What do you think?" Sammy said. He moved around his captive, standing in front of him again. He moved to Isabella and stroked a hand over her face, a soft and caressing touch. With his forefinger still caressing her cheek, he tilted his eyes up at Michael and grinned, then he pulled back an arm and drove a fist into her face.

She barely flinched. Michael snapped against the restraints with a violent and snarling menace that nearly ripped the wooden supports out from under him.

"You fucking prick!" he roared, a froth of spit squirting onto his chin.

Sammy laughed childishly. "Don't worry, Michael," he said softly. He walked past. Michael tried to lash out but only managed to shake the chair underneath him. "She's sedated, she won't feel a thing. This is not about her; it's about you."

He disappeared into the kitchen, leaving Michael alone to study his failures. He had dealt with death more than he ever imagined he would, but these two were his fault. Without his intervention, they'd still be smiling and stealing hearts; they'd still be singing, dancing, laughing, and joking.

Sammy returned with a large knife and an even wider smile etched on his smarmy face. He flashed it at Michael as he sat there, helpless and horrified.

"Don't do this," Michael said. "Whatever you want . . ."

"What?" Sammy asked. "Whatever I want, what?"

"Your issue is with me, right? So, take it out with me."

Sammy laughed. "Truth be told, Mr. Reaper Man, I don't have an issue with you at all. I mean, sure, some people do." He waved the knife at Michael. "It seems you have a habit of making enemies. But me? I just want to have fun."

"I'll give you whatever you want. I'll do whatever you ask. Just leave them alone."

"And what if what I want is to kill these two girls and then cause you a world of pain? What then?"

Michael didn't reply. The desperation in his eyes gradually turned to anger as he realized he was helpless and that Sammy wasn't in the mood for negotiation.

"I thought as much," Sammy said. He turned back to the girls, and then he got to work.

Janie was first. Like Isabella, she didn't seem to feel him when he straddled her, or when he grasped her neck to twist her head this way and that—as if examining the stitching on a torn doll—but her eyes did burst open when he stuck the blade into her throat. There was no sound, no scream, but her eyes remained open as he drove the knife in to the hilt and held it there until a torrent of blood pooled on the floor beneath her.

It was messy and it was horrific, but he reveled in it. Michael could see the enjoyment in his eyes, the almost orgasmic twitch in the corners of his mouth.

Janie slipped into the sedated sleep of death. Michael could have found solace in the fact that she hadn't suffered, but he didn't.

He wasn't there before he had drugged her. He didn't know what ordeal he had forced her through, what tricks he employed as she flirted with him and practically begged him.

"Tell me. Why these two?" Michael asked. "Why are you doing this?"

Sammy stood up quickly, the blood-drenched blade in his hand flicked droplets of crimson around the room. Janie's soul was already standing beside him. She looked him up and down with a blank expression on her ethereal face. She looked at the blade, then at the face of her killer, then at Michael.

He couldn't bring himself to meet her gaze.

"It would have been any girls," Sammy said with a grin. "It's not about them."

"If this is about me then leave them out of it."

He laughed, an energetic laugh that faded into a breathless snicker. He wiped a stream of moisture from his lips and grinned. "Don't try to be the fucking hero, Michael," he said with a shake of his head. "It doesn't suit you."

Sammy watched Michael squirm as he moved onto Isabella. Michael tried to kick and scream his way out of the chair, to force every inch of energy and effort he had into finding a way out. All the while Sammy just stood there watching, knife in hand, looming over Isabella.

When Michael finished, spent, beaten, and breathless, Sammy simply said, "Finished?"

"You'll fucking pay for this," Michael growled at him, spitting every syllable through gritted teeth.

He smiled, "I doubt it."

He was careful with her, like a doctor looking after a loving patient and not a psychotic killer about to rip her apart. Michael screamed and rocked until his throat tore and his body ached. Sammy didn't respond, he didn't even flinch. He was in a world of his own and had completely tuned his captive out.

Michael couldn't bring himself to watch. He saw it, he heard it. But the part of him that should have been registering all of that information had died. He blocked it out, pushed it away into a place he would, hopefully, never access again.

It was hell. He had experienced death himself. He had watched many people being murdered, committing suicide, and otherwise completing their journey. None of that came close to what happened just a few feet from him in that house on that rain-drenched evening.

He didn't have much left to give, but Sammy took a little part of him anyway.

Sammy stopped when Isabella was breathing her last breaths. She was covered in her own blood and had awakened to experience her own final sputters. Her eyes were watching Michael, caught in a silent and terrified embrace. She couldn't talk, couldn't utter anything more than a desperate gurgle. Michael couldn't look away. He had strained every last cell of energy out of his body in trying to stop the carnage. He just watched, feeling just as lifeless as she was about to become.

Sammy liked that moment—for him that was the essence of why he did what he did. He was grinning like an excited kid who pins his nose to the television to absorb himself in his favorite cartoon.

There was a clumsy clatter from the kitchen. The delighted expression faded from Sammy's face; the television had been switched off. He looked above Michael's head, his wide-eyed expression aimed toward the back of the house, his ears pinned to the air to catch the sound of an intruder.

Michael was beaten. He couldn't even gather the energy to hold his head up straight anymore; it lolled depressingly against his chest. But seeing him with the smile wiped off his face, no matter how briefly it may have been, stirred something inside of him.

"You heard that as well, eh?" Michael asked, raising his voice, hoping to annoy and distort his silence. His voice cracked and groaned and what he wanted to say didn't come out coherently, but it didn't matter.

Sammy snapped his eyes to his captive, a startling look of aggression on his face. "Shut up!" he spat.

"Fuck you," came the bitter reply. Michael's larynx was chewing gravel and spitting the wastage onto the back of his tongue. He could barely utter a sound without great effort. "I'll talk as much as I fucking—"

"Shut up!" Sammy snapped again, louder this time. He moved toward the reaper, waving the knife near his face, his ear still aimed toward the kitchen.

The initial, insignificant sound was followed by another, less innocuous sound; a pattering of intrusive mischief. Someone or something was in the kitchen; even Michael could hear them through the sound of his own blood rushing in his ears.

"That won't hurt me," Michael reminded him, feeling spurred on by the chance that he could save what was left of Isabella. "I'm already dead. A dickhead just like you already killed—"

Sammy whipped him around the head with the hand that cradled the knife. His clenched knuckles rapped a dull thud against Michael's temple. He budged past him into the darkness beyond the living room, and Michael watched him through the reflection in the window as he stalked into the blackness.

The portrait, the reflection that had so depressed Michael earlier, had changed. A veil of apathy had covered his features, a blank canvas devoid of emotion. He was still ragged and beaten, but he no longer cared. The killer, the cause of all this chaos, hovered over him, looming in the back of the reflected portrait like an anxious hunter on the prowl for deadly prey.

"Maybe it's your *friend*," Michael said. "Is he the one who put you up to this? Did you need someone holding your hand throughout it, is that it?"

Sammy merely growled in reply, clearly agitated, desperate for silence so he could hear the intruder clearly.

"Or is that all in your head? Let me guess, you wanted every-one to know that you're not really a sad, lonely bastard and that you really do have friends?"

The growl was louder this time. Michael watched the reflec-tion as Sammy turned, glared, raised the knife above his head to consider another strike, and then turned back to the kitchen.

"Then again, it all makes sense," Michael said, each word a struggle. "You probably needed their help. You're just a fucking musician, and not even a very good one. What the fuck do you know about tracking down a reaper?"

"Fuck off!" Sammy spat, moving away from the chair, away from Michael. He was annoyed, someone or something had inter-rupted his moment in the sun, but there was also a touch of trepi-dation in his step. That spurred Michael on.

"And what kind of self-respecting demon has to drug his vic-tims before he kills them? Worried they would fight back? Prefer to hunt in cages, do you?"

Sammy snapped on the light in the hallway. The reflection in the window ahead increased in intensity; Michael could see clearly as Sammy raised a threatening hand to the darkness and called menacingly. "Who's there?"

Michael laughed, recalling the killer's own outburst of delight at his previous discomfort. "Sounds like someone's come to spoil the party!" he yelled.

Sammy halted. He looked back at Michael as if about to say something, to snap at him again, and then remembered himself and concentrated back on the darkness. He stammered forward.

Michael was feeling stronger. He had been boxed into a cor-ner, hanging off the ropes, but now he had found a weak spot and had pushed his opponent back. He gathered his spirits and yelled at him again, "Probably just a cat. You're not scared of a little pussycat are you, *big man*?" He finished with another laugh, a stuttering, coughing laugh.

Sammy spun around angrily. He waved the knife at Michael, his mouth open to form a yell, to tell him to shut up. He uttered the beginnings of an aggressive rebuttal and then quickly fell silent. Something quick and surprisingly agile darted up behind him and struck him over the head.

Michael had been about to offer another pointless remark, but he swallowed his own words in bemusement. He watched through the reflection in the window as Sammy staggered. He swayed this way and that before collapsing with a thick thud, lifting a veil of dust and fibers from the floor as he crashed into it. For a moment, Michael wondered if there really was someone else involved, and if they had simply grown tired of Sammy taking all of the glory. But those concerns didn't stay for long.

Chip was standing in his wake. A broad smile on his little face; a sturdy bat in his grubby hand. He looked down at Sammy and hit him again, before striking him in the face with a sturdy wallop from his steal-capped shoes.

He was the last person Michael had expected to see standing there; he would have been less shocked if the battering perpetrator *had* been a cat. Chip muttered something, stopped beating the unconscious Sammy, and then trudged over, releasing Michael from his restraints.

"Phone an ambulance," Michael sputtered.

The apathy disappeared in an instant, replaced by a rush of adrenaline. Now that Chip had saved him, he knew there was a chance he could save Isabella.

Chip paused, gave him a puzzled look. "But you can't . . . how hard did he hit you exactly?"

"Not for me!" He motioned toward Isabella. Chip hadn't seen her until that point; crumpled and crippled in silence, seeping into her surroundings, it was forgivable not to notice her. Her smell was prominent, but distinguishing bad smells wasn't in Chip's repertoire.

Chip looked at her, did a double take. His beady eyes switched to Janie, first to her bloodied body and then to her lost soul. He mumbled to himself, actively twitching on the spot in a moment of mad hesitation.

Michael shifted off the seat, tossed the ropes aside, and glanced back toward Sammy. He was still down, grumbling into the carpet as his concussed mind struggled to return to reality.

"Check the kitchen," Michael said, breathlessly.

"Hmm?"

"Phone!"

He darted away, and Michael turned back to Isabella. Her eyes had closed and she was trying and failing to open them, as if fighting sleep. Her lips were parted; a thin trickle of blood ran a course from the corner of her mouth, down her chin, and onto the sofa. She was mumbling something soft and incoherent, her lowly voice fading further with every struggled sound.

Michael wanted to go to her, to comfort her and to try to save her, but something stopped him. He just stood there, staring at her as she lay staring back. He didn't know what she was trying to tell him. He hoped that she was delirious and spouting random outbursts, or that she was forgiving him—if she felt, as he did, that he needed forgiving—but there was also a chance that she was cursing him for leading her to her death.

Chip burst back into the room holding a phone. "It's dead!" he said, waving it around.

Michael looked into his startled expression and then glanced back at Isabella. "It doesn't matter," he said. "So is she."

She had joined her friend. They were both waiting for Michael to do his job. The horror that had painted their pretty faces during the night had vanished and had been replaced with a look of simple serenity. Whatever Isabella had been trying to tell him in life wouldn't be on her mind in death. The delirium and the bitterness wouldn't remain, and if it *was* forgiveness on her dying tongue, he didn't want to hear it from her spirit; he didn't think that he deserved it.

He didn't even want to look at them. He had failed them. It didn't matter that they were happy now, because he couldn't promise that they were going to a better place, he couldn't assure them that their eternities in death would be any less traumatic than their last few hours alive.

Chip had acknowledged Isabella, but he too seemed unwilling to talk to her.

"How did you find me?" Michael asked, keen to divert his attention.

"The guy at the bar. He knew the girls; he gave me their address." He smiled and laughed softly. "The poor sod was asleep, I had to—" he noticed that his friend wasn't paying attention. "Never mind," he finished, sensing Michael's pain.

Sammy was groaning back to life like a zombie awaking from the crypt. Michael stumbled slowly over to him, feeling the adrenaline rush into his body and revitalize his weakened muscles.

He looked up at him and sniggered. The smile had returned to his face, and it made Michael feel sick.

"Ah, well," Sammy propped himself up on his elbows and gave a defeated shrug. "Looks like you win this round, Michael."

There were no winners, Michael knew that, only a collection of losers and one sick fucker who had killed them.

Michael kicked the knife—still fresh with Isabella's blood—away and watched it scupper into the blackness. He knelt down beside Sammy. Chip stood over him, the bat in his hands once more, a mean look on his face.

"Why did you do this?" Michael asked.

"For a laugh?" Sammy coughed, laughed, and then flopped back to the floor, not even flinching as the back of his head hit the solid ground. "It's not about me, Michael. You made someone very angry. You took control away from a controlling man. He wanted to do the same to you."

"Who?"

Sammy slowly shook his head, the base of his skull rocking to and fro on the solid flooring. "I can't tell you that. I don't really know."

"Bollocks!" Chip spat.

Sammy didn't flinch. "It's true. All I know is that he helped to rouse me from my slumber. He gave me motivation, a target, and he helped to track you down. I kill, Michael, it's what I do. I enjoy causing mayhem. He gave me another reason, another incentive. He promised me more power, more victims—impunity. I mean, between you and me, I quite like the chase, and I'm not averse to punishment, but it's nice to have a choice, right?"

Michael and Chip exchanged a glance. They knew who it was. Michael had made enemies in life and death. There was no shortage of people out there who despised him either. But there was only one he had wronged to this degree, only one who would want to make him suffer, seemed to know everything about him, and had the power to do all of this and more. And the worst thing was, he didn't know that person's name, job, location, or purpose.

"If you take me to him, I'll spare your life," Michael said, feeling sick at the mere thought.

Sammy laughed. "I can read you like a book, Michael. You want nothing more than to kill me right now, and quite frankly, I don't blame you. But I'm not helping you." He coughed, turned his head to spit. "This is between you and him. He'll show himself to you in time. And when that happens, tonight will look like a fucking picnic by comparison."

Michael, clearly pained, struck with a desperation to find the person who had set this up and an unwillingness to let the person who had caused it live any longer, turned to Chip, hoping to find an answer in his friend's eyes.

"Let's just kill him," Chip said, answering the question Michael's eyes had asked. "Let's make him suffer. We caught the Bastard. He's the one that did this, not some fat prick behind a desk. Let's kill the fucker."

Michael pondered Chip's words, a smile gradually creeping back into the corners of his mouth. He was right. It didn't matter who was involved. It didn't matter what they would do. He was already dead, he was already at rock bottom. They couldn't hurt him; they couldn't drag him down any further. Whatever they had planned, he would deal with when it came. Right now, he wanted vengeance. He wanted blood.

"You're right," he said, turning back to Sammy.

"You can kill me," Sammy said with a grin. "But I'll come back."

"When?" Michael asked as he loomed over him, delighting in the role reversal.

"Thirty years. Fifty years. A hundred. It doesn't matter. I'll be back and more will die. Killing me now will be pointless."

"You're right."

There was still an empty smile on Michael's face, and judging by the look Sammy was giving him, it unnerved him. He could read him like a book. He was scared at what the reaper would do.

Michael knew there was nothing he could do to eradicate him, that job was for whoever had let such an entity exist in the first place. Whether that was God, the Devil, or something in between, it didn't matter. In time, he could try to find out. He could try to make sure he never returned and never killed again. He could put everything he had into making sure he was banished to the bowels of hell with the sick bastard that had brought him to Brittleside, the same sick bastard who had violated the souls of Martin Atkinson and Angela Washington and had made a mockery of Michael in the process.

However, that, like everything else in this world that Michael called home, was probably out of reach for him. It was beyond him. It was part of a great unknown that seemed to encompass everything he saw, everything he experienced, and everything that tried to hurt, kill, or mock him.

I'm just a lowly reaper after all, he thought bitterly to himself. The worst of the worst. A man with little power, few answers, and no respect.

Michael's smile blossomed into something a little less ambiguous, a little more menacing. "But I'm still going to kill you."

A momentary glint in Sammy's eye told Michael that he hadn't expected that. It suggested that he thought he could talk the reaper into submission, that he could still be the dominant one, the one with control. That glint gave Michael all the satisfaction he needed as he killed Sammy.

He enjoyed every bit of it. And he knew that it didn't matter if he wasn't able to stop him or his boss. It didn't matter if he wasn't able to stop him from being reborn and causing more chaos. Because he would just kill him again. Whether it took fifty years or a hundred, whether he was killing him on and off for the rest of eternity, it didn't matter. He would do his bit and he would do it as many times as he needed to—that much he *could* do, that much he *did* have control over.

A veil of silence flattened the atmosphere in the psychiatrist's office. Outside, the world had turned black; the light in the room had dimmed to a deathly shade. Only the beam of light from the waiting room, screaming under a slit in the door, washed any sense of daylight inside.

Doctor Khan cleared her throat and put her pen and notepad on her desk. She hadn't written anything more down.

"That's it," Michael said softly, his voice fading along with the light. He looked up at the doctor, offered a meek smile and a weakened shrug of his tired shoulders, and then lowered his head to his chest again.

"This has been a very traumatic experience for you," the doctor said warmly.

"No shit."

She nodded slowly, staring at the top of his downed head. "If you need any *help* . . ."

"Help?" he lifted his head, his eyes glimmering at her in the darkness.

"Antidepressants or—"

"Really?" he said, a breath short of a laugh. "I'm immortal and you want to pump me full of *Prozac*?"

"It works the same for you as for—"

"Ah, for fuck's sake," he shook his head and stood. "I think that's my call to leave."

"Michael, you came here for my help, right?"

He nodded. "But I don't want pills."

"Then what do you want from me?"

He laughed. "This is the afterlife," he opened up his arms, "the great fucking unknown. Heaven. Hell. God. Satan. This is fantasy, for fuck's sake. A world of mythical creatures, of dreams and legends. A world where you can make me live forever, a world where a psychiatrist is a fucking mind reader!" his voice increased in volume with each syllable. "Antidepressants? Seriously?" he opened his mouth, screeched out a disbelieving breath and then strangled any further complaints with a shake of his head. "*Idontfuckingbelieveit.*"

"I don't know what to tell you," the doctor said.

Michael stared at her for a moment. His frustration faded, turned to a smile. "You know what?" he said with another incredulous head shake. "Believe it or not, I *do* actually feel better. Getting it all out there," he held his head and thrust his palms outward, "it helped, ya know?"

The doctor remained still.

"I'll see you next week," Michael moved to leave.

"Is that it?" she asked his back. "What will you do now?"

He turned back to face her. "What can I do? No one will tell me who's behind it. No one will even admit that this prick wasn't working alone. I need proof, can you believe that? Apparently, there's a guy out there with God knows what power doing whatever the hell he wants, raising demons, facilitating the death of innocents. And I need fucking proof? Whatever happened to the all-seeing and the all-knowing? Sometimes I wonder if everyone is just as fucking clueless as I am and that the only reason they're not telling me is because they are too embarrassed to admit it."

Doctor Khan didn't seem to have a reply for that. Michael turned back around. He opened the door, spilling a flood of light into the room. "Now," he said, looking at her once more, "it's back to the grindstone, back to the countless other bastards who litter these streets. There may not be anyone as evil as *him* out there, but there're dozens of fuckers being just as annoying."

He slammed the door behind him, shrouding the doctor in a blanket of darkness.

Acknowledgments

In previous books, I've thanked everyone who has helped me with my career. I've thanked editors, agents, publishers, designers, and accountants. I've thanked my family, my in-laws, my friends, and my pets. In my last book, I even thanked a stray duck. The majority of people I've thanked have received a copy of my book and an extra note of gratitude (except the duck, she didn't leave a return address) so I'm sure they already understand how much I appreciate their help.

This time, I want to thank my mother. *Just* my mother. She's the only person on that list no longer alive to see these superfluous messages of appreciation, yet without her, none of these books would exist. She had fifty-five great years on this earth and five bad ones. She was one of the kindest, sweetest, and most compassionate people I have ever known, and she was also one of the few people in this world who had my back and supported me no matter what.

She was a fighter. My enduring memories growing up are of a woman who worked herself sick for her family and passed out cold at least twice a month. Hearing a loud thump interrupt frenzied activity, and spending the next ten minutes trying to rouse her with a wet cloth, only for her to get straight back to work when she was back on her feet, was just part of the routine in our household.

She managed to survive the high blood pressure, the stress and the diabetes, and she didn't seem inconvenienced by any of the other ailments that threatened her health. But she was powerless to the ALS. It turned a strong, beautiful, effervescent human being into a depressed, vulnerable, and reliant shell. In the end, it took her life, but only after it had taken her soul.

In my childhood, I relied on you. In my adolescence, I made life difficult for you. In my adulthood, I watched you suffer. You were there when no one else was, when everyone else had given up. You made me the person I am today, and I'll never forget that, even though I still can't quite accept that you'll never read these words.

So, to everyone I have thanked before, I still appreciate your help and support and you *will* be thanked again. But this one's for someone who will never truly understand how much I loved her, how much I appreciated her, and how much I will miss her.